THE MEDIEVAL WORLD
OF
KATHRYN LE VEQUE
THE OFFICIAL GUIDE

A Reader's guide to family groups, characters, and other information to connect the great and wide world of Kathryn Le Veque Medieval Romance Novels.

WINTER 2020

Author's Note

In the beginning, when there were only twenty or thirty novels, it was a bit easier to explain the connections on a page on my website entitled "Chronological Order". While that page is still valuable as a cursory explanation of what has become the very big Medieval world of Le Veque, it was time to start writing all of this down so readers can share a more in-depth explanation of who belongs where.

Each House will be broken down by name, connected novels, and connected characters. Everything is in alphabetical order. Some Houses are much bigger than others. Additionally, this book in of itself will be updated a few times a year with addendums to incorporate new books. It's a work in progress, and always will be as long as I continue writing.

There are more than thirty Houses contained within these pages. This is only the male hero line; the female heroine line will not be covered because I don't think it's necessary at this point. There are also many secondary houses from secondary characters and perhaps one day, I will go into even more detail with them, but at this point, it's enough to deal with the major family groups.

I have always said that you do NOT need to read my books in any order to understand what is going on. They are all stand alones. But it's always helpful to know the players with this score card!

With that, enjoy the detailed look into the Medieval World of Kathryn Le Veque.

Hugs,
Kathryn

RATINGS OF THE HOUSES BY SIZE

Rating Houses by Size (how many times they appear in Le Veque novels, how many secondary or primary characters they have within the scope of all novels, how many novels in their series, etc.):

The Biggest Houses:

De Wolfe

De Lara

De Lohr

De Russe

Big Houses:

De Nerra

De Reyne

De Shera

De Velt

Du Bois

St. Hever

Wellesbourne

Medium Houses:

De Moray

De Poyer

De Royans

De Winter

Du Reims

Forbes

Hage

Le Bec

Pembury

Smaller houses:

Ashbourne

Connaught

D'Aurilliac

D'Vant

Da Derga

De Bermingham

De Bretagne

De Dere

De Garr

De Llion

De Titouan

Le Brecque

Le Mon

Munro

St. John

Summerlin

CONTENTS

CLAN MUNRO

Novels in this House:

The Red Lion

Deep Into Darkness

Sub-Category (novel where the name appears or where cross over characters appear):

- Devil's Dominion

Castles:

Foulis Castle (The Red Lion)

Four Crosses Castle (The Red Lion)

Findlater Castle, also known as Whitecliff Castle (Deep Into
    Darkness)

Hero:

Jamison Munro (Younger version in The Red Lion, Older version in
    Deep Into Darkness)

Heroine:

Havilland de Llion (Younger version in The Red Lion, Older version
    in Deep Into Darkness)

Connections:

- This is a smaller house. Readers will see some familiar family names of de Llion and de Lohr.
- Jamison and Havilland were first introduced in the "ONCE UPON A HAUNTED CASTLE" USA Today bestselling collection released in September 2016. I wrote a novella for the collection entitled DEEP INTO DARKNESS.
- THE RED LION has the first highland hero and includes the introduction of the next three members of the Lions of the Highlands series – The White Dragon, The Gray Fox, and The Black Falcon.
- The de Llion sisters, Havilland, Madeline, and Amaline, and their father, Roald de Llion, from THE RED LION, are descendants of de Llion family from DEVIL'S DOMINION.
- Becket, Tobias, Brend, and Thad de Lohr appear in THE RED LION. These are grandsons of Christopher de Lohr (RISE OF THE DEFENDER). Their fathers appear in SILVERSWORD.
- Havilland de Llion Munro is the heroine of THE RED LION and DEEP INTO DARKNESS. She is the oldest daughter of Roald de Llion. Her father raised her and her two sisters as warriors.
- Jamison Munro is the hero of THE RED LION and DEEP INTO DARKNESS. He is one of the four Lions of the Highlands, and is called "The Red Lion." He is the second son of George the Elder Munro. He became chief of Clan Munro upon the death of his elder brother, George the Younger Munro.

CLAN MUNRO FAMILY TREE

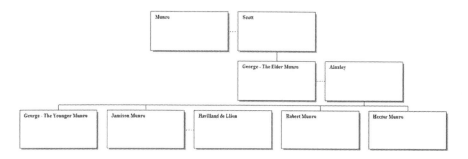

THE HOUSE OF ASHBOURNE

Novels in this House:

Upon a Midnight Dream

Sub-Category (novel where the name appears or where cross over characters appear):

Castles:

Thulston Manor

Hero:

Rennington of Ashbourne

Heroine:

Holly St. Maur

Connections:

- This is a small house.
- Bentley Ashbourne in GODSPEED changes his last name and becomes the Duke of Savernake.
- Payne St. Maur is a small secondary character in TENDER IS THE KNIGHT

THE HOUSE OF CONNAUGHT

Novels in this House:

The Darkland

Sub-Category (novel where the name appears or where cross over characters appear):

- Black Sword
- Great Protector
- Serpent
- The Thunder Lord (Lords of Thunder: The de Shera Brotherhood)

Castle:

Anchorsholme Castle

Hero:

Kirk Connaught

Heroine:

Mara le Bec

Connections:

- This is a smaller house, not tremendously used. Readers will see an occasional secondary character with the name Connaught, as in BLACK SWORD.

- The House of le Bec is the house that spawned Richmond le Bec, hero of GREAT PROTECTOR. Mara le Bec is from an off-shoot of that house about one hundred years after GREAT PROTECTOR takes place.
- Christopher Connaught is a legacy knight in BLACK SWORD.
- Drake Connaught is an Irish knight in THE DARK ONE: DARK KNIGHT.
- Spencer de Shera is a secondary character in THE DARKLAND with undefined family ties to SERPENT and THE THUNDER LORD. THE DARKLAND is where the de Shera name first appeared.

CONNAUGHT FAMILY TREE

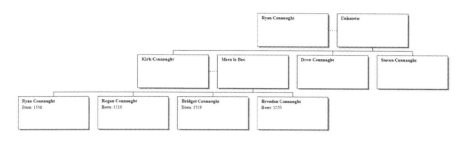

THE HOUSE OF D'AURILLIAC

Novels in this House:

Valiant Chaos

Castle:

None

Hero:

Brogan d'Aurilliac

Heroine:

Avalyn du Brant

Connections:

- This is a smaller house, only used in this novel. There is a powerful secondary character in William Inglesbatch but this is the only novel he, or the Inglesbatch name, appears in.
- Barton St. John is the Captain of the Guard at Geurdley Cross, the castle Avalyn's first husband owns.
- Hans d'Aurilliac is one of Andrew d'Vant's generals in THE RED FURY.

D'Aurilliac/du Brant Family Tree

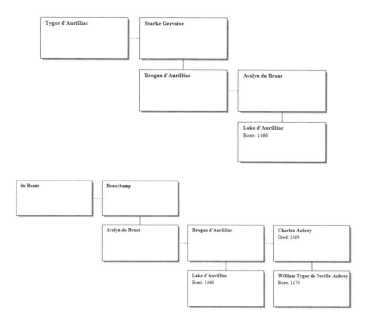

THE HOUSE OF D'VANT

Novels in this House:

Tender is the Knight

The Red Fury

Sub-Category (novel where the name appears):

- Nighthawk
- The Wolfe

Castle:

St. Austell Castle (Tender is the Knight)

Torridon Castle & Haldane Castle (The Red Fury)

Hero:

Denys d'Vant (Tender is the Knight)

Andrew d'Vant (The Red Fury)

Heroine:

Ryan de Bretagne (Tender is the Knight)

Josephine de Carron (The Red Fury)

Connections:

- This is a smaller house.

- De Bretagne is the name of the hero in THE QUESTING and there is a character named Andrew d'Vant (The Red Fury) in THE WOLFE. Other than bearing the same name, there is no other connection to this house or this book from either of these connections, as these characters do not appear in any other novels nor is there any cross-reference to them.

- Dacian d'Vant is a Captain of the Guard at Winchester Castle in VESTIGES OF VALOR.

- Damian d'Vant appears in NIGHTHAWK as a knight serving Patrick de Wolfe.

- Dirk d'Vant appears as King Henry's Guard of Six in SILVERSWORD.

- Felix d'Vant, from the House of d'Vant, appears in LEADER OF TITANS and SEA WOLFE.

- Hans d'Aurilliac is one of Andrew d'Vant's generals.

- Ridge de Reyne appears in THE RED FURY.

- Roan d'Vant is part of King Henry's Household troops in THE WOLFE, and is cousin to Andrew d'Vant, the Red Fury, in THE WOLFE.

- Tallis d'Vant, firstborn son of Denys & Ryan d'Vant, hero and heroine of TENDER IS THE KNIGHT, appears in THE THUNDER KNIGHT.

- Thane Alraedson is Andrew d'Vant's second-in-command and appears in THE WOLFE and THE RED FURY.

DE BRETAGNE/D'VANT FAMILY TREE

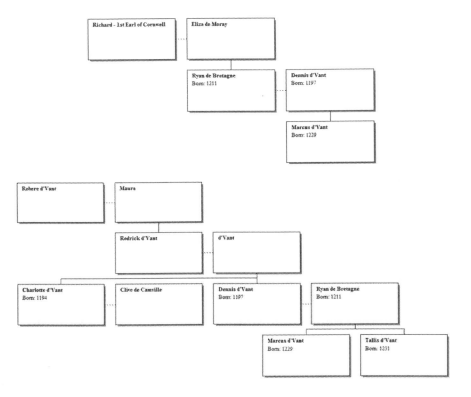

De Carron/d'Vant Family Tree

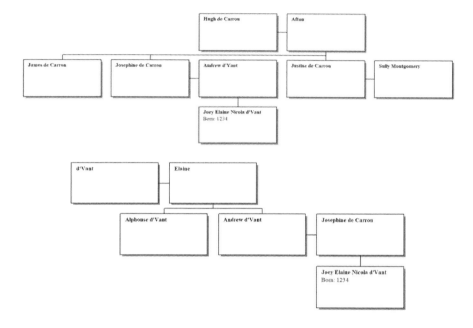

THE HOUSE OF DA DERGA

Novels in this House:

Echoes of Ancient Dreams Part One

Castle:

None

Hero:

Conor da Derga

Heroine:

Destry Caldbeck

Connections:

- This is a smaller house, an ancient Irish royal house, and is not used in any other novel at this time.

THE HOUSE OF DE BERMINGHAM

Novels in this House:

Black Sword

Sub-category (novels where this name also appears):

- Devil's Dominion (spelled de Birmingham in that family line)

Castle:

Black Castle

Hero:

Devlin de Bermingham

Heroine:

Emllyn de Fitzgerald

Connections:

- This is a smaller house, Irish nobility. The name de Bermingham appears in Devil's Dominion, but it is a distant relation. The name Connaught also appears in Black Sword, a distant relation to the hero of THE DARKLAND.
- Conor de Birmingham serves Kenton le Bec in WALLS OF BABYLON and is known as one of the "Trouble Trio."
- Dallan de Birmingham is an Irish knight in DEVIL'S DOMINION.
- Trevor le Mon is a knight in BLACK SWORD.

- Victor St. John is a commander for the Earl of Kildare, and is the father of Emllyn Fitzgerald, heroine of BLACK SWORD.
- William du Reims appears in BLACK SWORD.

DE BIRMINGHAM/FITZGERALD FAMILY TREE

THE HOUSE OF DE BRETAGNE

Novels in this House:

The Questing

Sub-Category (novel where the name appears):

- Tender is the Knight

Castles:

Sherborne Castle

Corfe Castle

Hero:

Cortez de Bretagne

Heroine:

Diamantha de Bocage Edlington de Bretagne

Connections:

- This is a smaller house.
- The name de Bretagne appears in TENDER IS THE KNIGHT as a distant relation.
- Cortez de Bretagne also appears in SCORPION and SWORDS AND SHIELDS.

- Diamantha's father is Michael de Bocage, a secondary character in THE WOLFE.
- Diamantha's grandfather is a de Velt, a son of Ajax de Velt of THE DARK LORD.
- Diamantha's grandmother on her mother's side is a de Lohr, a granddaughter to Christopher de Lohr of RISE OF THE DEFENDER.
- Jorrin de Bretagne appears in THE IRON KNIGHT. He is a legacy knight and garrison commander for Sherborne Castle. He is a direct descendant of Cortez de Bretagne.
- Lyla de Bretagne is a secondary character in TENDER IS THE KNIGHT.
- Michael of Pembury is a knight serving Keir St. Hever. He appears in FRAGMENTS OF GRACE and THE QUESTING.
- Peter Albert Brian Summerlin is the oldest son of Alec and Peyton Summerlin and serves as Cortez de Bretagne's squire in THE QUESTING.

DE BRETAGNE FAMILY TREE

Explore the Genealogy Charts below at
http://kathrynleveque.com/genealogy-charts/
The de Lara Line – Master File
The de Llion – de Titouan – de Velt Line – Master File
The de Velt – de Bocage – Edlington – de Lara Line – Master File

THE HOUSE OF DE DERE

Novels in this House:

Of Love and Legend (part of the Ever My Love collection)

Starless

Sub-Category (novel where the name appears):

- Steelheart

Castles:

Fourstones Castle

Aysgarth Castle

Hero:

Tyren de Dere

Achilles de Dere

Heroine:

Valeria de Velt

Susanna de Tiegh

Connections:

- Achilles de Dere, hero of STARLESS, is part of the "Unholy Trinity" in Juston de Royans' army in LORD OF WINTER. He also appears in BY THE UNHOLY HAND and THE MOUNTAIN DARK.

- Brickley "Brick" de Dere was a major secondary character in STEELHEART, as the captain of the Earl of Canterbury.
- Christopher de Lohr, hero of RISE OF THE DEFENDER, appears in STARLESS.
- Etienne de Gare is a knight serving the House of de Dere.
- Kevin de Lara, brother of Sean de Lara, appears in STARLESS.
- Morgan de Wolfe, nephew of the Earl of Wolverhampton, is a knight serving Caius d'Avignon in STARLESS.
- Tristiana de Dere de Moray is the wife of Rickard de Moray in SHIELD OF KRONOS.
- Tyren de Dere was the Greenhead Ghost, an outlaw in the story "Of Love and Legend."
- Tyren de Dere's best friend is Mars de Velt, brother of Valeria de Velt.
- Valeria de Velt's father is Romulus de Velt.

DE VELT/DE DERE FAMILY TREE

THE HOUSE OF DE LARA

Novels in this House:

Dragonblade

Lord of the Shadows

Sub-Category (Novels of the Dragonblade Series where the name appears or there is cross over characters):

- Beast
- Devil's Dominion
- Dragonblade
- Fragments of Grace
- Island of Glass
- Queen of Lost Stars
- The Fallen One
- The Savage Curtain
- The Thunder Warrior
- Warwolfe
- Dark Steel

Castles:

Harbottle Castle (Dragonblade)

Tower of London (Lord of the Shadows)

Heroes:

Tate de Lara (Dragonblade)

Sean de Lara (Lord of the Shadows)

Heroines:

Elizabetha "Toby" Cartington de Lara (Dragonblade)

Sheridan St. James de Lara (Lord of the Shadows)

Connections:

- This is one of the biggest houses.
- Earls of Carlisle.
- The name de Lara appears in DRAGONBLADE, FRAGMENTS OF GRACE, ISLAND OF GLASS, THE SAVAGE CURTAIN, THE FALLEN ONE, LORD OF WAR: BLACK ANGEL, BEAST, and ARCHANGEL.
- There are two branches of the de Lara family. The first branch is the Lords of the Trilaterals, which stemmed from Luc de Lara, who came over with the Duke of Normandy (see WARWOLFE for this character). The de Laras come from Spain, and Luc de Lara was the Count of Boucau. One of the direct descendants of this branch is Sean de Lara (LORD OF THE SHADOWS). You also meet Sean's father and brother in ARCHANGEL, and the Lords of the Trilaterals are discussed a bit in that book, too. The second branch of the de Lara family is the Earls of Carlisle (DRAGONBLADE), because Tate de Lara was adopted by the de Lara family. Being the bastard son of Edward I, the king sent his infant son to the de Laras to both shield him and take care of him, so that branch of the family is de Lara in name only – by blood, they are Plantagenet. Therefore, Shrewsbury is not the Dragonblade/Earl of Carlisle branch, but the Sean de Lara branch. DARK STEEL takes place three hundred years after Lord of the

Shadows, but I think it's particularly cool that Dane Stoneley de Russe is now the Lord of the Trinity Castles as well as the Duke of Shrewsbury. Sean de Lara's family properties and family legacy are in the hands of a competent de Russe.

- In BEAST, the hero's mother is a de Lara and his cousin, also a de Lara, serves with him.

- Alexander de Lara, twin son of Tate & Toby de Lara, appears in THE FALLEN ONE and LORD OF WAR: BLACK ANGEL.

- Cathlina de Lara de Reyne is the heroine in THE FALLEN ONE. She is a cousin of Tate de Lara. Her sisters, Abechail and Roxane de Lara also appear in THE FALLEN ONE.

- Colm de Lara appears in NIGHTHAWK, as a knight in service to Patrick de Wolfe.

- Dylan de Lara, twin son of Tate & Toby de Lara, appears in THE FALLEN ONE, THE SAVAGE CURTAIN, and LORD OF WAR: BLACK ANGEL.

- Grier de Lara de Russe, heroine of DARK STEEL, is the last of the de Lara family, the Lords of the Trinity Castles (or Lords of the Trilaterals, as they are also called). There are two branches of the de Lara family.

- The first branch is the Lords of the Trilaterals, which stemmed from Luc de Lara, who came over with the Duke of Normandy (see WARWOLFE for this character). The de Laras come from Spain, and Luc de Lara was the Count of Boucau. One of the direct descendants of this branch is Sean de Lara (LORD OF THE SHADOWS). You also meet Sean's father and brother in ARCHANGEL, and the Lords of the Trilaterals are discussed a bit in that book, too.

- The second branch of the de Lara family is the Earls of Carlisle (DRAGONBLADE), because Tate de Lara was adopted by the de Lara family. Being the bastard son of Edward I, the king sent his infant son to the de Laras to both shield him and take care of him, so that branch of the family is de Lara in name only – by blood, they are Plantagenet.

- Therefore, Shrewsbury is not the Dragonblade/Earl of Carlisle branch, but the Sean de Lara branch. This book takes place three hundred years after Lord of the Shadows, but I think it's particularly cool that Dane is now the Lord of the Trinity Castles as well as the Duke of Shrewsbury. I think Sean de Lara would have been very proud, and comforted, knowing that his family properties and family legacy are in the hands of a competent de Russe. Since my books cover approximately 450 years (the entire stretch of the High Middle Ages), sometimes there are centuries between books, especially with descendants, and the House of de Russe is my latest (most recent) house. They kind of close up the Medieval World and take us into the Tudor World.

- Heath de Lara is a knight serving Weston de Royans in TO THE LADY BORN.

- Isadora de Lara, sister of heroine Courtly de Lara de Shera in THE THUNDER KNIGHT and in THE THUNDER WARRIOR, marries Kirk St. Hever, second-in-command to Kellen de Lara.

- Jasper de Lara appears in DARK DESTROYER, and is the son of Liam de Lara, who is Tate de Lara's (DRAGONBLADE) adoptive brother.

- Kellen de Lara, father of Courtly de Lara, heroine of THE THUNDER WARRIOR, is Lord Sherriff of the Southern Marches.

- Kevin de Lara, Sean de Lara's brother, is a secondary character in Archangel.

- Kevin de Lara appears in BY THE UNHOLY HAND and STARLESS.

- Luc de Lara and his wife, Verity de Shera, are the ancestors of the de Lara family in England, and they appear in WARWOLFE.

- Lucas de Lara is a knight in the service of Bastian de Russe in BEAST.
- Marcus de Lara is the commander at Beeston Castle in FRAGMENTS OF GRACE.
- Rosamund de Lara, Jasper de Lara's wife in DARK DESTROYER, is a du Bois from Rhys du Bois' mother's family (SPECTRE OF THE SWORD).
- Sean de Lara is Tate de Lara's ancestor – but not by blood. There is about 150 years between them. Remember that Tate was 'adopted' by the Marcher lords of de Lara because he was the bastard son of Edward I. Sean and Tate are related in name only. Also, the blood relatives of the de Lara family have dark blond hair/blue eyes. Tate is black haired because of his Welsh mother. Any de Laras post-1333 A.D. may have Tate's black hair and Welsh coloring because of his bloodline now throughout the family lines.
- Sean de Lara appears in BY THE UNHOLY HAND.
- Stephen de Lara, father of Sean and Kevin de Lara, appears in ARCHANGEL.
- Stephen of Pembury is a knight serving Tate de Lara, and is the hero of THE SAVAGE CURTAIN. He appears in DRAGONBLADE and THE FALLEN ONE.
- Tate de Lara is the bastard eldest son of Edward I.
- Tate de Lara was a young page in FRAGMENTS OF GRACE.
- Tate de Lara is the premier hero of the Dragonblade Series, a five-book series.
- Teague de Lara is a secondary character in DEVIL'S DOMINION.
- Wesleigh de Lara de Norville appears in THE BEST IS YET TO BE, and is married to Adonis de Norville, son of Paris and Jemma de Norville.

DE LARA FAMILY TREE

Explore the Genealogy Charts below at
http://kathrynleveque.com/genealogy-charts/
Tate de Lara – English Royalty Illegitimate Line
The de Lara Line – Master File
The de Velt – de Bocage – Edlington – de Lara Line – Master File

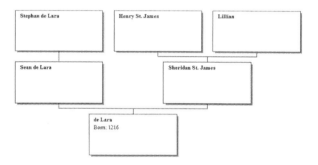

THE HOUSE OF DE LLION

Novels in this House:

Devil's Dominion

Sub-category (novels where the name appears):

- Deep Into Darkness
- Spectre of the Sword
- The Red Lion

Castle:

Comen Castle

Hero:

Bretton de Llion

Heroine:

Allaston de Velt

Connections:

- This is a smaller house.
- The name de Llion also appears in SPECTRE OF THE SWORD and THE RED LION.
- The name du Bois does not appear in DEVIL'S DOMINION.

- The de Llion sisters, Havilland, Madeline, and Amaline, and their father, Roald de Llion, from THE RED LION, are descendants of de Llion family from DEVIL'S DOMINION.

- Allaston de Velt's parents are Ajax & Kellington de Velt, hero and heroine of THE DARK LORD.

- Grayton du Reims is Bretton de Llion's second-in-command, and appears in DEVIL'S DOMINION.

- Havilland de Llion Munro is the heroine of THE RED LION and DEEP INTO DARKNESS. She is the oldest daughter of Roald de Llion. Her father raised her and her two sisters as warriors.

- Rod de Titouan, a secondary character, appears in Spectre of the Sword and Devil's Dominion. The House of de Titouan is related to the House of de Llion and the House of du Bois by marriage and by blood.

- Rod de Titouan is the brother of the hero of Spectre of the Sword, Rhys du Bois.

- William Wellesbourne is a knight serving Keller de Poyer. He appears in NETHERWORLD and DEVIL'S DOMINION.

DE LLION/MUNRO FAMILY TREE

Explore the Genealogy Charts below at
http://kathrynleveque.com/genealogy-charts/
The de Llion – de Titouan – de Velt Line – Master File

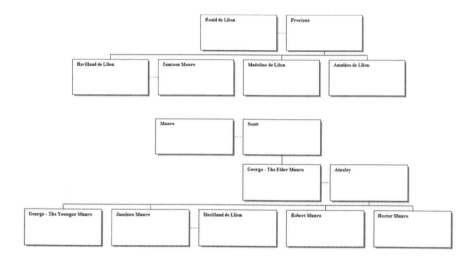

THE HOUSE OF DE LOHR

Novels in this House:

Rise of the Defender

Steelheart

A Blesed de Lohr Christmas

Shadowmoor

Silversword

Sub-category (novels where this name appears or cross-over characters appear):

- Archangel
- Devil's Dominion
- Great Protector
- Netherworld
- Shield of Kronos
- Spectre of the Sword
- Tender is the Knight
- The Questing
- The Thunder Knight
- The Thunder Lord
- The Thunder Warrior
- The Wolfe

- Unending Love
- Warwolfe
- While Angels Slept

Castles:

Lioncross Abbey Castle (Rise of the Defender)

Canterbury Castle (Steelheart and Silversword)

Lioncross Abbey (A Blessed de Lohr Christmas)

Shadowmoor Castle (Shadowmoor)

Heroes:

Christopher de Lohr (Rise of the Defender)

David de Lohr (Steelheart)

Daniel de Lohr (Shadowmoor)

Chadwick de Lohr (Silversword)

Heroines:

Dustin Barringdon de Lohr (Rise of the Defender)

Emilie de Lohr (Steelheart)

Liselotte de Lohr (Shadowmoor)

Alessandria de Lohr (Silversword)

Connections:

- This is one of the biggest houses.
- Earls of Hereford and Worcester.
- The name de Lohr is in many novels as secondary characters.
- The House of de Lohr is the name of secondary characters in GREAT PROTECTOR. There is a familial relationship, but it is distant and undefined.

- In GODSPEED, Christopher and David de Lohr make an appearance.
- In SHIELD OF KRONOS, Christopher de Lohr and David de Lohr appear.
- In STEELHEART, knights from Christopher de Lohr's stable make brief appearances or are briefly mentioned: Max and Anthony de Velt, Jeffrey Kessler, Nicholas de Burg, Sean de Lara, and Guy de la Rosa
- In SHADOWMOOR, the de Royans family features prominently. Their son, Brighton de Royans, was the antagonist in Unending Love.
- In SILVERSWORD, the following characters make an appearance: Bose de Moray, Gallus de Shera, Maximus de Shera, Tiberius de Shera, Davyss de Winter, and Daniel de Lohr.
- The parents of David and Christopher, Myles de Lohr and Valeria du Reims de Lohr, are secondary characters in WHILE ANGELS SLEPT.
- Adalind de Lohr de Aston is the granddaughter of David de Lohr, and she's the heroine of UNENDING LOVE.
- Aidric St. John is a knight serving in King Henry's Guard of Six in SILVERSWORD.
- Alexander de Lohr appears in DARK DESTROYER.
- Alys de Titouan appears in ShadowWolfe.
- Andra, a Welshwoman from the village, appears in A BLESSED DE LOHR CHRISTMAS.
- Anthony and Max de Velt, twin brothers, are in service to Christopher de Lohr and appear in RISE OF THE DEFENDER and STEELHEART.
- Becket, Tobias, Brend, and Thad de Lohr appear in THE RED LION.

- Brentford le Bec is a knight in STEELHEART.
- Cabot de Venter is a new knight in service of Christopher de Lohr in A BLESSED DE LOHR CHRISTMAS.
- Cassian de Velt, son of Ajax and Kellington de Velt, appears in A BLESSED DE LOHR CHRISTMAS.
- Charlotte "Honey" de Lohr, youngest daughter of Christopher & Dustin de Lohr, hero and heroine of RISE OF THE DEFENDER, is the matriarch of Gallus, Maximus, and Tibierius de Shera. She appears in THE THUNDER LORD and THE THUNDER WARRIOR.
- Christopher de Lohr has a major secondary role in DEVIL'S DOMINION.
- Christopher de Lohr is a young general in Juston de Royans' army in LORD OF WINTER.
- Christopher de Lohr appears in BY THE UNHOLY HAND, THE MOUNTAIN DARK, and STARLESS.
- Christopher de Lohr, grandson of Christopher de Lohr (RISE OF THE DEFENDER) appears in ShadowWolfe.
- Daniel de Lohr is an older man when he appears in NIGHTHAWK.
- David de Lohr is a major secondary character in RISE OF THE DEFENDER, ARCHANGEL, and UNENDING LOVE.
- David de Lohr is a young knight serving in Juston de Royans' army in LORD OF WINTER.
- David de Lohr appears in BY THE UNHOLY HAND.
- Dirk d'Vant appears as King Henry's Guard of Six in SILVERSWORD.
- Douglas de Lohr is a secondary character in TENDER IS THE KNIGHT.

- Edward de Wolfe, one of Christopher's closest friends, is the father of William de Wolfe (THE WOLFE).

- Gabrielle de Havilland Burton, former wife of Charles de Havilland, Earl of Fenwark, marries Marcus Burton in RISE OF THE DEFENDER. She also appears in STEELHEART and A BLESSED DE LOHR CHRISTMAS.

- Gerid du Reims is second-in-command of the Canterbury troops, and appears in SHADOWMOOR.

- James de Lohr appears in SWORDS AND SHIELDS.

- James de Lohr is a secondary character in THE QUESTING as a grandson of Christopher de Lohr.

- Jorden de Russe is a knight and friend to Chad de Lohr in SILVERSWORD.

- Kerk le Sander, hero of IMMORTAL SEA, appears as a knight in NIGHTHAWK.

- Kristoph de Lohr, the ancestor of the de Lohrs in England, appears in WARWOLFE.

- Leeton de Shera is a knight in service to Christopher de Lohr. He appears in RISE OF THE DEFENDER and STEELHEART.

- Luc Summerlin served Simon de Montfort as King Henry III's primary jailor in SILVERSWORD.

- Maddoc du Bois is still Captain of the Guard for David de Lohr.

- Marc de Russe is a knight serving Christopher de Lohr in SHADOWMOOR.

- Marcus Burton appears in RISE OF THE DEFENDER, STEELHEART, and A BLESSED DE LOHR CHRISTMAS.

- Max de Velt appears in RISE OF THE DEFENDER, STEELHEART, and A BLESSED DE LOHR CHRISTMAS. He is a knight in service to Marcus Burton.

- Myles de Lohr, the father of Christopher and David de Lohr, first appears in WHILE ANGELS SLEPT.
- Rhun du Bois, son of Maddoc du Bois (UNENDING LOVE) appears in SILVERSWORD.
- Valeria du Reims de Lohr, the mother of Christopher and David, is a female knight in WHILE ANGELS SLEPT.

DE LOHR FAMILY TREE

Explore the Genealogy Chart below at
http://kathrynleveque.com/genealogy-charts/
du Reims, De Lohrs, Hage – Wall Chart
Cassian de Velt – Brielle de Lohr Family
Myles de Lohr Family Line – Master File

THE HOUSE OF DE LONG

Novels in this House:

By the Unholy Hand

Sub-category (novels where the same name or cross-over characters appear):

- The Promise
- The Mountain Dark

Castles:

Chalford Hill Castle

Heroes:

Maxton de Long

Heroines:

Andressa du Bose

Connections:

- This is a small house.
- Part of the Unholy Trinity, Executioner Knights series.
- Maxton de Long is also known as Maxton of Loxbeare.
- Achilles de Dere is one of the Executioner Knights, and appears in BY THE UNHOLY HAND.

- Alexander "Sherry" de Sherrington is one of the Executioner Knights and appears in BY THE UNHOLY HAND.

- Bric MacRohan appears in BY THE UNHOLY HAND.

- Christopher de Lohr appears in BY THE UNHOLY HAND.

- Cullen de Nerra appears in BY THE UNHOLY HAND.

- Dashiell du Reims appears in BY THE UNHOLY HAND.

- David de Lohr appears in BY THE UNHOLY HAND.

- Gart Forbes appears in BY THE UNHOLY HAND.

- Kevin de Lara appears in BY THE UNHOLY HAND.

- Kress de Rhydian is one of the Executioner Knights, and appears in BY THE UNHOLY HAND.

- Sean de Lara appears in BY THE UNHOLY HAND.

Maxton of Loxbeare – De Long Family Tree

Explore the Genealogy Chart below at
http://kathrynleveque.com/genealogy-charts/
Loxbeare Family File

THE HOUSE OF DE MORAY

Novels in this House:

Shield of Kronos

The Gorgon

Sub-category (novels where this name appears or cross-over characters appear):

- Fragments of Grace
- Silversword
- The Lords of Thunder Trilogy
- Warwolfe

Castle:

Chaldon Castle (The Gorgon)

Hero:

Garret de Moray (Shield of Kronos)

Bose de Moray (The Gorgon)

Heroine:

Lyssia du Bose (Shield of Kronos)

Summer du Bonne (The Gorgon)

Connections:

- This is a smaller house.
- (See House of Pembury) Bose is the great-grandfather of Stephen of Pembury.
- Bose and his son, Garran de Moray, feature prominently in SILVERSWORD.
- Bose is the father-in-law to Tiberius de Shera (THUNDER KNIGHT) through his daughter Douglass.
- Bose appears in THE THUNDER WARRIOR and THE THUNDER KNIGHT.
- Christopher de Lohr, hero of RISE OF THE DEFENDER, is in SHIELD OF KRONOS.
- David de Lohr (STEELHEART) is in SHIELD OF KRONOS.
- Garren de Moray, son of Bose & Summer de Moray, appears in THE THUNDER LORDS Trilogy.
- Garret de Moray, hero of SHIELD OF KRONOS, is the father of Bose de Moray.
- Gart Forbes, hero of ARCHANGEL, is in SHIELD OF KRONOS.
- Gavin de Nerra, of the House of de Nerra, is in SHIELD OF KRONOS.
- Juliana de Nerra, of the House of de Nerra, is in SHIELD OF KRONOS.
- Knox Penden, from the Stewards of Rochester, related to the House of du Reim, is in SHIELD OF KRONOS.
- Marc de Moray marries Atia de Shera, and they become the ancestors of the de Moray family in England. They appear in WARWOLFE.
- Max de Velt appears in SHIELD OF KRONOS.
- Rhys du Bois, hero of SPECTRE OF THE SWORD, is in SHIELD OF KRONOS.

- Rickard de Moray, older brother of Garret de Moray, is in SHIELD OF KRONOS.

- Rolf de Moray is captain of King Henry's Household Troops in THE WOLFE.

- Sable de Moray, daughter of Bose & Summer, marries Cassius de Shera in THE THUNDER KNIGHT.

- Remy de Moray, from the House of de Moray, appears in LEADER OF TITANS and SEA WOLFE.

- Tristiana de Dere de Moray is the wife of Rickard de Moray in SHIELD OF KRONOS.

DE MORAY FAMILY TREE

Explore the Genealogy Chart below at
http://kathrynleveque.com/genealogy-charts/
The de Moray – de Shera – Pembury Line – Master File

THE HOUSE OF DE NERRA

Novels in this House:

The Falls of Erith

Vestiges of Valor

The Promise

Sub-category (novels where the name appears):

- Beast
- Lord of War: Black Angel
- Realm of Angels

Castle:

Erith Castle (The Falls of Erith)

Selborne Castle (Vestiges of Valor)

Cerenbeau Castle (The Promise)

Hero:

Braxton de Nerra (The Falls of Erith)

Valor "Val" de Nerra (Vestiges of Valor)

Cullen de Nerra (The Promise)

Heroine:

Gray de Montfort Serroux (The Falls of Erith)

Vesper d'Avignon (Vestiges of Valor

Theodora de Rivington de Nerra (The Promise)

Connections:

- This is a big house with moderate connections.
- Brandt de Russe, hero of LORD OF WAR: BLACK ANGEL, marries Braxton and Gray's granddaughter.
- Braxton is the great-great-great grandfather of Bastian de Russe, hero of BEAST.
- A young Cullen de Nerra appears briefly in REALM OF ANGELS.
- Cullen de Nerra, the son of Valor de Nerra, appears in BY THE UNHOLY HAND.
- Dacian d'Vant is Captain of the Guard at Winchester Castle in VESTIGES OF VALOR.
- Gavin de Nerra appears in SHIELD OF KRONOS and GODSPEED. He is the son of Valor de Nerra.
- Geoff de Mandeville is a knight serving Braxton de Nerra.
- Gray de Montfort Serroux is the granddaughter of Simon de Montfort.
- Juliana de Nerra de Garr, heroine of REALM OF ANGELS, is the sister of Gavin de Nerra and appears in SHIELD OF KRONOS.
- Kenan de Poyer is a knight serving Val de Nerra in VESTIGES OF VALOR.
- Mayne de Garr is a knight serving Valor de Nerra in VESTIGES OF VALOR.
- Olivier d'Avignon is a knight in DEVIL'S DOMINION.
- Sean de Lara appears in THE PROMISE.
- Stephan d'Avignon is a knight serving Jasper de Lara in DARK DESTROYER.
- Tobias Aston, who is the grandson of Dallas Aston (THE FALLS OF ERITH) appears in DARK DESTROYER.
- Valor, Vesper, Gabriel, Charlotte, Cullen, Sophia, and Theo de Nerra appear in REALM OF ANGELS.

DE NERRA/DE RUSSE FAMILY TREE

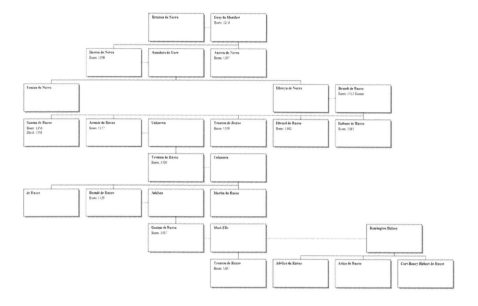

Aston Family Tree

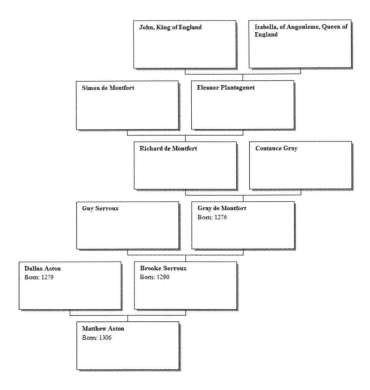

De Nerra/d'Avignon/de Garr Family Tree

Explore the Genealogy Chart below at
http://kathrynleveque.com/genealogy-charts/
The de Nerra Line

THE HOUSE OF DE POYER

Novels in this House:

Netherworld

Sub-category (novels where this name or same characters appear):

- Devil's Dominion
- The Whispering Night

Castle:

Nether Castle

Hero:

Keller de Poyer

Heroine:

Chrystobel d'Einen

Connections:

- This is a smaller house.
- The de Lohr brothers are mentioned in NETHERWORLD.
- Ewan de Poyer is a knight serving Kaspian St. Hever in QUEEN OF LOST STARS.
- Gart Forbes, hero of ARCHANGEL, appears in NETHERWORLD as a young man.

- Keller de Poyer also appears in DEVIL'S DOMINION and THE WHISPERING NIGHT.
- Kenan de Poyer is a knight serving Valor de Nerra in VESTIGES OF VALOR.
- Reece de Poyer is a knight serving Kaspian St. Hever in QUEEN OF LOST STARS.
- Rhys du Bois, hero of SPECTRE OF THE SWORD, appears in NETHERWORLD.
- William Wellesbourne, a forefather of Matthew Wellesbourne of THE WHITE LORD OF WELLESBOURNE, appears in DEVIL'S DOMINION.

DE POYER FAMILY TREE

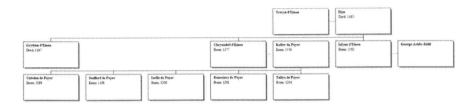

THE HOUSE OF DE REYNE

Novels in this House:

Guardian of Darkness

The Fallen One

With Dreams Only of You – Series

Sub-category (novels where the same name or cross-over characters appear):

- Lord of War: Black Angel
- Warwolfe

Castles:

Prudhoe Castle (Guardian of Darkness)

No castle (The Fallen One)

Heroes:

Creed de Reyne (Guardian of Darkness)

Mathias de Reyne (The Fallen One)

Eryx de Reyne (With Dreams Only of You Series)

Heroines:

Carington Kerr de Reyne (Guardian of Darkness)

Cathlina de Lara de Reyne (The Fallen One)

Frederica de Titouan (With Dreams Only of You Series)

Connections:

- This is a big house.
- Beauson de Velt is a knight serving Saer de Lara in THE FALLEN ONE.
- Broderick de Velt appears in WITH DREAMS ONLY OF YOU Series.
- Brodie de Reyne appears in DARKWOLFE.
- Cathlina de Lara de Reyne is a cousin to Tate de Lara of DRAGONBLADE.
- Frederica de Titouan de Reyne is a cousin to the de Velt family at Pelinom Castle.
- Hayes de Reyne is a big knight in the service of William de Wolfe in BLACKWOLFE.
- Lancelot "Lance" de Reyne is the ancestor of the de Reyne family in England, and appears in WARWOLFE.
- Magnus de Reyne, firstborn son of Mathias & Cathlina de Reyne, marries Brandt de Russe's daughter (LORD OF WAR: BLACK ANGEL), Rosalind de Russe.
- Ridge de Reyne, personal bodyguard to King Alexander, appears in THE RED FURY.
- Scott de Wolfe, twin son of William & Jordan de Wolfe from THE WOLFE, appears in WITH DREAMS ONLY OF YOU Series.

DE REYNE/DE LARA FAMILY TREE

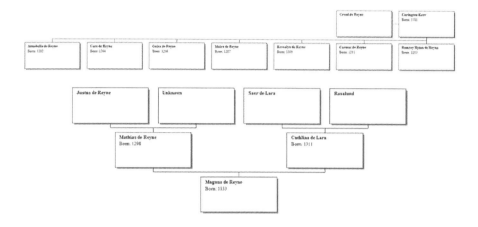

THE HOUSE OF DE RHYDIAN

Novels in this House:

The Mountain Dark

Sub-category (novels where the same name or cross-over characters appear):

- By the Unholy Hand
- The Promise

Castles:

Castle Rising (The Mountain Dark)

Seton Castle (The Mountain Dark)

Heroes:

Kress de Rhydian

Heroines:

Cadelyn "Cadie" of Vendotia

Connections:

- This is a small house.
- The De Rhydian family is related to the St. Hever family in Cumbria.
- Part of the Unholy Trinity, Executioner Knights series.

- Kress de Rhydian, hero of The Mountain Dark, also appears in BY THE UNHOLY HAND.

- Achilles de Dere, part of the Unholy Trinity and Executioner Knights, appears in THE MOUNTAIN DARK.

- Alexander "Sherry" de Sherrington, part of the Unholy Trinity and Executioner Knights, appears in THE MOUNTAIN DARK.

- Antoninus de Shera, the father of Gallus, Maximus, and Tiberius (the Lords of Thunder), appears as a young man in THE MOUNTAIN DARK.

- Atilius de Shera appears in THE MOUNTAIN DARK.

- Bric MacRohan appears in THE MOUNTAIN DARK.

- Christopher de Lohr appears in THE MOUNTAIN DARK.

- Delesse de Winter Summerlin is the garrison commander's wife at Castle Rising.

- Edward de Wolfe, the father of William de Wolfe (THE WOLFE) appears in THE MOUNTAIN DARK.

- Fabius de Shera appears in THE MOUNTAIN DARK.

- Max de Velt appears in THE MOUNTAIN DARK.

- Padriag Summerlin is garrison commander at Castle Rising.

- Tatius de Shera appears in THE MOUNTAIN DARK.

DE RHYDIAN FAMILY TREE

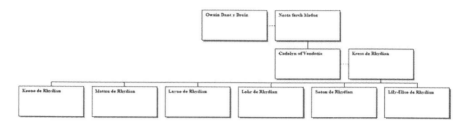

THE HOUSE OF DE ROYANS

Novels in this House:

To The Lady Born (Lords of de Royans Book 1)

Lord of Winter (Lords of de Royans Book 2)

Sub-category (novels where the same name or cross-over characters appear):

- The Iron Knight
- Unending Love

Castles:

Hedingham Castle (To The Lady Born)

Netherghyll Castle (To The Lady Born and Lord of Winter)

Bowes Castle (Lord of Winter)

The Lyceum (The Centurion)

Makendon Castle (The Centurion)

Heroes:

Weston de Royans (To the Lady Born)

Juston de Royans (Lord of Winter)

Torston de Royans (The Centurion)

Heroines:

Amalie de Vere de Royans (To The Lady Born)

Emera la Marche de Royans (Lord of Winter)

Alyx de Ameland (The Centurion)

Connections:

- This is a medium House.
- All of the de Royans men have names ending in 'ton'.
- Achilles de Dere is part of the "Unholy Trinity" in Juston de Royans' army in LORD OF WINTER.
- Alys de Royans de Wolfe, in BLACKWOLFE, is the wife of Gerard de Wolfe. He is the nephew of William de Wolfe. Alys de Royans' parents are Torston and Alyx de Royans, the hero and heroine of THE CENTURION.
- Brighton de Royans appears in UNENDING LOVE as the antagonist. His siblings, Caston and Glennie, and father, Easton de Royans, appear in SHADOWMOOR.
- Christopher de Lohr is a young general in Juston de Royans' army in LORD OF WINTER.
- Colton de Royans marries Emmaline de Gournay, stepdaughter of Lucien de Russe, at the end of THE IRON KNIGHT.
- David de Lohr is a young knight serving in Juston de Royans' army in LORD OF WINTER.
- Erik de Russe appears in LORD OF WINTER. He is the best friend of Gart Forbes, and is the brother of Emberley de Russe. Gart & Emberley de Russe is the hero and heroine of ARCHANGEL.
- Gart Forbes, hero of ARCHANGEL, is Juston de Royans' squire in LORD OF WINTER.
- Heath de Lara is a knight serving Weston de Royans in TO THE LADY BORN.
- Juston de Royans is a young knight in THE LION OF THE NORTH.

- Kenneth of Pembury is a knight appearing in TO THE LADY BORN.
- Paeton de Royans, the right-hand man of Simon de Montfort, appears in THE THUNDER WARRIOR.
- Marcus Burton is a young general in Juston de Royans' army in LORD OF WINTER.
- Range de Winter is a knight appearing in TO THE LADY BORN.
- Richmond le Bec, hero of Great Protector, makes an appearance in TO THE LADY BORN.
- Simon Wellesbourne is a knight appearing in TO THE LADY BORN.
- Uriah de Royans is a knight serving the de Gare family in THE WARRIOR POET.
- Weston de Royans becomes Baron Cononley in 1392, and Constable of North Yorkshire and of the Northern Dales.
- Weston & Amalie de Royans appear in THE IRON KNIGHT, as their son, Colton de Royans, is a major secondary character in that novel.
- William de Wolfe appears in THE CENTURION as a young knight.
- Paris de Norville appears in THE CENTURION as a young knight.

DE RUSSE/DE ROYANS FAMILY TREE

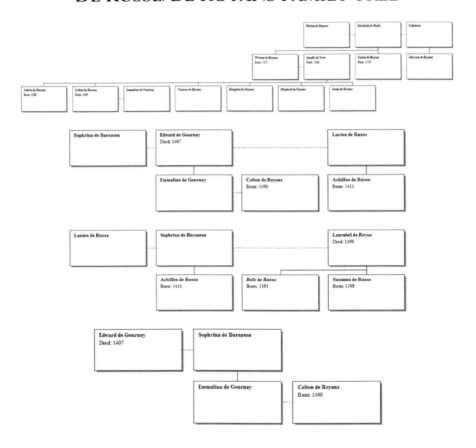

THE HOUSE OF DE RUSSE

Novels in this House:

Lord of War: Black Angel

The Iron Knight

Beast

The Dark One: Dark Knight

Dark Moon

Dark Steel

A De Russe Christmas Miracle

Emma

Sub-category (novels where the same name or cross-over characters appear):

- Great Protector
- The White Lord of Wellesbourne
- To The Lady Born
- Warwolfe

Castles:

Guildford Castle (Lord of War: Black Angel)

Melesse Castle (Lord of War: Black Angel)

Spelthorne Castle (The Iron Knight)

Braidwood Manor (Beast)

Mt. Holyoak Castle (The Dark One: Dark Knight)

Dorset Castle (Dark Moon)

Stretford Castle (Dark Moon)

Devrill Castle (Dark Moon and A De Russe Christmas Miracle)

Stretford Castle (Dark Steel)

Blackmoor Hall (Emma)

Heroes:

Brandt de Russe (Lord of War: Black Angel)

Lucien de Russe (The Iron Knight)

Bastian de Russe (Beast)

Gaston de Russe (The Dark One: Dark Knight)

Trenton de Russe (Dark Moon)

Dane Stonely de Russe (Dark Steel)

Asher "Ash" de Russe (Emma)

Heroines:

Ellowyn de Nerra de Russe (Lord of War: Black Angel)

Sophina de Barenton de Russe (The Iron Knight)

Gisella le Bec de Russe (Beast)

Remington Stoneley de Russe (The Dark One: Dark Knight)

Lysabel Wellesbourne de Russe (Dark Moon)

Grier de Lara de Russe (Dark Steel)

Emma Fairweather (Emma)

Connections:

- This is one of the biggest houses.
- This house has the most heroes with their own novels.
- Because they come chronologically very late in the timeline of Le Veque novels, there aren't many opportunities to use cross-over

characters. The de Russe family dominates the courts of the Black Prince, Henry VI, and Henry Tudor.

- Through battle and falling out of favor, several nobility titles have passed through their hands including the Duke of Warminster and the Duke of Exeter.

- The de Russes are intertwined with the House of Wellesbourne. They are related (established in BEAST and DARK MOON).

- Grier de Lara de Russe is the last of the de Lara family, the Lords of the Trinity Castles (or Lords of the Trilaterals, as they are also called). There are two branches of the de Lara family. The first branch is the Lords of the Trilaterals, which stemmed from Luc de Lara, who came over with the Duke of Normandy (see WARWOLFE for this character). The de Laras come from Spain, and Luc de Lara was the Count of Boucau. One of the direct descendants of this branch is Sean de Lara (LORD OF THE SHADOWS). You also meet Sean's father and brother in ARCHANGEL, and the Lords of the Trilaterals are discussed a bit in that book, too. The second branch of the de Lara family is the Earls of Carlisle (DRAGONBLADE), because Tate de Lara was adopted by the de Lara family. Being the bastard son of Edward I, the king sent his infant son to the de Laras to both shield him and take care of him, so that branch of the family is de Lara in name only – by blood, they are Plantagenet. Therefore, Shrewsbury is not the Dragonblade/Earl of Carlisle branch, but the Sean de Lara branch. DARK STEEL takes place three hundred years after Lord of the Shadows, and Dane Stoneley de Russe is now the Lord of the Trinity Castles as well as the Duke of Shrewsbury. Sean de Lara's family properties and family legacy are in the hands of a competent de Russe.

- Aramis de Russe and his wife, Lygia de Shera, are the ancestors of the de Russes in England, and they appear in WARWOLFE.

KATHRYN LE VEQUE

- Augustine de Russe, from the House of de Russe is a quartermaster and appears in LEADER OF TITANS and SEA WOLFE.
- Brennan St. Hever is a knight serving Brandt de Russe. He is the firstborn son of Kenneth and Aubrielle St. Hever from ISLAND OF GLASS.
- Colton de Royans first made his appearance at the age of two in TO THE LADY BORN, and is a major secondary character in THE IRON KNIGHT. His parents, Weston & Amalie de Royans, also make an appearance in that novel.
- Dallan le Mon is a knight in service to Brandt de Russe, and appears in LORD OF WAR: BLACK ANGEL.
- Darrien de Russe is a knight serving Simon de Montfort in LESPADA.
- Daston du Reims is the Captain of Shrewsbury's army, and he appears in DARK STEEL.
- Emberley de Russe de Moyans marries Gart Forbes in ARCHANGEL.
- Ellowyn de Nerra is the great-granddaughter of Simon de Montfort.
- Erik de Russe, brother of Emberley de Russe, appears in LORD OF WINTER. His sister, Emberley, marries Gart Forbes, and they are the hero and heroine of ARCHANGEL.
- Evan St. Hever, younger brother of Brennan, also serves Brandt de Russe towards the end of LORD OF WAR: BLACK ANGEL.
- Gabriel of Pembury appears in THE IRON KNIGHT, as a knight in service to Lucien de Russe.
- Garreth de Lara, Duke of Shrewsbury and Lord of the Trinity Castles, is Grier de Lara's father in DARK STEEL. Grier is the heiress so her husband, Dane Stoneley de Russe, becomes the next Duke of Shrewsbury.

68

- Gaston de Russe appears as a young knight in WALLS OF BABYLON.
- Gaston de Russe appears in THE WHITE LORD OF WELLESBOURNE.
- Hughston de Russe appears in THE THUNDER LORDS Trilogy.
- Jorden de Russe is a knight and friend to Chad de Lohr in SILVERSWORD.
- Jorrin de Bretagne appears in THE IRON KNIGHT. He is a direct descendant of Cortez de Bretagne.
- Lucas de Lara is a knight serving Bastian de Russe in BEAST.
- Marc de Russe is a knight serving Christopher de Lohr in SHADOWMOOR.
- Maxim de Russe, son of Bastian de Russe (BEAST), appears in THE LION OF THE NORTH.
- Patrick de Russe, cousin of Gaston de Russe, appears in THE WHITE LORD OF WELLESBOURNE.
- Richmond le Bec (GREAT PROTECTOR) is the father of Gisella le Bec and makes an appearance in BEAST and in THE IRON KNIGHT.
- Stefan le Bec is a knight in service to Brandt de Russe, and appears in LORD OF WAR: BLACK ANGEL.
- Syler de Poyer is in service to the Duke of Shrewsbury, and he appears in DARK STEEL.

DE NERRA/DE RUSSE FAMILY TREE

Explore the Genealogy Chart below at
http://kathrynleveque.com/genealogy-charts/
De Russe – le Bec – Wellesbourne #2
Le Bec – de Russe – Wellesbourne #1
The de Russe Line – Master File

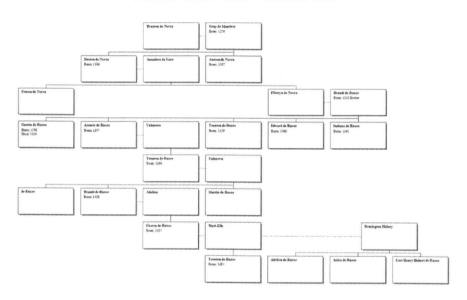

THE HOUSE OF DE SHERA

Novels in this House:

Serpent

The Thunder Lord (Lords of Thunder: The de Shera Brotherhood
    trilogy)

The Thunder Warrior (Lords of Thunder: The de Shera Brotherhood
    trilogy)

The Thunder Knight (Lords of Thunder: The de Shera Brotherhood
    trilogy)

**Sub-category (novels where the same name or cross-over characters
appear):**

- DarkWolfe
- Lespada
- Rise of the Defender
- Silversword
- The Gorgon
- The Wolfe
- Warwolfe

Castles:

Rhydilian Castle (Serpent)

Isenhall Castle (The Lords of Thunder Trilogy)

Heroes:

Bhrodi ap Gaerwen de Shera (Serpent)

Gallus de Shera (The Thunder Lord)

Maximus de Shera (The Thunder Warrior)

Tiberius de Shera (The Thunder Knight)

Heroines:

Penelope de Wolfe de Shera (Serpent)

Jeniver ferch Gaerwen de Shera (The Thunder Lord)

Courtly de Lara de Shera (The Thunder Warrior)

Douglass de Moray de Shera (The Thunder Knight)

Connections:

- This is a smaller house even though they are related to de Wolfe. At some point, other books will bear the de Shera name but as of this edition, de Shera is still a smaller house.
- Hereditary kings of Anglesey (Welsh house of ap Gaerwen)
- Serpent has the distinction of having two major secondary characters from THE WOLFE in it – Kieran Hage and Paris de Norville.
- In SILVERSWORD, Gallus, Max, and Tiberius are major secondary characters.
- Antillius de Shera is the ancestor of the de Shera family in England, and he appears in WARWOLFE.
- Antoninus de Shera, the father of Gallus, Maximus, and Tiberius (Lords of Thunder) appears as a young man in THE MOUNTAIN DARK.
- Atia de Shera, and her husband, Marc de Moray, are the ancestors of the de Moray family in England, and they appear in WARWOLFE.

- Atilius de Shera commands the de Shera armies in THE MOUNTAIN DARK.

- Bose de Moray, hero of THE GORGON, appears in THE THUNDER WARRIOR and THE THUNDER KNIGHT.

- Bowen de Shera is a young squire serving his cousin, William de Wolfe, in SWORDS AND SHIELDS. His parents are Bhrodi and Penelope de Shera.

- Cassius de Shera, bastard son of Maximus de Shera, and husband to Sable de Moray de Shera, appears in DARKWOLFE.

- Charlotte "Honey" de Lohr, youngest daughter of Christopher & Dustin de Lohr, hero and heroine of RISE OF THE DEFENDER, is the matriarch of Gallus, Maximus, and Tibierius de Shera. She appears in THE THUNDER LORD and THE THUNDER WARRIOR.

- Davyss de Winter appears in THE THUNDER LORDS Trilogy.

- Douglass de Moray, heroine of THE THUNDER KNIGHT, is the daughter of Bose & Summer de Moray, hero and heroine of THE GORGON.

- Fabius de Shera appears in THE MOUNTAIN DARK.

- Garren de Moray, son of Bose & Summer de Moray, hero and heroine of THE GORGON, appears in THE THUNDER LORDS Trilogy.

- Grayson de Winter, father of Davyss de Winter, appears in THE THUNDER LORDS Trilogy.

- Hughston de Russe appears in THE THUNDER LORDS Trilogy.

- Isobeau de Shera de Wolfe, heroine of THE LION OF THE NORTH, is a descendant of Maximus de Shera (THE THUNDER WARRIOR).

- Kellen de Lara, father of Courtly de Lara, heroine of THE THUNDER WARRIOR, is Lord Sherriff of the Southern Marches.

- Lancelot "Lance" de Reyne is the ancestor of the de Reyne family in England, and appears in WARWOLFE.

- Leeton de Shera is a knight in service to Christopher de Lohr. He appears in RISE OF THE DEFENDER and STEELHEART.

- Lygia de Shera and her husband Aramis de Russe are the ancestors of the de Russes in England, and they appear in WARWOLFE.

- Paeton de Royans, the right-hand man of Simon de Montfort, appears in THE THUNDER WARRIOR.

- Sable de Moray, daughter of Bose & Summer de Moray, marries Cassius de Shera in THE THUNDER KNIGHT.

- Sable de Moray de Shera appears in DARKWOLFE.

- Scott de Wolfe, twin son of William & Jordan de Wolfe, hero and heroine of THE WOLFE, appears in THE LORDS OF THUNDER Trilogy.

- Spencer de Shera appears in THE DARKLAND. He marries Micheline le Bec, sister of Mara le Bec, who is the heroine of THE DARKLAND.

- Stefan du Bois, son of Maddoc & Adalind du Bois, hero and heroine of UNENDING LOVE, appears in THE THUNDER LORDS Trilogy.

- Summer de Moray, heroine of THE GORGON, appears in THE THUNDER KNIGHT.

- Tatius de Shera is the Earl of Ellesemere and appears in THE MOUNTAIN DARK.

- Troy de Wolfe, twin son of William & Jordan de Wolfe, hero and heroine of THE WOLFE, appears in THE LORDS OF THUNDER Trilogy.

- Verity de Shera and her husband, Luc de Lara, are the ancestors of the de Lara family in England, and they appear in WARWOLFE.

- William de Wolfe, hero of THE WOLFE, appears in THE THUNDER LORDS Trilogy.

GALLUS DE SHERA FAMILY TREE

Explore the Genealogy Chart below at
http://kathrynleveque.com/genealogy-charts/
The de Moray – de Shera – Pembury Line – Master File
The Lords of Thunder Family Line – Master File

THE HOUSE OF DE TITOUAN

Novels in this House:

None

Sub-category (novels where the same name or cross-over characters appear):

- Devil's Dominion
- ShadowWolfe
- Spectre of the Sword
- Tender is the Knight

Connections:

- This is a smaller house – only secondary characters at this point (1/2017).
- Alys de Titouan appears in SHADOWWOLFE.
- Dylan de Titouan is the youngest son of Renard and Orlaith de Titouan. Appears in SPECTRE OF THE SWORD.
- Effington de Velt de Titouan is the daughter of Jax & Kellington de Velt, and marries Rod de Titouan in DEVIL'S DOMINION.
- Frederica de Titouan de Reyne, the heroine of WITH DREAMS ONLY OF YOU Series, is a cousin to the de Velts at Pelinom Castle.

- Orlaith de Llion de Titouan is the mother of Rhys du Bois from her forced liaison with the Duke of Navarre. She married Renard de Titouan and they became the parents of Rod, Carys, and Dylan. She appears in SPECTRE OF THE SWORD.

- Renard de Titouan is the stepfather to Rhys du Bois, and appears in SPECTRE OF THE SWORD.

- Rhett de Titouan is the older brother of Renard de Titouan and appears in SPECTRE OF THE SWORD.

- Riston de Titouan is a knight serving Dennis d'Vant in TENDER IS THE KNIGHT.

- Rod de Titouan is the first cousin to Bretton de Llion (DEVIL'S DOMINION) and is the younger half-brother of Rhys du Bois. He appears in DEVIL'S DOMINION and SPECTRE OF THE SWORD.

DE TITOUAN FAMILY TREE

Explore the Genealogy Chart below at

http://kathrynleveque.com/genealogy-charts/
The de Llion – de Titouan – de Velt Line – Master File

THE HOUSE OF DE VELT

Novels in this House:

The Dark Lord (Book One in The Titans Series – it is the only book in
the series published as of 2014)

The Dark Lord's First Christmas

Bay of Fear

**Sub-category (novels where the same name or cross-over characters
appear):**

- Devil's Dominion
- Fragments of Grace
- The Questing

Castle:

Pelinom Castle (The Dark Lord and The Dark Lord's First Christmas)

Baiadepaura Castle (Bay of Fear)

Hero:

Ajax "Jax" de Velt (The Dark Lord and The Dark Lord's First
Christmas)

Tenner de Velt (Bay of Fear)

Heroine:

Kellington Coleby de Velt (The Dark Lord and The Dark Lord's First Christmas)

Annalyla St. Lo de Velt (Bay of Fear)

Connection:

- This is a big house.
- Jax de Velt is a major secondary character in DEVIL'S DOMINION.
- In the contemporary romance DARKLING, I LISTEN, the hero (Archer de Velt Phipps) is descended from the House of de Velt through his mother.
- In THE QUESTING, the heroine's grandfather was Jax de Velt's youngest son.
- Anthony and Max de Velt, twin brothers, are knights in service to Christopher de Lohr, and appear in RISE OF THE DEFENDER and STEELHEART.
- Beauson de Velt is a knight serving Saer de Lara in THE FALLEN ONE.
- Broderick de Velt appears in WITH DREAMS ONLY OF YOU Series.
- Cassian de Velt, son of Ajax and Kellington de Velt, appears in A BLESSED DE LOHR CHRISTMAS.
- Julia de Velt Seton is the mother of Joselyn de Velt Seton Pembury, heroine of THE SAVAGE CURTAIN.
- Lucan de Velt is a secondary character in FRAGMENTS OF GRACE. He is part of the House of de Velt but it is never specified how.
- Max de Velt also appears separately in A BLESSED DE LOHR CHRISTMAS and THE MOUNTAIN DARK.

- Morgan de Velt appears in THE SAVAGE CURTAIN, and is the first cousin of Julia de Velt Seton, mother of Joselyn de Velt Seton Pembury.

- Raleigh "Leigh" MacBeth – He is the Scottish pirate captain of the "Beast of the Sea" and appears in BAY OF FEAR.

- Valeria de Velt de Dere is the heroine in OF LOVE AND LEGEND (part of the Ever My Love collection). Her brother is Mars de Velt, best friend of her husband, Tyren de Dere.

DE VELT FAMILY TREE

Explore the Genealogy Charts below at
http://kathrynleveque.com/genealogy-charts/
The de Velt – de Bocage – Edlington – de Lara Line – Master File
Ajax de Velt Family
Cassian de Velt – Brielle de Lohr Family

THE HOUSE OF DE WINTER

Novels in this House:

Lespada

Swords and Shields

Sub-category (novels where the same name or cross-over characters appear):

- Silversword
- The Questing
- Warwolfe

Castles:

Norwich Castle (Lespada)

Castle Acre Castle (Lespada)

Breckland Castle (Lespada)

Wintercroft Castle (Lespada)

Hollyhock Manor (Lespada)

Thetford Castle (Swords and Shields)

Heroes:

Davyss de Winter (Lespada)

Drake de Winter (Swords and Shields)

Heroines:

Devereux d'Arcy de Winter (Lespada)

Elizaveta du Reims de Winter (Swords and Shields)

Connections:

- This is a medium house but probably the wealthiest of the bunch.
- The secondary knights in LESPADA – de Nogaret, Catesby, and de Ros – are from houses not found anywhere else in Le Veque novels.
- Adam Wellesbourne, father of Matthew Wellesbourne (THE WHITE LORD OF WELLESBOURNE), appears in THE LION OF THE NORTH.
- Alec le Bec appears in THE LION OF THE NORTH.
- Bowen de Shera is a young squire serving his cousin, William de Wolfe, in SWORDS AND SHIELDS. His parents are Bhrodi and Penelope de Shera.
- Darrien de Russe is a knight in service to Simon de Montfort in LESPADA.
- Davyss de Winter and Hugh de Winter are secondary characters in SILVERSWORD.
- Davyss de Winter appears in THE THUNDER LORDS Trilogy.
- Denis de Winter brings his sword, Lespada, with him to fight with William the Conqueror. He is the ancestor of the de Winter family in England and appears in WARWOLFE.
- Delesse de Winter Summerlin appears in THE MOUNTAIN DARK.
- Drake de Winter, son of Davyss and Devereux, is a secondary character in THE QUESTING. He is in the service of Cortez de Bretagne.

- Elizaveta du Reim de Winter's ancestors are from WHILE ANGELS SLEPT.
- Grayson de Winter, father of Davyss de Winter, appears in THE THUNDER LORDS Trilogy.
- James de Lohr appears in SWORDS AND SHIELDS.
- Oliver St. John, son of Christian and Gaithlin of THE WARRIOR POET, appears in SWORDS AND SHIELDS.
- Range de Winter is a knight appearing in TO THE LADY BORN.
- Warenne de Winter, Earl of Thetford, is a descendant of Davyss de Winter, and appears in THE LION OF THE NORTH.
- William de Wolfe, grandson of William de Wolfe (THE WOLFE), through his son Scott de Wolfe, appears in SWORDS AND SHIELDS.

DE WINTER/DU REIMS FAMILY TREE

Explore the Genealogy Charts below at
http://kathrynleveque.com/genealogy-charts/
Katharine de Warrene de Winter – Wall Chart
The du Reims & de Winter Lines
The de Winter Dynasty

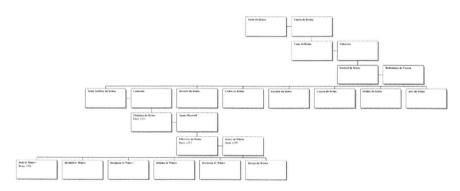

THE HOUSE OF DE WOLFE

Novels in this House:

Warwolfe

The Wolfe

Nighthawk

ShadowWolfe

DarkWolfe

A Joyous de Wolfe Christmas

BlackWolfe

Serpent

A Wolfe Among Dragons

Scorpion

StormWolfe

Sea Wolfe

The Lion of the North

The Best is Yet to Be

Sub-category (novels where the same name or cross-over characters appear):

- Rise of the Defender
- Dark Destroyer
- The Thunder Lords Trilogy

- Unending Love
- Walls of Babylon

Castles:

Warstone Castle (Warwolfe)

Northwood Castle (The Wolfe, Blackwolfe, The Best is Yet to Be)

Castle Questing (The Wolfe, Nighthawk, Blackwolfe, The Best is Yet to Be)

Berwick Castle/Wolfe's Teeth (Nighthawk)

Kale Castle/Wolfe's Den (Nighthawk)

Wark Castle/Wolfe's Eye (Nighthawk)

Monteviot Tower (DarkWolfe)

Canaan Castle (ShadowWolfe)

Castle Questing (A Joyous de Wolfe Christmas)

Carmarthen (A Wolfe Among Dragons)

Hyssington Castle (Dark Destroyer)

Perran Castle (Sea Wolfe)

Rule Water Castle/Wolfe's Lair (The Lion of the North, Nighthawk)

Wark Castle (Stormwolfe)

Heroes:

Gaetan de Wolfe (Warwolfe)

William de Wolfe (The Wolfe)

Patrick de Wolfe (Nighthawk)

Troy de Wolfe (DarkWolfe)

Scott de Wolfe (ShadowWolfe)

James de Wolfe/Blayth the Strong (A Wolfe Among Dragons)

Gates de Wolfe (Dark Destroyer)

Rhoan de Wolfe "Lucifer" (Sea Wolfe)

Atticus de Wolfe (The Lion of the North)

Thomas de Wolfe (Stormwolfe)

Edwarwd de Wolfe (Blackwolfe)

Paris de Norville (The Best is Yet to Be)

Heroines:

Ghislaine of Mercia (Warwolfe)

Jordan Scott de Wolfe (The Wolfe)

Brighton "Bridey" de Favereux de Wolfe (Nighthawk)

Rhoswyn Whitton Kerr de Wolfe (DarkWolfe)

Avrielle du Rennic de Wolfe (ShadowWolfe)

Asmara ferch Cader de Wolfe (A Wolfe Among Dragons)

Kathalin de Wolfe (Dark Destroyer)

Genevieve Efford de Wolfe (Sea Wolfe)

Isobeau de Shera de Wolfe (The Lion of the North)

Maitland de Ryes Bowlin de Wolfe (Stormwolfe)

Cassiopeia de Norville de Wolfe (Blackwolfe)

Jemma Scott Hage de Norville (The Best is Yet to Be)

Connections:

- This is one of the biggest houses.
- The name de Wolfe isn't used as widely throughout Le Veque novels as other names; hence, it is only a 'big' house and not a 'biggest' house. This will change, as future novels have de Wolfe descendants as heroes.
- In SERPENT, we meet most of William and Jordan's children as well as several children from secondary knights in THE WOLFE.
- Adam Wellesbourne is a young knight in THE LION OF THE NORTH.
- Alec le Bec is a knight in THE LION OF THE NORTH.

- Alexander de Lohr appears in DARK DESTROYER.
- Alys de Royans de Wolfe, in BLACKWOLFE, is the wife of Gerard de Wolfe, and he's the nephew of William de Wolfe. Alys' parents are Torston and Alyx de Royans, and are the hero and heroine in THE CENTURION.
- Antillius de Shera is the ancestor of the de Shera family in England, and he appears in WARWOLFE.
- Aramis de Russe and his wife, Lygia de Shera, are the ancestors of the de Russes in England, and they appear in WARWOLFE.
- Atticus de Wolfe is the hero of THE LION OF THE NORTH.
- Bartholomew Wellesbourne is the ancestor of the Wellesbourne family in England, and he appears in WARWOLFE.
- Brodie de Reyne appears in DARKWOLFE.
- Caria de Wolfe is a Welsh princess, born from Tacey ap Gruffydd, sister of Bhrodi de Shera. Tacey's late husband was the last prince of Wales. Caria was given to William and Jordan de Wolfe to raise and for safekeeping.
- Cassius de Shera appears in DARKWOLFE.
- Christopher de Lohr, grandson of Christopher de Lohr (RISE OF THE DEFENDER) appears in SHADOWWOLFE and A WOLFE AMONG DRAGONS.
- Colm de Lara appears in NIGHTHAWK as a knight serving Patrick de Wolfe.
- Corbett Payton-Foster, son of William Payton-Foster from THE WOLFE, appears in A WOLFE AMONG DRAGONS.
- Damian d'Vant appears in NIGHTHAWK as a knight serving Patrick de Wolfe.
- Denis de Winter brings his sword, Lespada, with him to fight with William the Conqueror. He is the ancestor of the de Winter family in England and appears in WARWOLFE.

- Edward de Wolfe, William de Wolfe's father, was Christopher de Lohr's (RISE OF THE DEFENDER) best friend and confidant.

- Edward de Wolfe from THE WOLFE, also appears in GODSPEED and THE MOUNTAIN DARK.

- Felix d'Vant appears in SEA WOLFE.

- Hayes de Reyne, in BLACKWOLFE, is a knight in service of William de Wolfe.

- Isobeau de Shera de Wolfe, heroine of THE LION OF THE NORTH, is a descendant of Maximus de Shera (THE THUNDER WARRIOR).

- Jasper de Lara appears in DARK DESTROYER, and is the son of Liam de Lara, who is Tate de Lara's (DRAGONBLADE) adoptive brother.

- Jean-Pierre du Bois appears in SHADOWWOLFE.

- Kenton le Bec appears in THE LION OF THE NORTH.

- Kristoph de Lohr, the ancestors of the de Lohrs in England, appears in WARWOLFE.

- Kye St. Hever is the ancestor of the St. Hever family in England, and he appears in WARWOLFE.

- Luc de Lara and Verity de Shera, are the ancestors of the de Lara family in England, and they appear in WARWOLFE.

- Marc de Moray marries Atia de Shera, and they become the ancestors of the de Moray family in England. They appear in WARWOLFE.

- Maxim de Russe, son of Bastian de Russe (BEAST), appears in THE LION OF THE NORTH.

- Morgan de Wolfe, the nephew of the Earl of Wolverhampton, is a knight serving Caius d'Avignon in STARLESS.

- Remy de Moray appears in SEA WOLFE.

- Rhoan de Wolfe, of the House of de Wolfe, is the hero of SEA WOLFE, and is otherwise known as 'Lucifer.'
- Rik du Reims, son of the earl of East Anglia, appears in THE LION OF THE NORTH.
- Roan d'Vant is part of King Henry's Household troops in THE WOLFE, and is cousin to Andrew d'Vant, the Red Fury, in THE WOLFE.
- Rolf de Moray appears in THE WOLFE.
- Rosamund de Lara, wife of Jasper de Lara, in DARK DESTROYER, is a du Bois from Rhys du Bois' mother's family (SPECTRE OF THE SWORD).
- Sable de Moray de Shera, daughter of Bose and Summer de Moray, and wife to Cassius de Shera, appears in DARKWOLFE.
- Shaun Summerlin is a knight and brother-in-law to Warenne de Winter in THE LION OF THE NORTH.
- Scott de Wolfe, twin son of William & Jordan de Wolfe, appears in THE THUNDER LORDS Trilogy. He also appears in WITH DREAMS ONLY OF YOU Series.
- Teo du Reims is the ancestor of the du Reims family in England, and he appears in WARWOLFE.
- Thane Alraedson appears in THE WOLFE and is the second-in-command to Andrew d'Vant in THE RED FURY.
- Tobias Aston, in DARK DESTROYER, is the grandson of Dallas Aston (THE FALLS OF ERITH).
- Troy de Wolfe, twin son of William & Jordan de Wolfe, appears in THE THUNDER LORDS Trilogy.
- Warenne de Winter, Earl of Thetford, is a descendant of Davyss de Winter, and appears in LION OF THE NORTH.
- Wesleigh de Lara de Wolfe appears in THE BEST IS YET TO BE, and is married to Adonis de Norville.

- William de Wolfe, hero of THE WOLFE, appears in THE THUNDER LORDS Trilogy.
- William de Wolfe, Paris de Norville, Kieran Hage, and Michael de Bocage are young knights in UNDENDING LOVE.
- William de Wolfe's grandson, through his son Scott de Wolfe, appears in SWORDS AND SHIELDS.
- Sons of de Wolfe – Patrick, Scott, Troy, James, Edward, and Thomas appear in NIGHTHAWK. This novel takes place thirty years after THE WOLFE and is only one generation removed.

De Wolfe Ancestor:	Year they became Earl of Warenton:
Gaetan	1066
Robert	1100
Edward (Robert's son)	1130
Thomas (Son of Edward)	1150
Padraig	Abt 1152
Robert	1155
James (Robert's son)	1160
Robert (James' son)	1180
Edward (Robert's son/William de Wolfe's father)	1200
Robert (Edward's oldest son/William's older brother)	1210

DE WOLFE FAMILY TREE

Explore the Genealogy Charts below at
http://kathrynleveque.com/genealogy-charts/
William de Wolfe Family File
De Norville Wall Chart
The de Moray – de Shera – Pembury Line – Master File
The de Wolfe Line – Master File
The du Reim Family Line – Master File
The Hage Line – Master File

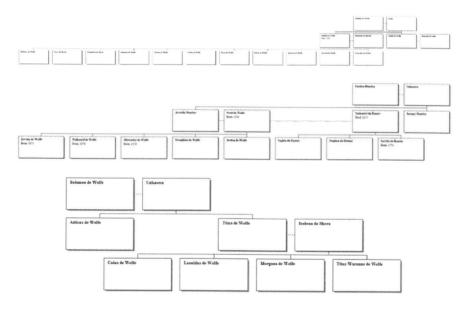

THE HOUSE OF DU BOIS

Novels in this House:

Spectre of the Sword

Unending Love

Sub-category (novels where the same name or cross-over characters appear):

- Kingdom Come
- Netherworld
- Silversword

Castles:

Lioncross Abbey (Spectre of the Sword)

St. Briavel's Castle (Spectre of the Sword)

Ludlow Castle (Spectre of the Sword)

Canterbury Castle (Unending Love)

Heroes:

Rhys du Bois (Spectre of the Sword)

Maddoc du Bois (Unending Love)

Heroines:

Elizabeau du Bois (Spectre of the Sword)

Adalind de Lohr du Bois (Unending Love)

Connections:

- This is a big house

- This his house has the distinction of being the only Le Veque family group that has a father and then a son as heroes in their own novels.

- The name du Bois makes an appearance in RISE OF THE DEFENDER, but it is not from this House.

- Adalind de Lohr de Aston is the granddaughter of David de Lohr.

- Avarine du Bois is the mother of twin girls born out of wedlock from her affair with Davyss de Winter.

- Brydon Forbes, son of Gart & Emberley Forbes, hero and heroine of ARCHANGEL, appears in UNENDING LOVE.

- Gart Forbes, hero of ARCHANGEL, appears in UNENDING LOVE.

- Jean-Pierre du Bois appears in SHADOWWOLFE.

- Maddoc du Bois' mother was a Welsh noblewoman who died during his birth (she was Rhys' first wife).

- Maddoc du Bois is still Captain of the Guard for David de Lohr.

- Maddoc du Bois also appears in SILVERSWORD.

- Margaret "Marble-Head Maggie" du Bois is a secondary character in THE WARRIOR POET. There is an undefined family relationship.

- Jasper de Lara's wife, Rosamund de Lara, in DARK DESTROYER, is a du Bois from Rhys du Bois' mother's family (SPECTRE OF THE SWORD).

- Rhun du Bois, son of Maddoc du Bois, appears in SILVERSWORD.

- Rhys du Bois is a very young man in KINGDOM COME and SHIELD OF KRONOS.

- Rhys du Bois is the bastard son of the Duke of Navarre.

- Rhys du Bois makes an appearance in Netherworld about two years before SPECTRE OF THE SWORD.
- Stefan du Bois, son of Maddoc & Adalind du Bois, hero and heroine of UNENDING LOVE, appears in THE THUNDER LORDS Trilogy.

Du Bois Family Tree

Explore the Genealogy Charts below at
http://kathrynleveque.com/genealogy-charts/
du Reims, De Lohrs, Hage – Wall Chart
The de Llion – de Titouan – de Velt Line – Master File

THE HOUSE OF DU REIMS

Novels in this House:

While Angels Slept

Godspeed

Sub-category (novels where the same name or cross-over characters appear):

- (See House of De Lohr)
- (See House of Hage)
- Devil's Dominion
- Warwolfe

Castle:

Rochester Castle (While Angels Slept)

Ramsbury Castle (Godspeed)

Hero:

Tevin du Reims (While Angels Slept)

Dashiell du Reims (Godspeed)

Heroine:

Cantia du Bexley Penden du Reims (While Angels Slept)

Belladonna de Vaston (Godspeed)

Connections:

- This is a medium house.
- Earls of East Anglia.
- The House of du Reims is related to the House of Hage, as Tevin and Cantia's daughter, Eleanor, married Sir Jeffrey Hage and became the mother of Kieran Hage of THE CRUSADER and KINGDOM COME. (See House of Hage for more information).
- Tevin du Reims is the uncle of Christopher and David de Lohr.
- Tevin's sister, Val, is the mother of Christopher and David de Lohr.
- Christopher and David's father, Myles, is a secondary character in this novel.
- Aston Summerlin appears in GODSPEED.
- Bentley Ashbourne appears in GODSPEED.
- Bric MacRohan appears in GODSPEED.
- Bruis, Edmund, and Glenn de Mandeville appear in SWORDS AND SHIELDS and are the bitter enemies of the du Reims family.
- Dashiell du Reims appears in BY THE UNHOLY HAND.
- Edward de Wolfe, from THE WOLFE, appears in GODSPEED.
- Elizaveta du Reims de Winter was the only child of Christian & Agnes du Reims, and married Drake de Winter in SWORDS AND SHIELDS.
- Eloise du Bexley and her mother Felicia du Bexley appear in SILVERSWORD. There is an undefined relationship to Cantia du Bexley du Reims.
- Gart Forbes from ARCHANGEL, appears in GODSPEED.
- Gavin de Nerra appears in GODSPEED.
- Gerid du Reims is Maddoc du Bois' second-in-command at Canterbury Castle in UNENDING LOVE and SHADOWMOOR.

- Grayton du Reims is Bretton de Llion's second-in-command, and appears in DEVIL'S DOMINION.

- Knox Penden, from the Stewards of Rochester, appears in SHIELD OF KRONOS.

- Marcus Burton from RISE OF THE DEFENDER appears in GODSPEED.

- Myles de Lohr appears in WHILE ANGELS SLEPT, and marries Valeria du Reims. They become the parents of Christopher de Lohr and David de Lohr.

- Rik du Reims, son of the earl of East Anglia, appears in THE LION OF THE NORTH.

- Teo du Reims is the ancestor of the du Reims family in England, and he appears in WARWOLFE.

- Valeria du Reims de Lohr, a female knight serving her brother Tevin du Reims, is the mother of Christopher and David de Lohr.

- William du Reims appears in BLACK SWORD.

DU REIMS FAMILY TREE

Explore the Genealogy Chart below at
http://kathrynleveque.com/genealogy-charts/
du Reims, De Lohrs, Hage – Wall Chart
de Vaston – du Reims – Ashbourne Wall Chart

DE VASTON/DU REIMS/DE WINTER FAMILY TREE

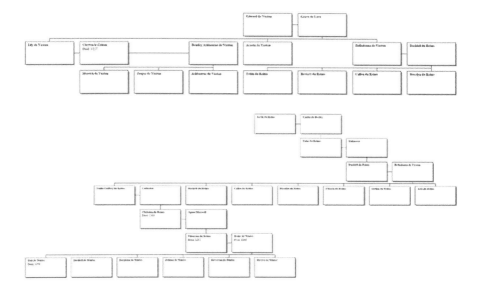

THE HOUSE OF FORBES

Novels in this House:

Archangel

The Highlander's Hidden Heart

Sub-category (novels where the same name or cross-over characters appear):

- Netherworld
- Unending Love

Castles:

Dunster Castle – Archangel and The Highlander's Hidden Heart

Belham Place – Archangel

Braelaw Manor, Scotland – The Highlander's Hidden Heart

Blackbog Castle – Scotland – The Highlander's Hidden Heart

Hero:

Gabriel "Gart" Forbes (Archangel)

Jackston Forbes (The Highlander's Hidden Heart)

Heroine:

Emberley de Russe de Moyon (Archangel)

Rora of Lonmay (The Highlander's Hidden Heart)

Connections:

- This is a medium house.
- Ackerley Forbes is a knight serving Kenton le Bec as one of the "Trouble Trio" in WALLS OF BABYLON.
- Brydon Forbes, son of Gart & Emberley Forbes, appears in UNENDING LOVE.
- Donnan Forbes is the son of Jackston & Rora Forbes, and is the 3rd Lord Daviot.
- Erik de Russe, Emberley's brother, is Gart Forbes' best friend. They served together in LORD OF WINTER.
- Gart Forbes is a squire serving Juston de Royans in LORD OF WINTER.
- Gart Forbes appears in SHIELD OF KRONOS, GODSPEED, and BY THE UNHOLY HAND.
- Gart Forbes makes an appearance in UNENDING LOVE as an older knight.
- Gart's appearance in NETHERWORLD is pre-Archangel by about a year.
- Gregoria de Moyon le Brecque is the sister of Baron Buckland, from Julian de Moyon's family from ARCHANGEL.
- Jackston Forbes is the hero of THE HIGHLANDER'S HIDDEN HEART and becomes the 2nd Lord Daviot.

GART FORBES FAMILY TREE/DE MOYON FAMILY TREE

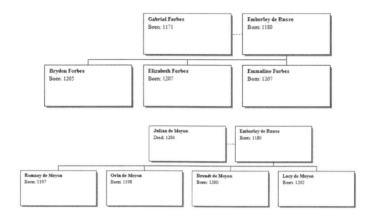

THE HOUSE OF DE GARE

Novels in this House:

None – it ties in with the Warrior Poet (The St. John and de Gare
  Clans)

Connections:

- Gaithlin de Gare is the heroine of THE WARRIOR POET. She
  marries Christian St. John.

- Alicia de Gare, Gaithlin's mother, appears in THE WARRIOR
  POET.

- Malcolm de Gare is the adopted son of Alicia de Gare and appears
  in THE WARRIOR POET.

- Etienne de Gare is a knight serving in the House of de Dere in OF
  LOVE AND LEGEND.

- Uriah de Royans is a knight serving the de Gare family in THE
  WARRIOR POET.

THE HOUSE OF DE GARR

Novels in this House:

Lord of Light

Realm of Angels

Castle:

None

Hero:

Roane de Garr (Lord of Light)

Rhogan de Garr (Realm of Angels)

Heroine:

Alisanne du Soulant (Lord of Light)

Juliana de Nerra (Realm of Angels)

Connections:

- This is a small house.
- There are no cross over characters or names from, or in, any other novel.
- This is a novella, smaller than any other Le Veque novel.
- Paranormal elements, rare for a Le Veque novel.
- Britt de Garr appears in SILVERSWORD.

- Mayne de Garr is a knight serving Valor de Nerra in VESTIGES OF VALOR.
- Valor de Nerra, hero of VESTIGES OF VALOR, is in REALM OF ANGELS.

DE GARR/DE NERRA/D'AVIGNON FAMILY TREE

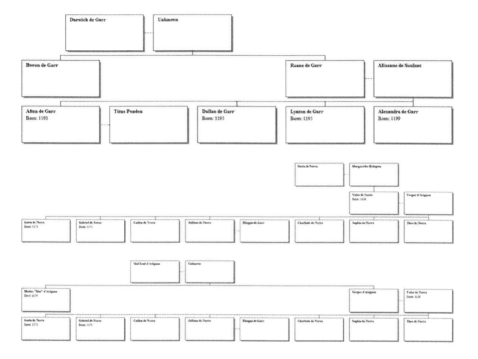

THE HOUSE OF DE LA HAYE

Novels in this House

The Jewel's Embrace (Novella)

Castle:

Arcmare Castle – Property of the Earl of Drumburgh

Hero:

River de la Haye

Heroine:

Emerald "Emmie" Linhope

Connections:

- This is a small house.
- There are no cross over characters or names from, or in, any other novel.
- This is a novella and part of the HOW TO WED A WILD LASS, a duo with Emma Prince.
- River de la Haye is a twin of Falcon de la Haye.
- Roget de la Haye is the Earl of Drumburgh (father of the twins)

Book Links for this House:

How To Wed a Wild Lass

THE HOUSE OF HAGE

Novels in this House:

Kingdom Come (Kieran Hage the Elder)

The Crusader (Kieran Hage the Elder)

Scorpion (Kevin Hage)

Sub-category (novels where the same name or cross-over characters appear):

- Great Protector (secondary character Gavan Hage)
- Scorpion (Kevin Hage)
- Serpent (secondary character, Kieran Hage the Nephew)
- The Wolfe (secondary character, Kieran Hage the Nephew)

Castles:

Southwell Castle (Kingdom Come and The Crusader)

Ilchester Castle (Scorpion)

Heroes:

Kieran Hage the Elder (Kingdom Come and The Crusader)

Kevin Hage (Scorpion)

Heroines:

Rory Osgrove Hage (Kingdom Come and The Crusader)

Annavieve ferch Rhodri de Ferrers Hage (Scorpion)

Connections:

- This is a medium house but it is the most complex house.
- The Crusader Series, which is a two-book series with The Crusader and Kingdom Come, is a Medieval Time-Travel series.
- The House of Hage has the distinction of being the only house with two characters – on hero and one popular secondary character – of the same name yet they are not the same man. It gets confusing, so let's explain:
  - Kieran Hage the Elder is the hero from THE CRUSADER and KINGDOM COME. If you recall in KINGDOM COME, which is a time-travel novel dealing with Rory and Kieran being back in Medieval Times, there's a big twist at the end of the book. Not want to blow this twist for those of you who haven't read it (and you MUST read it because it's a killer twist), Kieran 'disappears' from Medieval England at that point. He leaves behind his young son, Tevin, who was named after Tevin du Reims of WHILE ANGELS SLEPT, who was his mother's father (Kieran's grandfather). If you recall, Tevin from WHILE ANGELS SLEPT was the UNCLE of Christopher de Lohr because Tevin's sister, Val, married Myles de Lohr, a knight. These two became parents to Christopher and David de Lohr, making Christopher and David distantly related to both Kieran Hages.
  - Kieran Hage the Elder, having left Medieval England at the end of KINGDOM COME, left behind his son, Tevin, whom his brother Sean raised as his own. Tevin Hage was a great man, a powerful knight, and he was told that his father, Kieran, had been killed, as had his mother. Both of his parents are gone.

Therefore, he knew his father was Kieran Hage the Elder and that Sean, even though he raised him, was his uncle. Sean then had three sons of his own that were younger than his nephew Tevin, and it was Sean's youngest son, Jeffrey (named for Kieran Hage the Elder and Sean's father) who had Kieran Hage the Nephew, named for Kieran Hage the Elder. Kieran Hage the Nephew is the Kieran who appears in The Wolfe and Serpent.

Therefore – Kieran Hage the Nephew from THE WOLFE is Kieran Hage the Elder's great-nephew.

Kevin Hage is Kieran Hage the Nephew's son (SERPENT, SCOR-PION)

Gavan Hage is a secondary character in GREAT PROTECTOR, an undefined relation to the House of Hage.

HAGE FAMILY TREE

Explore the Genealogy Chart below at
http://kathrynleveque.com/genealogy-charts/
The Hage Line – Master File

THE HOUSE OF LE BEC

Novels in this House:

Great Protector

Walls of Babylon

Sub-category (novels where the same name or cross-over characters appear):

- (See House of de Lohr)
- Beast
- Lord of War: Black Angel
- The Iron Knight
- To The Lady Born

Castles:

Lambourn Castle (Great Protector)

Babylon Castle (Walls of Babylon)

Heroes:

Richmond le Bec (Great Protector)

Kenton le Bec (Walls of Babylon)

Heroines:

Arissa de Lohr le Bec (Great Protector)

Nicola Aubrey-Thorne le Bec (Walls of Babylon)

Connections:

- This is a medium house.
- The de Lohr name appears with secondary characters but it is an undefined relationship to the House of de Lohr.
- Richmond and Arissa are parents of Gisella le Bec, the heroine in BEAST. Through their son, Gannon, who marries a Summerlin, they are related by marriage to the House of Summerlin.
- Ackerley Forbes is a knight serving Kenton le Bec as one of the "Trouble Trio" in WALLS OF BABYLON.
- Alec le Bec appears in THE LION OF THE NORTH.
- Brentford le Bec is a knight in STEELHEART.
- Conor de Birmingham, Gerik le Mon, and Ackerley Forbes serve Kenton le Bec in WALLS OF BABYLON, and are known as the Trouble Trio.
- Gannon le Bec is a knight serving Bastian de Russe in BEAST. His sister is Gisella le Bec de Russe, heroine of BEAST, and is the son of Richmond le Bec.
- Gaston de Russe (THE DARK ONE: DARK KNIGHT) and Matthew Wellesbourne (THE WHITE LORD OF WELLESBOURNE) appear as younger knights in WALLS OF BABYLON.
- Gavan Hage is a secondary character in GREAT PROTECTOR, an undefined relation to the House of Hage.
- Gerik le Mon is a knight serving Kenton le Bec in WALLS OF BABYLON, and is one of the "Trouble Trio."
- Kenton le Bec, hero of WALLS OF BABYLON, and grandson of Richmond le Bec, appeared as a young knight in THE LION OF THE NORTH.
- Richmond le Bec appears as a younger knight in TO THE LADY BORN.

- Richmond le Bec appears as an older man in THE IRON KNIGHT.
- Stefan le Bec is a knight in service to Brandt de Russe, and appears in LORD OF WAR: BLACK ANGEL.

LE BEC FAMILY TREE

Explore the Genealogy Charts below at

http://kathrynleveque.com/genealogy-charts/

Arissa & Richmond le Bec – Royal Line

Le Bec – de Russe – Wellesbourne #1

De Russe – le Bec – Wellesbourne #2

THE HOUSE OF LE BRECQUE

Novels in this House:

Lady of the Moon

Leader of Titans

Sea Wolfe

Sub-category (novels where the same name or cross-over characters appear):

- The Immortal SEA

Castles:

Tyringham Castle (Lady of the Moon)

Perran Castle (Leader of Titans)

Perran Castle (Sea Wolfe)

Heroes:

Rhodes de Leybourne (Lady of the Moon)

Constantine le Brecque (Leader of Titans)

Rhoan de Wolfe (Sea Wolfe)

Heroines:

Sammara le Brecque de Leybourne (Lady of the Moon)

Gregoria de Moyon le Brecque (Leader of Titans)

Genevieve Efford de Wolfe (Sea Wolfe)

Connections:

- This is a small house.
- Samarra le Brecque de Leybourne is a female mercenary, and is the sister of pirate Constantine le Brecque.
- Gregoria de Moyon le Brecque is the sister of Baron Buckland, from Julian de Moyon's family from ARCHANGEL.
- Kerk le Sander from THE IMMORTAL SEA is a character in LEADER OF TITANS.
- Augustine de Russe, from the House of de Russe is a quartermaster and appears in LEADER OF TITANS and SEA WOLFE.
- Remy de Moray, from the House of de Moray, appears in LEADER OF TITANS and SEA WOLFE.
- Felix d'Vant, from the House of d'Vant, appears in LEADER OF TITANS and SEA WOLFE.
- Rhoan de Wolfe, of the House of de Wolfe, is the hero of SEA WOLFE, and is otherwise known as 'Lucifer.'

THE HOUSE OF LE MON

Novels in this House:

The Whispering Night

Sub-category (novels where the same name or cross-over characters appear):

- Netherworld

Castle:

Cilgarren Castle

Hero:

Garren le Mon

Heroine:

Derica de Rosa le Mon

Connections:

- This is a smaller house.
- There is one or two minor characters with the le Mon last name in other Le Veque novels, but their relationship to the House of le Mon is undefined.
- Dallan le Mon is a knight in service to Brandt de Russe, and appears in LORD OF WAR: BLACK ANGEL.

- Garren le Mon is heir to the ancient Saxon kingdom of Anglecynn and Ceri.
- Gerik le Mon is a knight serving Kenton le Bec in WALLS OF BABYLON, and is one of the "Trouble Trio."
- Gerik le Mon is one of the Trouble Trio knights serving Kenton le Bec, and appears in WALLS OF BABYLON.
- Trevor le Mon is a knight in BLACK SWORD.

LE MON/DE ROSA FAMILY TREE

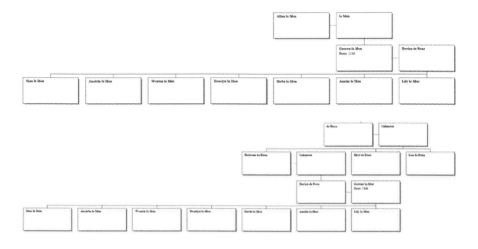

THE HOUSE OF PEMBURY (CULPEPPER)

Novels in this House:

The Savage Curtain

Fragments of Grace (secondary character Michael of Pembury)

Sub-category (novels where the same name or cross-over characters appear):

- (See House of de Lara/Dragonblade Series)

Castle:

Berwick Castle

Hero:

Stephen of Pembury

Heroine:

Joselyn de Velt Seton

Connections:

- A medium house
- Barons of Pembury (family name is Culpepper but they are known by Pembury).
- Cade Seton Pembury, adopted son of Stephen & Joselyn Pembury, marries Catherine de Lara, daughter of Tate & Toby de Lara.

- Gabriel Pembury appears in THE IRON KNIGHT. He is a knight in service to Lucien de Russe.

- Julia de Velt Seton is the mother of Joselyn de Velt Seton Pembury.

- Kenneth Pembury is a knight appearing in TO THE LADY BORN.

- Michael Pembury is a knight serving Keir St. Hever. He appears in FRAGMENTS OF GRACE and THE QUESTING.

- Morgan de Velt appears in THE SAVAGE CURTAIN. He is a first cousin of Julia de Velt Seton.

- Stephen Pembury also served Tate de Lara in DRAGONBLADE and THE FALLEN ONE.

- Stephen Pembury's father, Michael and his mother, Summer, meet in FRAGMENTS OF GRACE. Summer's father is Garran de Moray, son of Bose and Summer de Moray (THE GORGON). Therefore, Stephen is the great-grandson of Bose de Moray.

PEMBURY FAMILY TREE

Explore the Genealogy Chart below at

http://kathrynleveque.com/genealogy-charts/

The de Moray – de Shera – Pembury Line – Master File

THE HOUSE OF ROHAN

Novels in this House

High Warrior

Sub-category (novels where this name appears or cross-over characters appear):

- GODSPEED
- BY THE UNHOLY HAND

Castles:

Narborough Castle – (High Warrior)

Heroes:

Bric MacRohan – (High Warrior)

Heroines:

Eiselle de Gael MacRohan – (High Warrior)

Connections:

- This is a small house.
- The heroine of HIGH WARRIOR, Eiselle de Gael MacRohan is the bastard great-granddaughter of the Earl of East Anglia (Geoffrey de Gaeil from WHILE ANGELS SLEPT). She is also a cousin to Dashiell du Reims.

- Bric MacRohan appears in BY THE UNHOLY HAND, THE MOUNTAIN DARK, and STARLESS.
- Dashiell du Reims, hero of GODSPEED, appears in HIGH WARRIOR.
- Daveigh de Winter appears in HIGH WARRIOR.
- Keeva de Goish de Winter, wife of Daveigh de Winter, appears in HIGH WARRIOR. She is also cousin to Bric MacRohan.
- Peerce de Dere appears in HIGH WARRIOR.
- Sean de Lara, hero of LORD OF THE SHADOWS, appears in HIGH WARRIOR.
- Zara de Dere appears in HIGH WARRIOR.

ROHAN FAMILY TREE

Explore the Genealogy Charts below at
http://kathrynleveque.com/genealogy-charts/
MacRohan & du Reims Line
The de Winter Dynasty
The du Reims & de Winter Lines

THE HOUSE OF ST. HEVER

Novels in this House:

Island of Glass

Fragments of Grace

Queen of Lost Stars

Sub-category (novels where this name appears or cross-over characters appear):

- (See House of de Lara/Dragonblade Series)
- Lord of War: Black Angel
- The Thunder Warrior
- Warwolfe

Castles:

Kirk Castle (Island of Glass)

Pendragon Castle (Fragments of Grace)

Lavister Crag Castle (Queen of Lost Stars)

Heroes:

Kenneth St. Hever (Island of Glass)

Keir St. Hever (Fragments of Grace)

Kaspian St. Hever (Queen of Lost Stars)

Heroines:

Aubrielle St. Hever (Island of Glass)

Chloe de Geld St. Hever (Fragments of Grace)

Madelayne St. Hever (Queen of Lost Stars)

Connections:

- This is a medium house.
- St. Hever appears all through the DRAGONBLADE series
- A secondary character in THE THUNDER WARRIOR is an undefined St. Hever relation.
- Hero in FRAGMENTS OF GRACE is Kenneth St. Hever's uncle. Kenneth's father, Kurtis, and his mother Cassandra are also secondary characters in FRAGMENTS OF GRACE.
- Brennan St. Hever is a knight serving Brandt de Russe. He is the firstborn son of Kenneth and Aubrielle St. Hever from ISLAND OF GLASS.
- Evan St. Hever, younger brother of Brennan, also serves Brandt de Russe towards the end of LORD OF WAR: BLACK ANGEL.
- Ewan and Reece de Poyer, brothers, serve Kaspian St. Hever in QUEEN OF LOST STARS.
- Kaspian (QUEEN OF LOST STARS), is a cousin to Kenneth St. Hèver (ISLAND OF GLASS) from the Dragonblade saga. Since Kenneth's father, Kurtis, only had one brother, we will assume that Kaspian's father was a cousin to Kurtis and his brother, Keir (FRAGMENTS OF GRACE).
- Keenan St. Hever is the firstborn son of Kirk & Isadora St. Hever in THE THUNDER KNIGHT.
- Kirk St. Hever, second-in-command to Kellen de Lara in THE THUNDER KNIGHT and THE THUNDER WARRIOR, marries Isadora de Lara, sister of Courtly de Lara de Shera.

- Kye St. Hever is the ancestor of the St. Hever family in England, and he appears in WARWOLFE.
- Marcus de Lara appears in FRAGMENTS OF GRACE.

ST. HEVER FAMILY TREE

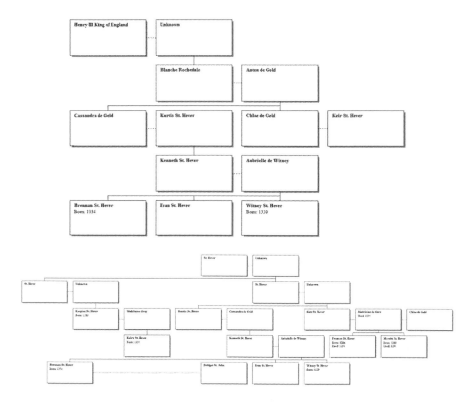

THE HOUSE OF ST. JOHN

Novels in this House:

The Warrior Poet

Sub-category (novels where this name appears or cross-over characters appear):

- The Questing

Castles:

Winding Cross Castle

Rougham Castle

Eden Castle

Hero:

Christian St. John

Heroine:

Gaithlin de Gare

Connections:

- This is a small house.
- Aidric St. John is a knight serving in King Henry's Guard of Six in SILVERSWORD.

- Barton St. John is the Captain of the Guard at Geurdley Cross in VALIANT CHAOS.
- Brome St. John and his sister, Katryne St. John, appear in WALLS OF BABYLON.
- Oliver St. John is a secondary character in THE QUESTING and is a son of Christian and Gaithlin. He also appears in SWORDS AND SHIELDS.
- Victor St. John is a commander for the Earl of Kildare, and is the father of Emllyn Fitzgerald, heroine of BLACK SWORD.

St. John/de Gare Family Tree

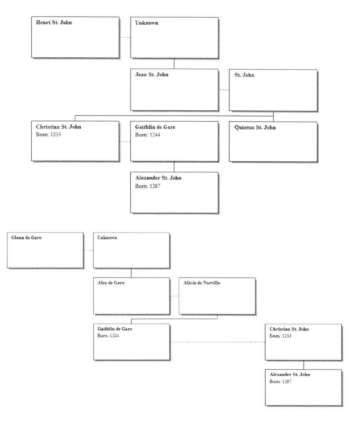

THE HOUSE OF SUMMERLIN

Novels in this House:

The Legend

Sub-category (novels where this name appears or cross-over characters appear):

- Beast

Castles:

Blackstone Castle

St. Cloven Manor

Hero:

Alec Summerlin

Heroine:

Peyton de Flournoy Summerlin

Connections:

- This is a smaller house.
- Aston Summerlin is a senior knight to Dashiell du Reims in GODSPEED.
- Sparrow Summerlin, a descendant, is a secondary character in BEAST and mother, it is assumed, of another Alec named after

her ancestor. This character would be Alec le Bec since her husband is a son of Richmond le Bec.

- Luc Summerlin served Simon de Montfort as King Henry III's primary jailor in SILVERSWORD.

- Deleese de Winter Summerlin is the wife of the garrison commander at THE MOUNTAIN DARK.

- Padriac Summerlin is the garrison commander at Castle Rising in THE MOUNTAIN DARK.

- Peter Albert Brian Summerlin is the oldest son of Alec and Peyton Summerlin and serves as Cortez de Bretagne's squire in THE QUESTING.

- Shaun Summerlin is a knight and brother-in-law to Warenne de Winter in THE LION OF THE NORTH.

SUMMERLIN/DE FLUOURNEY FAMILY TREE

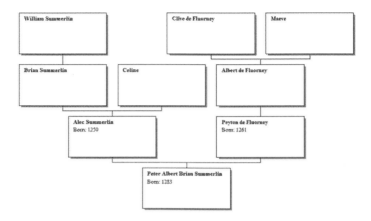

THE HOUSE OF WELLESBOURNE

Novels in this House:

The White Lord of Wellesbourne

Sub-category (novels where this name appears or cross-over characters appear):

- Beast
- Netherworld
- The Dark One: Dark Knight
- Warwolfe

Castle:

Wellesbourne Castle

Hero:

Matthew Wellesbourne

Heroine:

Alexandrea St. Ave Wellesbourne

Connections:

- This is a bigger house.
- Adam Wellesbourne is a young knight in THE LION OF THE NORTH.

- Andrew Wellesbourne is a secondary character in BEAST. He is Adam Wellesbourne's father and Adam is Matthew Wellesbourne's father.

- Audrey de Russe Wellesbourne, Matthew's mother, is the daughter of Bastian and Gisella le Bec de Russe from BEAST. The fact that Matthew is a cousin to Gaston is never mentioned in The Dark One: Dark Knight or The White Lord of Wellesbourne.

- Bartholomew Wellesbourne is the ancestor of the Wellesbourne family in England, and he appears in WARWOLFE.

- Gaston de Russe appears in THE WHITE LORD OF WELLESBOURNE.

- Matthew Wellesbourne appears as a young knight in WALLS OF BABYLON.

- Matthew Wellesbourne is a secondary character in THE DARK ONE: DARK KNIGHT.

- Patrick de Russe, cousin to Gaston de Russe, also appears in THE WHITE LORD OF WELLESBOURNE.

- Simon Wellesbourne is a knight appearing in TO THE LADY BORN.

- William Wellesbourne is a knight serving Keller de Poyer. He appears in NETHERWORLD and DEVIL'S DOMINION.

- William Wellesbourne is a secondary character in NETHERWORLD. He is an undefined ancestor.

WELLESBOURNE FAMILY TREE

Explore the Genealogy Charts below at
http://kathrynleveque.com/genealogy-charts/
Arissa & Richmond le Bec – Royal Line
Le Bec – de Russe – Wellesbourne #1
De Russe – le Bec – Wellesbourne #2
Wellesbourne Wall Chart

THE MARCUS BURTONS

This is a complex situation, but let me see if I can explain it –

Marcus Burton was originally in RISE OF THE DEFENDER. I loved his character and was sad when Marcus didn't get the girl. After I finished RISE OF THE DEFENDER, I was working on a modern-day adventure series and thought it would be a perfect vehicle for Marcus Burton reincarnated, so I put Marcus Burton into the present day where he did, in fact, get the girl.

Therefore, here's the way I look at it – the Marcus Burton in the Trent/Burton romance adventure series is Marcus Burton reincarnated. It's Marcus, but with a few personality differences. Modern Marcus is much more of an asshole than Medieval Marcus. He's meaner, brusquer, and just generally more unpleasant at times.

Medieval Marcus is more amiable, more willing to play second banana to Christopher de Lohr, but he has honesty issues. He'll steal a man's wife and then try to justify it, which Modern Marcus would never do.

So, there you have it – the best way I have of explaining The Marcuses.

Other medieval Burton characters:

- Gabrielle de Havilland Burton, first wife of Charles de Havilland, Earl of Fenwark. She later marries Marcus Burton in RISE OF

THE DEFENDER. She also appears in STEELHEART and A BLESSED DE LOHR CHRISTMAS.

- Marcus Burton also appears as a young general in Justin de Royans' army in LORD OF WINTER. He also appears in GODSPEED, STEELHEART, and A BLESSED DE LOHR CHRISTMAS.

- Peter de Lohr, Christopher de Lohr's illegitimate son, fosters at Somerhill with Marcus Burton. Christopher also sends some of his and Dustin's sons to foster with their older half-brother at Marcus' home.

- Rickard Burton, cousin of Marcus Burton, appears in RISE OF THE DEFENDER briefly, but this character is killed.

- Rickard Burton, a knight with a mean temperament, known for his violent competitiveness. Appears in THE FALLS OF ERITH.

- Trent Burton, a cousin to Marcus Burton, and is a knight in Marcus' service. Appears in RISE OF THE DEFENDER and STEELHEART.

BOOKS CHRONOLOGICALLY BY YEAR.

This is a list of every novel and the year it is set in. This list is for all families, all novels, and is not grouped by families. It is grouped by year. Since some people like to read books chronologically by the year they are set in, regardless of family groups or series, this will be helpful to see where each book in the Kathryn Le Veque Medieval World sits.

Book Title	Year Book Took Place	Series or House
The Legend of the Spirit Waters	891	Highland Wishes
Warwolfe	1066	De Wolfe Pack
Kingdom by the Sea	1101	The Lore Chronicles
While Angels Slept	1139	De Lohr Dynasty
Of Love and Legend	1145	De Dere
Vestiges of Valor	1170	De Nerra
Devil's Dominion	1179	De Llion
The Dark Lord	1180	De Velt
The Dark Lord's First Christmas	1180	De Velt
Lord of Winter	1187	The Lords of de Royans
The Crusader	1192-Present	The Crusader
Kingdom Come	1192-Present	The Crusader
Rise of the Defender	1192	De Lohr Dynasty
Steelheart	1192	De Lohr Dynasty
Lord of Light	1192	House of de Garr
Upon a Midnight Dream	1194	Ashbourne

Shield of Kronos	1196	Great Knights of de Moray
The Whispering Night	1197	Le Mon
Netherworld	1197	De Poyer
Realm of Angels	1197	House of de Garr
Guardian of Darkness	1200	De Reyne
By the Unholy Hand	1200	De Long
Spectre of the Sword	1203	De Lohr Dynasty
Archangel	1204	De Lohr Dynasty
The Mountain Dark	1206	De Rhydian
Starless	1206	The Executioner Knights
The Promise	1208	Noble Line of De Nerra
A Blessed de Lohr Christmas	1210	De Lohr Dynasty
Lord of the Shadows	1215	De Lara
Godspeed	1216	Earls of East Anglia
High Warrior	1217	High Warriors of Rohan
Tender is the Knight	1228	D'Vant Bloodlines
The Wolfe	1231	De Wolfe Pack
The Red Fury	1233	D'Vant Bloodlines
Unending Love	1234	De Lohr Dynasty
The Gorgon	1235	De Moray
Shadowmoor	1236	De Lohr Dynasty
The Centurion	1240	Lords of de Royans
The Thunder Lord	1258	De Shera Brothers
The Thunder Warrior	1258	De Shera Brothers
The Thunder Knight	1258	De Shera Brothers
Lespada	1264	House of de Winter
The Warrior Poet	1266	St. John
Silversword	1266	De Lohr Dynasty
Bay of Fear	1268	Battle Lords of de Velt
Nighthawk	1271	De Wolfe Pack

With Dreams	1272	De Velt
DarkWolfe	1272	De Wolfe Pack
ShadowWolfe	1273	De Wolfe Pack
A Joyous de Wolfe Christmas	1274	De Wolfe Pack
Blackwolfe	1279	De Wolfe Pack
The Legend	1282	Summerlin
Serpent	1283	De Wolfe Pack
A Wolfe Among Dragons	1287	De Wolfe Pack
The Red Lion	1288	Highland Warriors of Munro
Scorpion	1289	De Wolfe Pack
Deep Into Darkness	1290	Highland Warriors of Munro
StormWolfe	1292	De Wolfe Pack
The Best is Yet to Be	1293	De Wolfe Pack
Fragments of Grace	1294	St. Hever
The Questing	1298	De Bretagne
Swords and Shields	1300	House of de Winter
The Falls of Erith	1305	De Russe Legacy
Queen of Lost Stars	1320	House of St. Hever
Black Sword	1323	De Birmingham
Dragonblade	1326	De Lara
The Jewel's Embrace	1330	Wild Lass Duet
The Fallen One	1331	De Reyne
Island of Glass	1333	St. Hever
The Savage Curtain	1333	Pembury
The Highlander's Hidden Heart	1335	Warrior House of Forbes
Lord of War: Black Angel	1356	De Russe Legacy
Dark Destroyer	1357	De Wolfe/De Winter
To The Lady Born	1388	Lords of de Royans

Great Protector	1402	Le Bec
The Iron Knight	1408	De Russe Legacy
Beast	1431	De Russe Legacy
Lady of the Moon	1444	Pirates of Britannia
Leader of Titans	1445	Pirates of Britannia
Sea Wolfe	1447	Pirates of Britannia
The Lion of the North	1461	De Wolfe Pack
Valiant Chaos	1469	D'Aurilliac
Walls of Babylon	1471	De Wolfe Pack
The White Lord of Wellesbourne	1485	De Russe Legacy
The Dark One: Dark Knight	1486	De Russe Legacy
The Darkland	1515	Linked to Black Sword
Dark Moon	1518	De Russe Legacy
Dark Steel	1519	De Russe Legacy
A De Russe Christmas Miracle	1520	De Russe Legacy
Emma	1811	De Russe Legacy
Echoes of Ancient Dreams	Time Travel	Da Derga
Valley of the Shadow	Present	Kathlyn Trent
Canyon of the Sphinx	Present	Kathlyn Trent
The Eden Factor	Present	Kathlyn Trent
Lady of Heaven	Present	Contemporary
Darkling, I Listen	Present	Contemporary
Resurrection	Present	American Heroes
Fires of Autumn	Present	American Heroes
Purgatory	Present	American Heroes
Sea of Dreams	Present	American Heroes
Evenshade	Present	American Heroes
In the Dreaming Hour	Present	Contemporary

MASTER LIST OF
MAIN & SECONDARY CHARACTERS

This is a list of all main and secondary characters from Kathryn's novels.

A reference guide only.

All Characters are copyrighted.

Aentillius, Lucius Maximus – Hero of WITH DREAMS. He was the first husband of Theodosia, who was the heroine of OF LOVE AND LEGEND. He died in battle in England.

Aentillius, Lucia – The firstborn child of Lucius and Theodosia Aentillius. Appears in OF LOVE AND LEGEND.

Aentillius, Theodosia – Daughter of Tiberius Brutus. First wife of Lucius and then second wife of Gaius. Heroine in OF LOVE AND LEGEND.

Ainsley, Darren – Son of Lord Robert Ainsley. He is Christopher de Lohr's squire. Appears in RISE OF THE DEFENDER, STEELHEART, and SHIELD OF KRONOS.

Allington, St. Paul – Father of Devereux Allington. He is the Lord Mayor of Thetford and Sheriff of the Shire. He is not a particularly loving parent. Appears in LESPADA.

Allington-More, Mavia – Wife of Thomas Allington-More. Appears in QUEEN OF LOST STARS.

Allington-More, Thomas – A knight in service to Kaspian St. Hever. Husband of Mavia Allington-More. Appears in QUEEN OF LOST STARS.

Alraedson, Thane – Second-in-Command of Andrew d'Vant's mercenary army. Appears in THE RED FURY and THE WOLFE.

ap Athoe, Deinwald – Welshman and brother to Rolphe ap Athoe. He is related to the Princes of Wales. He and his brother are unwanted suitors for Adalind de Aston's hand. Appears in UNENDING LOVE.

ap Athoe, Rolphe – Welshman and brother to Deinwald ap Athoe. He is related to the Princes of Wales. He and his brother are unwanted suitors for Adalind de Aston's hand. Appears in UNENDING LOVE.

ap Gaerwen, Gaerwen – He is the father of Jeniver Gaerwen de Shera, wife of Gallus de Shera. He is the last hereditary king of Anglesey. He appears in THE THUNDER LORD.

ap Gruffydd, Howell – He is a Welsh warlord. He appears in A WOLFE AMONG DRAGONS.

ap Gruffyd, Tacey – Daughter of Bhrodi de Shera's sister, Tacey, who died giving birth to Lady Tacey. May be the last Welsh royal. She is sent to live with William and Jordan de Wolfe, for safekeeping. Appears in SERPENT.

ap Gruffydd, Tacey de Shera – Bhrodi de Shera's youngest sister. Widow of the youngest Prince of Wales and the mother of his heir. Appears in SERPENT.

ap Gwynwynwyn, Colvyn – He is a Welsh prince and is the illegitimate son of the last king of Powys, Gwynwynwyn ap Owain. Appears in NETHERWORLD.

ap Macsen, Cader – He is the father of Asmara and Fairynne. He is a Welsh warlord. He is also the youngest brother of Morys ap Macsen. He is descended from the last kings of Deheubarth. He appears in A WOLFE AMONG DRAGONS.

ap Macsen, Morys – Oldest brother of Cader ap Macsen, and uncle to Asmara and Fairynne. He is a Welsh warlord. He is descended from the last kings of Deheubarth. He is the warlord who found James de Wolfe/Blayth the Strong on the battlefield.

ap Maddoc, Davies – Eolande ferch Maddoc's brother. He is descended from the Lords of Godor; Welsh nobility. Appears in DARK STEEL.

ap Ninian, Aeddan – He is a Welsh warrior and friend to Blayth. He is the older brother of Pryce ap Ninian. He appears in A WOLFE AMONG DRAGONS.

ap Ninian, Pryce – He is a Welsh warrior and friend to Blayth. He is the younger brother of Aeddan ap Ninian. He appears in A WOLFE AMONG DRAGONS.

Arc, Joan of – An illiterate farm girl and French martyr. Appears in BEAST.

Archer-Phipps, Raphael – A knight in THE LION OF THE NOTH.

Armstrong, Alan – He is an older knight in service of Marcus Burton at Somerhill Castle. Appears in RISE OF THE DEFENDER.

Armstrong, Margaret – She is the wife of Alan Armstrong and resides at Somerhill Castle. Appears in RISE OF THE DEFENDER.

Arnsworth, Lewis – A knight in THE WOLFE.

Ashbourne, Hollen "Holly" St. Maur – Heroine of UPON A MIDNIGHT DREAM. Oldest daughter and heiress of Perot St. Maur. She is smart, diligent, and educated.

Ashbourne, Rennington – Hero of UPON A MIDNIGHT DREAM. He is from the Saxon House of Osmaston. He is a knight who just returned from The Levant. Through his wife, he will inherit the title of Lord Elvaston and Thulston Manor.

Ashby-Kidd, Aimery – Twin brother of George. He is a knight in the service of Keller de Poyer. He marries Rose Wellesbourne, daughter of William Wellesbourne. Appears in NETHERWORLD.

Ashby-Kidd, Douglas – He is older man and brother of Julia Ashby-Kidd de la Haye. He is also known as "Duchy." Appears in THE JEWEL'S EMBRACE.

Ashby-Kidd, George – A knight serving Keller de Poyer. Twin brother of Aimery. He marries Izlynn d'Einen. Appears in NETHERWORLD and DEVIL'S DOMINION.

Ashby-Kidd, Izlynn d'Einen – Appears in NETHERWORLD. Youngers sister of Gryfynn and Chrystobel. She marries George Ashby-Kidd, a knight in service to Keller de Poyer.

Aston, Alexandra – Twin daughter of Dallas & Brooke Aston. Appears in THE FALLS OF ERITH.

Aston, Andrew – Twin son of Dallas & Brooke Aston. Appears in THE FALLS OF ERITH.

Aston, Brooke Serroux – Only child and daughter of Gray and Guy Serroux. She marries Dallas Aston and appears in THE FALLS OF ERITH.

Aston, Dallas – Braxton de Nerra's second-in-command. He marries Brooke Serroux and is gifted Castle Erith as part of Brooke's dowry. Appears in THE FALLS OF ERITH.

Aston, Gillis – A knight serving King Edward, and also a royal messenger. He appears in SHADOWWOLFE.

Aston, Matthew – Firstborn child and son of Dallas & Brooke Aston. Appears in THE FALLS OF ERITH.

Aston, Tobias – He is a knight sworn to Jasper de Lara. Appears in DARK DESTROYER. He is the grandson of Dallas Aston from THE FALLS OF ERITH.

Aubrey, Charles – He is a land-wealthy baron from Merseyside, who owns Guerdley Cross. He is a young man in ill health, and was the first husband of Avalyn du Brant Aubrey d'Aurilliac. Appears in VALIANT CHAOS.

Auclair, Milo – A senior knight serving Scott de Wolfe in SHADOWWOLFE.

Balliol, Edward – A son of former King John Balliol, who was a descendant of Isabella of Angouleme and John de Warenne, the Earl of Surrey. He tries to usurp the throne from the infant King David. Appears in THE FALLEN ONE.

Barclay, Kristoph – A knight serving Nathaniel du Rennic in SHADOWWOLFE.

Barkley, Eldon – He is a knight in service to the de Gare family. He becomes Alicia de Gare's lover after her husband dies. Appears in THE WARRIOR POET.

Banbury, Hamilton – He is a knight who serves Preston de Lacy. Appears in THE PROMISE.

Barr, Oliver – Laird of Clan Barr. Appears in THE WOLFE.

Barringdon, Arthur – He is the father of Dustin Barringdon de Lohr and is husband to Mary Fitz Walter Barringdon. He went on the Crusade with King Richard the Lionheart. He is a distant cousin to King Richard and Prince John. Appears in RISE OF THE DEFENDER.

Barringdon, Mary Fitz Walter Barringdon – She is the wife of Arthur Barringdon and the mother of Dustin Barringdon de Lohr. She is a first cousin of Ralph Fitz Walter. Appears in RISE OF THE DEFENDER.

Beaufort, Margaret – She is the mother of King Henry VII. Appears in THE DARK ONE: DARK KNIGHT.

Becker, Uriah – Uncle to Rory Osgrove. He is the Dean of Archeology & Anthropology at San Marcos University. Appears in THE CRUSADER.

Bellerby, Henry – He is a knight serving Witton de Meynell. He appears in STARLESS.

Bigod, Hugh – He is a powerful baron, but he is a barbaric bully and a dangerous fool. He failed to have his daughter, Matilda, marry into the powerful de Shera family. He appears in THE THUNDER LORD, THE THUNDER WARRIOR, and THE THUNDER KNIGHT.

Bigod, Matilda – She is the daughter of Hugh Bigod. She appears in THE THUNDER LORD.

Bigod, Robert – He is also known as Father Manducor. He is the bastard son of the Earl of Norfolk. He was previously a knight for the Earl of Leicester. He joined the priesthood after his wife and children passed away. He appears in HIGH WARRIOR.

Bishop of Bath and Glastonbury, Jocelin – He helped guide Sheridan St. James after her father, the Earl of Bath and Glastonbury, passed away. Appears in LORD OF THE SHADOWS.

Blackwelder, John – He is the former troopmaster for the Earl of Langdon at Tickhill Castle, before he was displaced by Prince John. He saved the life of Christopher de Lohr as he lay dying near the battlefield. Appears in RISE OF THE DEFENDER.

Blainroe, Iver – Master of Men because he is calm and wise. He is a distant cousin of Devlin's. Appears in BLACK SWORD.

Blankynship, Edward – The young man who Mira de Velt left Jax de Velt for. She later marries Edward. Appears in THE DARK LORD.

Blankynship, Mira de Velt – Jax's first wife, who unbeknownst to Jax de Velt, fled her marriage to Jax with the help of Amadeo le Somes. Appears in THE DARK LORD.

Boltophdottter, Gunnora – She is the Lady of Westerham, and is a friend to Ghislaine of Mercia. She appears in WARWOLFE.

Boratu, Ali – A black soldier and best friend of Alec Summerlin. Appears in THE LEGEND.

Boratu, Ivy de Fluorney – Younger sister of Peyton de Fluorney. She marries Ali Boratu. Appears in THE LEGEND.

Boratu, Olphampa – Father of Ali Boratu and husband to Sula Boratu. They live at Blackstone Castle and serve the Summerlin family. Appears in THE LEGEND.

Boratu, Sula – Mother of Ali and wife of Olphampa. They live at Blackstone Castle and serve the Summerlin family. Appears in THE LEGEND.

Bordeleaux, Tertious – The head of the Order of the Hospitallers of St. John the Baptist. Appears in LORD OF LIGHT.

Botmore, Derek – A knight who loses against Gaston de Russe in a fight. He is the only heir of Keith Botmore of Rainton Castle. Appears in THE DARK ONE: DARK KNIGHT.

Botmore, Keith – A Yorkist ally of Guy Stoneley. He is the father of Derek Botmore. Appears in THE DARK ONE: DARK KNIGHT.

Brabrant, Princess Augusta – She is a young woman, the daughter of Marie, Princess of France, and the Duke of Brabrant. She appears in REALM OF ANGELS.

Branach, Frederick – Known as Blood Warrior, because he's a bloodthirsty person. Appears in BLACK SWORD.

Brimley, Clive – Lord Brimley's son. An ally to Guy Stoneley and now an ally to Gaston de Russe. Appears in THE DARK ONE: DARK KNIGHT.

Brimley, Lord – An older knight who owns Crayke Castle. An ally to Guy Stoneley and now ally to Gaston de Russe. Appears in THE DARK ONE: DARK KNIGHT.

Brimley, Walter – Lord Brimley's son. An ally to Guy Stoneley and now an ally to Gaston de Russe. Appears in THE DARK ONE: DARK KNIGHT.

Brittany, John – A son of the Duke of Brittany, and the favorite nephew of King Edward I. He is an untalented man with no military skill. Appears in SWORDS AND SHIELDS.

Brockenhurst, Charlotte – She is the daughter of Lance and Lygia Brockenhurst. She appears in THE CENTURION.

Brockenhurst, Lance – He is the Captain of the Guard at Makendon Castle. He appears in THE CENTURION.

Brockenhurst, Lygia – She is the wife of Lance Brockenhurst. She appears in THE CENTURION.

Brockenhurst, Steven – He is the Captain of the Guard from Deauxville Mount. Appears in THE WOLFE as a younger man, and as an older man in BLACKWOLFE.

Brundun, Cecily – Daughter of Lord Sudbury. She is a close friend of Amalie de Vere. Appears in TO THE LADY BORN.

Brutus, Tiberius – Father of Theodosia Aentillius. Appears in OF LOVE AND LEGEND.

Burleson, Galen – Captain of the Guard at Hexham Castle. Appears in GUARDIAN OF DARKNESS.

Burton, Gabrielle de Havilland – She was the wife of Charles de Havilland and is a friend to Dustin de Lohr. She later marries Marcus Burton. Appears in RISE OF THE DEFENDER and A BLESSED DE LOHR CHRISTMAS.

Burton, Marcus – He is a knight and the best friend of Christopher de Lohr. He became Baron Somerhill. He served under King Richard in the Crusades and was his general. He served with Christopher and David de Lohr. He marries Gabrielle de Havilland. Appears in RISE OF THE DEFENDER, STEELHEART, GODSPEED, and A

BLESSED DE LOHR CHRISTMAS. In LORD OF WINTER he is also a general in Juston de Royans' army, serving alongside Christopher and David de Lohr.

Burton, Rickard – A big knight with a mean temperament. He is known for his violent competitiveness. Appears in THE FALLS OF ERITH.

Burton, Trent – He is a cousin to Marcus Burton, and is a knight in Marcus' service. Appears in RISE OF THE DEFENDER and STEELHEART.

Cartingdon, Ailsa – Sister of Toby Cartingdon, and daughter of Balin and Judith. She is a frail girl, who is weak-bodied, and is sometimes bedridden. Appears in DRAGONBLADE.

Cartingdon, Balin – Mayor of Cartingdon and the father of Toby Cartingdon. He is a farmer of noble descent who amassed a great empire because of Toby's management. Appears in DRAGONBLADE.

Cartingdon, Judith – Mother of Toby and Ailsa, and wife of Balin Cartington. She suffered a stroke giving birth to Ailsa and is bedridden. Appears in DRAGONBLADE.

Cartingdon, Worth – He is an older, trusted knight serving Mars de Velt. He helps Valeria de Velt as she administers justice as Warden of the Tyne Vale. Appears in OF LOVE AND LEGEND.

Catesby, Andrew – A knight in the service of Davyss de Winter. He is the older brother of Edmund Catesby. Appears in LESPADA.

Catesby, Edmund – A knight in the service of Davyss de Winter. He is the younger brother of Andrew Catesby. Appears in LESPADA.

Chadlington, Bruce – He is Jillayne's father. Appears in GODSPEED.

Coleby, Keats – Garrison Commander of Pelinom Castle, and father of Kellington Coleby. Appears in THE DARK LORD. He serves William de Vesci, Baron of Northumberland.

Connaught, Brendan – Son of Kirk & Mara Connaught. Appears in THE DARKLAND.

Connaught, Bridget – Daughter of Kirk & Mara Connaught. Appears in THE DARKLAND.

Connaught, Christopher – A legacy knight for de Cleveley. Appears in BLACK SWORD.

Connaught, Drake – An Irish knight serving Lord Alex Ingilsby. Appears in THE DARK ONE: DARK KNIGHT.

Connaught, Drew – Brother of Kirk and Steven Connaught. Appears in THE DARKLAND.

Connaught, Kirk – Hero of THE DARKLAND. Captain of Anchorsholme Castle. Marries Mara le Bec.

Connaught, Mara le Bec – Heroine of THE DARKLAND. Wife of Kirk Connaught, Captain of Anchorsholme Castle.

Connaught, Regan – Son of Kirk & Mara Connaught. Appears in THE DARKLAND.

Connaught, Ryan – Firstborn son of Kirk & Mara Connaught. Appears in THE DARKLAND.

Connaught, Steven – Brother of Kirk and Drew Connaught. Appears in THE DARKLAND.

Corbin, Steven – The reincarnated version of Simon de Corlet, Kieran's assassin in THE CRUSADER. He is an attorney representing the modern-day Hage Family. Also appears in KINGDOM COME.

Cornwallis, Max – A knight in the service of Christopher de Lohr. Appears in DEVIL'S DOMINION and SPECTRE OF THE SWORD.

Crandall, Anne – Daughter of LeRoy Crandall. Appears in THE DARK LORD.

Crandall, LeRoy – Lord of White Crag Castle. Serves under Gilbert de Vesci. Appears in THE DARK LORD.

Cromford, Anthony – He is Lord Sherston. He marries Jillayne Chadlington. Appears in GODSPEED.

Cromford, Jillayne Chadlington – She is the daughter of Bruce Chadlington. Appears in GODSPEED.

Cropton, Eulalie – She was Asher's first love, and died in the phaeton accident. She appeared in EMMA.

Crosby-Denedor, Lavaine de Chambon – Lady-in-waiting to Kellington Coleby. Appears in THE DARK LORD. Her first husband was Sir Trevan de Chambon, one of Keat's Coleby's captains. She later marries Norjdul Crosby-Denedor. She also appears in THE DARK LORD'S FIRST CHRISTMAS.

Crosby-Denedor, Norjdul – The Commander of Alnwick Castle, serving Baron Gilbert de Vesci of Northumberland. Appears in THE DARK LORD. He later marries LaVaine de Chambon. He also appears in THE DARK LORD'S FIRST CHRISTMAS.

Crosby-Denedor, William "Will" – Son of Denedor, who is Commander of Alnwick Castle. Appears in THE DARK LORD.

Cuthbert, Audrey – She is the illegitimate daughter of Matthew Wellesbourne and his former love interest, Mena Cuthbert. She looks like her father, Matthew. She appears in THE WHITE LORD OF WELLESBOURNE.

Cuthbert, Mena – She is the cousin of Caroline Wellesbourne, and was the former love interest of Matthew Wellesbourne. She bore Matthew an illegitimate daughter and then married someone else. She appears in THE WHITE LORD OF WELLESBOURNE.

d'Athee, Gerard – One of two strong-arm personal protectors of King John, with Sean de Lara being the main strong-arm. Appears in LORD OF THE SHADOWS.

d'Aubigney, Hugh – He is the 4th Earl of Norfolk and liege of Brighton de Royans. He is married to Isabelle d'Aubigney. He appears in UNENDING LOVE.

d'Aubigney, Isabelle – She is the Countess of Norfolk, and is married to Hugh d'Aubigney. She appears in UNENDING LOVE.

d'Aurilliac, Avalyn du Brant Aubrey – Heroine of VALIANT CHAOS. She is the niece of "The Kingmaker," Richard de Neville.

d'Aurilliac, Brogan – Hero of VALIANT CHAOS. He is a Germanic foot soldier, sergeant of King Edward's infantry. He later becomes a knight in Saxony, Germany.

d'Aurilliac, Hans – He is a big German man, and is one of Andrew d'Vant's generals. He is also the father of Brogan d'Aurilliac. He appears in THE RED FURY.

d'Aurilliac, Lake – She was a street child when she was discovered, and was later adopted by Avalyn and Brogan d'Aurilliac. Appears in VALIANT CHAOS.

d'Aurilliac, Starke – Brogan d'Aurilliac's mother. Appears in VALIANT CHAOS.

d'Avignon, Caius – He is the commander at Richmond Castle. He is also known as The Britannia Viper. He appears in STARLESS.

d'Avignon, Matins "Mat" – He is the simple-minded older brother of Vesper d'Avignon. He appears in VESTIGES OF VALOR.

d'Avignon, McCloud – He is the father of Vesper d'Avignon. He is slovenly, old, and grizzled. He appears in VESTIGES OF VALOR.

d'Avignon, Olivier – Burly blond knight. Appears in DEVIL'S DOMINION.

d'Avignon, Stephan – He is a knight sworn to Jasper de Lara. He is nicknamed 'Bear.' Appears in DARK DESTROYER.

d'Einen, Gryfynn – Appears in NETHERWORLD. Oldest son and heir of Trevyn d'Einen, and brother to Chrystobel and Izlynn.

d'Einen, Trevynn – Father of Gryfynn, Chrystobel, and Izlynn. He is the former lord of Nether Castle. Appears in NETHERWORLD.

d'Eneas, Jory – A dishonorable knight in the service at Prudhoe Castle. Appears in GUARDIAN OF DARKNESS.

d'Evereux, Curtiz – He is a cutthroat mercenary serving Lucifer. He previously served de Nerra's mercenary army. Appears in SEA WOLFE.

d'Evereux, Gillem – A knight serving Juston de Royans. He appears in LORD OF WINTER.

d'Oro, Alphonse – Lord Ingilby's closest advisor and commander. He is a cunning and evil man. He appears in FRAGMENTS OF GRACE.

D'Savigniac, Orian – One of the Titan Generals. Appears in THE DARK LORD.

d'Umfraville, Anne – Wife of Richard d'Umfraville and parents to Gilbert & Edward d'Umfraville. Appears in GUARDIAN OF DARKNESS.

d'Umfraville, Edward – Youngest son of Richard & Anne d'Umfraville. Appears in GUARDIAN OF DARKNESS.

d'Umfraville, Gilbert – Oldest son of Richard & Anne d'Umfraville. Appears in GUARDIAN OF DARKNESS.

d'Umfraville, Richard – Lord of Prudhoe Castle. Husband to Anne d'Umfraville. They are the parents of Gilbert and Edward d'Umfraville. Appears in GUARDIAN OF DARKNESS.

d'Vant, Alphonse – He is the older brother of Andrew d'Vant, and is the Earl of Anan & Blackbank of Haldane Castle. He appears in THE RED FURY.

d'Vant, Andrew – Hero of THE RED FURY. His nickname is 'The Red Fury,' and is the leader of an almost one-thousand-man mercenary army. He later becomes the Earl of Anan & Blackbank of Haldane Castle, and holds the title of Viscount Brydekirk. Cousin to Roan d'Vant. He also appears in THE WOLFE.

d'Vant, Charlotte – She is the sister of Dennis d'Vant and is the niece of King Henry II and his brother, Richard, Earl of Cornwall. She was raised as a knight and fights like one too. She later marries Riston de Titouan. Appears in TENDER IS THE KNIGHT.

d'Vant, Dacian – He is the Captain of the Guard for King Henry II at Winchester Castle. He appears in VESTIGES OF VALOR.

d'Vant, Damian – He is a knight serving Patrick de Wolfe. Appears in NIGHTHAWK.

d'Vant, Dennis – Hero of TENDER IS THE KNIGHT. He is the nephew of King Henry III and his brother Richard, Earl of Cornwall. He becomes the Lord of St. Austell upon his father's death and marries Ryan de Bretagne.

d'Vant, Dirk – Serving King Henry III as part of his Guard of Six. Appears in SILVERSWORD.

d'Vant, Elaine – She is the mother of Alphonse and Andrew d'Vant, and appears in THE RED FURY.

d'Vant, Felix – He is a senior officer serving Constantine le Brecque and Lucifer. Appears in LEADER OF TITANS and SEA WOLFE.

d'Vant, Joey Elaine Nicola – She is the firstborn daughter of Andrew and Josephine d'Vant, and first appears in THE RED FURY.

d'Vant, Josephine de Carron – Heroine of THE RED FURY. She's the heiress of Torridon Castle, and leads her army as a fighter. Her titles are Countess of Ayr and Lady Ashkirk. Her nickname is "Joey." She later becomes the Countess of Anan & Blackbank.

d' Vant, Marcus – He is the firstborn son of Dennis & Ryan d'Vant. First appears in TENDER IS THE KNIGHT.

d'Vant, Roan – Part of King Henry's Household Troops. Cousin to The Red Fury, Andrew d'Vant. Appears in THE WOLFE.

d'Vant, Ryan de Bretagne – Heroine of TENDER IS THE KNIGHT. She is the illegitimate daughter of Richard, Earl of Cornwall, and brother to King Henry III. She is raised by her mother's husband, Thomas de Bretagne.

d'Vant, Tallis – Firstborn son of Dennis & Ryan d'Vant, the hero and heroine of TENDER IS THE KNIGHT. He appears in THE THUNDER KNIGHT.

Dalmellington, Colin – He is the mortal enemy of the de Carron family. He has been feuding with Castle Torridon for years. He appears in THE RED FURY.

Darlow, Justin – Senior Administrative Aid at the British Embassy in Tel Aviv. Appears in THE CRUSADER and KINGDOM COME.

de Ameland, Dyl – He is the oldest son and heir of Winslow de Ameland. He appears in THE CENTURION.

de Ameland, Winslow – He is lord at Makendon Castle. He is the father of Dyl and Alyx. He appears in THE CENTURION.

de Aston, Christina de Lohr – Oldest daughter of David & Emilie de Lohr. First appears in RISE OF THE DEFENDER and STEELHEART. Also appears in ARCHANGEL. In UNENDING LOVE she was married Merric de Aston, and they became the parents of Adalind de Aston du Bois and Willow de Aston de Foix.

de Aston, Markus – Captain of the Guard at Stretford Castle. He appears in DARK MOON.

de Aughton, Niclas – A knight in service to Thomas de Nerra. Appears in THE FALLS OF ERITH.

de Barenton, Rose – An older woman, her sister is the mother of Lyssia du Bose. She is the premiere lady-in-waiting to the Duchess of Colchester. Appears in SHIELD OF KRONOS.

de Barenton, Tor – One of the Titan Generals. Appears in THE DARK LORD. He is a cousin to Atreus le Velle.

de Beaumont, Henry – An opportunist. He fights for himself. Appears in THE FALLEN ONE.

de Beckett, Lawrence – He is a knight in service to Christopher de Lohr. He is the traitor in SPECTRE OF THE SWORD.

de Beckett, Lincoln – A knight serving Simon de Montfort. He appears in THE THUNDER KNIGHT.

de Bermingham, Corey – Third oldest son of Devlin & Emllyn de Bermingham. Appears in BLACK SWORD.

de Bermingham, Daven – Second oldest son of Devlin & Emllyn de Bermingham. Appears in BLACK SWORD.

de Bermingham, Devlin – Known as "Black Sword." Hero of BLACK SWORD. He is the firstborn and recognized bastard son of John de Birmingham, Earl of Louth. His mother is Elohn.

de Bermingham, Emllyn Fitzgerald – Also known as Catherine St. John. Heroine of BLACK SWORD. Daughter of Victor St. John.

de Bermingham, Flynn – Oldest son of Devlin & Emllyn de Bermingham. Appears in BLACK SWORD.

de Birmingham, Conor – A knight who serves Kenton le Bec in WALLS OF BABYLON. Known as part of the "Trouble Trio."

de Birmingham, Dallan – An Irish knight whose loyalty can be bought. He is greedy and shifty. Appears in DEVIL'S DOMINION.

de Bocage, Case – He is Michael de Bocage's younger son. He is a young knight serving the de Wolfes and appears in DARKWOLFE.

de Bocage, Corbin – He is Michael de Bocage's younger son. He is a young knight serving the de Wolfes and appears in DARKWOLFE.

de Bocage, Michael – A knight and main character in THE WOLFE. He also appears as a young knight in UNENDING LOVE, and as an older knight in DARKWOLFE. He is the father of the heroine of THE QUESTING, Diamantha de Bocage de Bretagne, and the father of Tobias de Bocage, Case de Bocage, and Corbin de Bocage.

de Bocage, Tobias – He is Michael de Bocage's oldest son and is a young knight serving the de Wolfes. He appears in DARKWOLFE.

de Bowland, Reid – A knight in the service of Kenneth St. Hever. Appears in ISLAND OF GLASS.

de Braose, Guy – A knight and heir of Reginald de Braose. His father is a very powerful Marcher lord, and he comes from the ruthless House of de Braose. Appears in LORD OF THE SHADOWS.

de Bretagne, Allegria – Oldest daughter of Cortez & Diamantha de Bretagne. First appears in THE QUESTING.

de Bretagne, Andres – He is the younger brother of Cortez de Bretagne and is in his brother's service. Appears in THE QUESTING.

de Bretagne, Cortez – Hero of THE QUESTING. Served as a squire for Kevin Hage and appears in SCORPION. He is the Garrison Commander of Sherborne Castle, and was Drake de Winter's liege. Also appears in SWORDS AND SHIELDS.

de Bretagne, Cruz – Fifth child of Cortez & Diamantha de Bretagne. First appears in THE QUESTING.

de Bretagne, Diamantha de Bocage Edlington – Heroine of THE QUESTING. She was previously married to Robert Edlington, but he perished in Scotland after the battle of Falkirk. Her father is Michael de Bocage, a knight who served William de Wolfe in THE WOLFE.

de Bretagne, Gorsedd – Father of Cortez de Bretagne and Andres de Bretagne from The QUESTING. He is a knight for the Earl of Salisbury. He appears in SCORPION.

de Bretagne, Isabella – Third oldest child of Cortez & Diamantha de Bretagne. First appears in THE QUESTING.

de Bretagne, Jorrin – He is a legacy knight and the garrison commander for Sherborne Castle, and is a direct descendant of Cortez de Bretagne from THE QUESTING. He appears in THE IRON KNIGHT.

de Bretagne, Juliana – Fourth oldest child of Cortez & Diamantha de Bretagne. First appears in THE QUESTING.

de Bretagne, Lyla – She is a cousin to Ryan de Bretagne, and was raised at Launceston Castle with Ryan. Appears in TENDER IS THE KNIGHT.

de Bretagne, Mateo (Matt) – Sixth and youngest child of Cortez & Diamantha de Bretagne. First appears in THE QUESTING.

de Bretagne, Rhordi – Oldest son of Cortez & Diamantha de Bretagne. First appears in THE QUESTING.

de Bretagne, Thomas – He is the captain of the Earl of Cornwall's army at Launceston Castle. His wife bore the illegitimate child from the Earl of Cornwall and raised Ryan as his own daughter. Appears in TENDER IS THE KNIGHT.

de Burg, Nicholas – He is a knight in the service of Christopher de Lohr. Appears in RISE OF THE DEFENDER.

de Burgh, Hubert – He is the elderly the Chief Justicar of England in SPECTRE OF THE SWORD.

de Burgh, Walter – Younger brother of Hubert de Burgh of the powerful de Burgh family. He is older than Adalind du Bois' grandfather, David de Lohr, and is her unwanted suitor. Appears in UNENDING LOVE.

de Cairon, Henley – One of Ajax de Velt's knights. Appears in THE DARK LORD.

de Camville, Clive – He is a knight serving Dennis d'Vant. He marries Charlotte d'Vant. Appears in TENDER IS THE KNIGHT.

de Chevington, Angela – Wife of Mylo Chevington. She appears in HIGH WARRIOR.

de Chevington, Edward – Only son and child of Mylo and Angela de Chevington. He is a spoiled child. He appears in HIGH WARRIOR.

de Chevington, Mylo – A senior knight to Bric MacRohan, and is in the service of Daveigh de Winter. He appears in HIGH WARRIOR.

de Clare, Roger – A wealthy baron whose seat is Elswick Castle. His cousin is Gilbert de Clare, 6th Earl of Gloucester. Father of William de Clare. Appears in THE FALLS OF ERITH.

de Clare, William – The eldest son and heir of Roger de Clare. Appears in THE FALLS OF ERITH.

de Clerc, Simon – A knight who served with Alec in the Crusades. He is now the owner of an inn. Appears in THE LEGEND.

de Cleveley, Edmund – Lord of Anchorsholme Castle. Demented first husband of Micheline le Bec, and step-brother to Johanne de Cleveley. Appears in THE DARKLAND.

de Cleveley, Johanne – The demented and psychotic step-sister to Edmund de Cleveley. Appears in THE DARKLAND.

de Comlach, Michael – One of Ajax de Velt's knights. Appears in THE DARK LORD.

de Cor, Lucius – Former and disgraced Captain of the Guard for Garson Mortimer. Appears in ISLAND OF GLASS.

de Corlet, Simon – A traitorous knight who used to be a friend of Kieran's. He is cruel and arrogant, and has a great sense of entitlement. He tried to assassinate Kieran several times. Appears in KINGDOM COME.

de Correa, Arlo – He is the second-in-command of Tiverton's army. Appears in BAY OF FEAR.

de Correa, Maude – She is the wife of Arlo de Correa. Appears in BAY OF FEAR.

de Dalyn, Nicholas – A cunning and manipulative knight, who is also arrogant and ambitious. He schemes to take over command of Lavister Crag Castle. Appears in QUEEN OF LOST STARS.

de Dere, Achilles – Hero of STARLESS. He is the muscle of Juston de Royans' core of knights, and is part of his Unholy Trinity. He appears in LORD OF WINTER. In BY THE UNHOLY HAND he is one of the Executioner Knights and part of the Unholy Trinity. He also appears in THE MOUNTAIN DARK.

de Dere, Alis – Youngest daughter of Achilles & Susanna de Dere. She first appears in STARLESS.

de Dere, Brickley – Captain of the Guard for the Earl of Canterbury, Lyle Hampton. Appears in STEELHEART.

de Dere, Brigit – Firstborn child and daughter of Achilles & Susanna de Dere. She first appears in STARLESS.

de Dere, Elizabeth "Libby" – Second oldest child of Achilles & Susanna de Dere. She first appears in STARLESS.

de Dere, Pearce – A senior knight to Bric MacRohan, and is in the service of Daveigh de Winter in HIGH WARRIOR.

de Dere, Susanna de Tiegh – Heroine of STARLESS. She was assigned by William Marshal to be the female bodyguard for Cadelyn of Vendotia during her childhood. She trained as a female warrior at Blackchurch for three years by the Lords of Exmoor, otherwise known as the pirates of Exmoor. Her father is Baron Coverdale

from Aysgarth Castle in Cumbria. She appears in THE
MOUNTAIN DARK.

de Dere, Tiegh – Oldest son of Achilles & Susanna de Dere. He first
appears in STARLESS.

de Dere, Tyren – Hero in OF LOVE AND LEGEND. Head of the
House of de Dere. He is also known as the Greenhead Ghost.

de Dere, Valeria de Velt – Heroine in OF LOVE AND LEGEND. She
is secretly the Warden of Tyne Vale when her father, Mars de Velt,
becomes incapacitated.

de Dere, Zara – Wife to Pearce de Dere in HIGH WARRIOR.

de Digge, Wallace – A younger brother of the Lord of Chilham Castle.
He appears in UNENDING LOVE.

de Edwin, Emyl – He is an aged knight and is Fergus de Edwin's
father. He appears in THE WHISPERING NIGHT.

de Edwin, Fergus – A bachelor knight and best friend to Garren le
Mon. He appears in THE WHISPERING NIGHT.

de Evereux, Piers – A French knight who's a paid assassin for the
Templars. Appears in SCORPION.

de Ferrar, Adam – He is a knight serving Nathaniel du Rennic. It is
was rumored that he was Nathaniel's illegitimate son. He appears
in SHADOWWOLFE.

de Ferrer, George – A knight at de Cleveley's settlement. Appears in
BLACK SWORD.

de Ferrers, Aland – He is a knight and childhood friend of Rhogan de
Garr. He is also known as Lord Hawkley. He appears in REALM
OF ANGELS.

de Ferrers, Daphne – Daughter of the Baron Albury. Appears in
LORD OF WAR: BLACK ANGEL.

de Ferrers, Kieran – Oldest son of Annavieve and Kevin Hage. He inherited the title Duke of Dorset at his birth since when his mother's first husband died. Appears in SCORPION.

de Ferrers, Sabine – Baroness Albury, wife to Baron Albury. Appears in LORD OF WAR: BLACK ANGEL.

de Ferrers, Victor – Duke of Dorset, close cousin to King Edward I. Annavieve Fitz Roderick's first husband. Appears in SCORPION.

de Ferrers, William – He is the young heir to the earldom of Derby. Appears in STEELHEART.

de Fey, Ossian – He is a knight in service to St. Michael du Pont in THE IRON KNIGHT.

de Fira, Beaufort – He is the best friend of Tenner de Velt. Appears in BAY OF FEAR.

de Fira, Jane FitzJohn – She is the daughter of Ivor FitzJohn. Appears in BAY OF FEAR.

de Fluorney, Jubil – Aunt of Peyton & Ivy de Fluorney. She is a self-proclaimed witch. Appears in THE LEGEND.

de Foix, Edward – Twin son of Rhys and Elizabeau (du Bois) de Foix. First appears in SPECTRE OF THE SWORD.

de Foix, Evan – He is the oldest twin son of Rhys and Elizabeau (du Bois) de Foix. He is the half-brother of Maddoc du Bois, and is the twin brother of Edward in SPECTRE OF THE SWORD. He appears as a young man in UNENDING LOVE.

de Foix, Geniver – Daughter of Rhys and Elizabeau (du Bois) de Foix. First appears in SPECTRE OF THE SWORD.

de Foix, Morgan – Daughter of Rhys and Elizabeau (du Bois) de Foix. First appears in SPECTRE OF THE SWORD.

de Foix, Rhiann – Daughter of Rhys and Elizabeau (du Bois) de Foix. First appears in SPECTRE OF THE SWORD.

de Foix, Trevor – Youngest son of Rhys and Elizabeau (du Bois) de Foix. He is a half-brother to Maddoc du Bois. He appears in UNENDING LOVE as a young man. Trevor later marries Willow de Aston, Adalind du Bois' younger sister.

de Foix, William – Younger son and child of Rhys and Elizabeau (du Bois) de Foix. First appears in SPECTRE OF THE SWORD.

de Foix, Willow de Aston – She is Adalind de Aston du Bois' younger sister. Appears in UNENDING LOVE. She later marries Trevor de Foix, the younger half-brother of Maddoc du Bois.

de Fortlage, Amanda – She is the mother of Christopher de Lohr's bastard son, Peter Myles de Vries. Her father is the Earl of Chaumont. Appears in RISE OF THE DEFENDER.

de Fortlage, Corin – A knight in THE WOLFE.

de Gael, Geoffrey – He is the Earl of East Anglia, until he perishes, and then the title went to Tevin du Reims. He appears in WHILE ANGELS SLEPT.

de Gare, Etienne – A knight serving the House of de Dere. Appears in OF LOVE AND LEGEND.

de Gare, Malcolm – Adopted orphan who Christian and Gaithlin found in Scotland. He's raised by Gaithlin's mother. Appears in THE WARRIOR POET.

de Garr, Afton – Roane & Alisanne de Garr's oldest daughter. She marries Titus Penden. First appears in LORD OF LIGHT.

de Garr, Alexandra – She is the youngest of Roane & Alisanne de Garr's children. First appears in LORD OF LIGHT.

de Garr, Alisanne de Soulant – Heroine of LORD OF LIGHT. She is the only child of Edward de Soulant, and heiress of Kinlet Castle and the Craven barony. She suffered from a blindness affliction for a short period.

de Garr, Bowen – The eldest son and heir of Darwich de Garr, who inherited the barony of Coniston when his father passed away. He is the older brother of Roane de Garr. Appears in LORD OF LIGHT.

de Garr, Britt – Serving King Henry III as part of his Guard of Six. Appears in SILVERSWORD.

de Garr, Dallan – Twin son of Roane & Alisanne de Garr. He is loud and aggressive. First appears in LORD OF LIGHT.

de Garr, Juliana de Nerra – Heroine of REALM OF ANGELS. She marries Rhogan de Garr. She is the younger sister of Gavin de Nerra, and a daughter of Valor de Nerra from VESTIGES OF VALOR. She is a lady-in-waiting to the Duchess of Colchester, and is a good friend to Lyssia du Bose. Appeared in SHIELD OF KRONOS.

de Garr, Mayne – He is a knight serving Valor de Nerra. He appears in VESTIGES OF VALOR. He is the father of Rhogan de Garr, who is the hero of REALM OF ANGELS.

de Garr, Lynton – Twin son of Roane & Alisanne de Garr. He is calm and calculating. First appears in LORD OF LIGHT.

de Garr, Rhogan – Hero of REALM OF ANGELS. He was a very handsome knight until his accident. He is the son of Mayne de Garr, who was in service to Valor de Nerra in VESTIGES OF VALOR.

de Garr, Roane – Hero of LORD OF LIGHT. He is a knight, a healer who served in the Order of the Hospitallers of St. John the Baptist. Through his wife's father he inherits the title of Baron Craven and Kinlet Castle.

de Gault, Amalia – Wife of Augustus de Gault. Appears in DEVIL'S DOMINION.

de Gault, Ares – One of the Titan Generals. Cousin to Jax de Velt. Appears in THE DARK LORD & DEVIL'S DOMINION. Father of Augustus de Gault.

de Gault, Augustus – Son of Ares de Gault. Appears in DEVIL'S DOMINION.

de Geld, Anton – Lord of Exelby, Baron Kirklington. He is married to Princess Blanche, daughter of King Henry III. They are the parents of Cassandra and Chloe de Geld. Appears in FRAGMENTS OF GRACE.

de Geld, Blanche – Daughter of King Henry III. She is a princess and the mother of Cassandra and Chloe de Geld. Wife to Anton de Geld. Appears in FRAGMENTS OF GRACE.

de Havilland, Charles – He is the Earl of Fenwark and is a supporter of Prince John. His wife is Gabrielle de Havilland. Appears in RISE OF THE DEFENDER.

de Havilland, Isobelle – She is the sister of Charles de Havilland and former sister-in-law to Gabrielle de Havilland Burton. Appears in RISE OF THE DEFENDER.

de Kirk, Hawys – Lady of Kirk Castle. She is the wife of Owain de Kirk. Appears in QUEEN OF LOST STARS.

de Kirk, Owain – Lord of Kirk Castle. He is a short man with black hair and black eyes. Appears in QUEEN OF LOST STARS.

de Lacy, Henry – Earl of Lincoln. Appears in FRAGMENTS OF GRACE.

de Lacy, Preston – He is Lord Barklestone, and was the first husband of Theodora de Rivington. He appears in THE PROMISE.

de la Chambre, Regal – Mother of Antoinette de Rivington. She is the grandmother of Theodora de Rivington. She appears in THE PROMISE.

de La Haye, Emerald "Emmie" Linhope – Heroine of THE JEWEL'S EMBRACE. She is the daughter of Lammy Linhope, and sister to Sapphire, Garnet, and Amethyst.

de la Haye, Falcon – Twin brother of River de la Haye. He is the heir to the Earl of Drumburgh. He appears in THE JEWEL'S EMBRACE.

de La Haye, Gilbert – He is the brother of Brighton's mother, Juliana de la Haye. Appears in NIGHTHAWK.

de la Haye, River – Hero of THE JEWEL'S EMBRACE. He is a twin son of Roget and Julia de la Haye.

de la Haye, Roget – Father of twin sons River and Falcon. He is the Earl of Drumburgh. Appears in THE JEWEL'S EMBRACE.

de la Londe, Denys – A big knight in service to King John. Appears in GUARDIAN OF DARKNESS.

de la Londe, Simon – A knight who served Titus de Wolfe. He later became a traitor and murdered Titus in THE LION OF THE NORTH.

de la Roarke, Brey – He was the garrison commander of Bowes Castle. He is known as the "Bloody Knight of Bowes." He killed and robbed travelers on the road who passed by his castle. He appears in LORD OF WINTER.

de la Roarke, Jessamyn la Marche – She is the oldest sister of Emera la Marche. She was married to the commander of Bowes Castle, Brey de la Roarke. She appears in LORD OF WINTER.

de la Roarke, Sloan – He is a friend of Bradford de Rivington. Appears in THE PROMISE.

de Lancaster, Eleanor – Wife of the Duke of Gloucester. Appears in BEAST.

de Lancaster, Humphrey – Duke of Gloucester. Brother of John de Lancaster and King Henry V. Uncle of King Henry VI. Gisella le

Bec lives in their household as she is a lady-in-waiting to the Duke of Gloucester's wife, Eleanor. He has been pursuing Gisella, and gave her lots of gifts privately, which included the white stallion that Gisella gifted to Bastian as a wedding gift. Appears in BEAST.

de Lancaster, John – Duke of Bedford. Bastian serves the duke. Brother was King Henry V. Uncle of King Henry VI. Appears in BEAST.

de la Pole, Thomas – Younger brother of the Earl of Suffolk. Antagonist in BEAST.

de Lara, Abechail – Youngest sister of Cathlina de Lara and Roxane de Lara. Appears in THE FALLEN ONE.

de Lara, Alexander – A twin son of Tate & Toby de Lara. Appears in DRAGONBLADE, THE SAVAGE CURTAIN, and THE FALLEN ONE. Along with his identical twin brother, he is a knight in service to Brandt de Russe. Alex marries Annabeth du Gare. Appears in LORD OF WAR: BLACK ANGEL.

de Lara, Annabeth du Gare – A lady-in-waiting for Ellowynn de Russe. She later marries Alex de Lara. Appears in LORD OF WAR: BLACK ANGEL.

de Lara, Arabella Mary – Daughter of Tate & Toby de Lara. Appears in DRAGONBLADE and THE SAVAGE CURTAIN.

de Lara, Catherine "Cate" Ailsa – Named after Tate's first wife who died in childbirth, and also after Toby's sister Ailsa. Appears in DRAGONBLADE and THE SAVAGE CURTAIN. She marries Cade Seton Pembury.

de Lara, Colm – He is a knight serving Patrick de Wolfe. Appears in NIGHTHAWK.

de Lara, Dane – Son of Toby & Tate de Lara. First appears in THE SAVAGE CURTAIN.

de Lara, Dylan – A twin son of Tate & Toby de Lara. Appears in DRAGONBLADE, THE SAVAGE CURTAIN, and THE FALLEN ONE. He is a knight who serves Brandt de Russe, and is his second-in-command in LORD OF WAR: BLACK ANGEL.

de Lara, Elizabetha de Tobins **"Toby"** Cartingdon – Heroine of DRAGONBLADE. Daughter of the Balin Cartingdon, who is the mayor of Cartingdon. She actually rules the town instead of her father. Also appears in THE FALLEN ONE, THE SAVAGE CURTAIN, and ISLAND OF GLASS.

de Lara, Ellice – Older sister of Kellen de Lara. She appears in THE THUNDER WARRIOR.

de Lara, Garreth – Duke of Shrewsbury and Lord of the Trinity Castles before his death. He is the father of Grier de Lara de Russe. Appears in DARK STEEL.

de Lara, Heath – He is a knight serving Weston de Royans. Appears in TO THE LADY BORN.

de Lara, Jasper – Appears in DARK DESTROYER. He is the father of Kathalin de Lara, and is the son of Liam de Lara, who is the adopted brother of Tate de Lara from DRAGONBLADE.

de Lara, Kellen – Lord Sheriff of the Southern Marches. He is the widowed father of Courtly and Isadora de Lara. He appears in THE THUNDER WARRIOR.

de Lara, Kevin – Serves David de Lohr and close friend of Gart Forbes. Younger brother of Sean de Lara of THE SHADOW LORD. Appears in ARCHANGEL, BY THE UNHOLY HAND, and STARLESS.

de Lara, Liam – He is the half-brother to Tate de Lara. His son is Jasper de Lara from DARK DESTROYER. Appears in DRAGONBLADE.

de Lara, Luc – He is a noble of Spanish blood, and is the Count of Boucau. He marries Verity Shericus (later de Shera). Luc and Verity become the ancestors of the de Lara family in England. He appears in WARWOLFE.

de Lara, Lucas – A knight serving Bastian. Appears in BEAST.

de Lara, Marcus – A big knight who is brilliant and well-spoken, but is rather mean. He is the commander at Beeston Castle. Appears in FRAGMENTS OF GRACE.

de Lara, Roman – Firstborn son of Tate & Toby de Lara. Appears in DRAGONBLADE, THE SAVAGE CURTAIN, and THE FALLEN ONE.

de Lara, Rosalund – Mother of Roxane, Cathlina, and Abechail. Wife of Saer de Lara. Appears in THE FALLEN ONE.

de Lara, Rosamund du Bois – Appears in DARK DESTROYER. She is the mother of Kathalin de Lara, and is from the de Titouan, de Llion, and du Bois family through Rhys du Bois (from SPECTRE OF THE SWORD). She has leprosy.

de Lara, Roxane – She is the older sister of Cathlina de Lara. Appears in THE FALLEN ONE.

de Lara, Saer – Father of Roxane, Cathlina, and Abechail. Husband of Rosalund de Lara. He used to be called "The Axe" in his younger days. Appears in THE FALLEN ONE.

de Lara, Sean – Hero of LORD OF THE SHADOWS. He is a double-agent posing as a spy/strong-arm/personal protector of King John. His deadly nickname is 'The Shadow Lord.' He is the great-grandfather many times over of Tate de Lara from DRAGONBLADE. He is the oldest son and heir of Viscount Trelystan, Stephan de Lara, a powerful Marcher Lord. He inherits the title of Viscount Darlignton and Stonegrave Castle. He also served Christopher de Lohr in RISE OF THE DEFENDER and

STEELHEART. He also appears in HIGH WARRIOR, BY THE UNHOLY HAND, and THE PROMISE.

de Lara, Sheridan St. James – Heroine of LORD OF THE SHADOWS. She is the daughter of Henry and Lillian St. James, and heiress to the earldom of Bath and Glastonbury. She is the oldest sister of Alys St. James.

de Lara, Sophie – Youngest child of Tate and Toby de Lara. Appears in THE FALLEN ONE and THE SAVAGE CURTAIN.

de Lara, Stephen – Viscount Trelystan. Father of Kevin and Sean de Lara. He commands the Trinity Castles on the Welsh Marshes. Appears in ARCHANGEL.

de Lara, Tate Crewys – Hero of DRAGONBLADE. Bastard firstborn son of King Edward I. Half-brother of Edward II. Uncle to Edward III. His mother was a princess of Wales. He was given to the Marcher Lords of de Lara to raise. He is Lord of Harbottle and Earl of Carlisle. He is also Baron of Workington and Consett, and Viscount Whitehaven. He is also the Lord Protector of Cumbria. His nickname is 'Dragonblade' because his sword hilt has a dragonhead on it and Tate is known to wield his sword with great power. Also appears in THE FALLEN ONE, THE SAVAGE CURTAIN, and ISLAND OF GLASS. Appears in FRAGMENTS OF GRACE as a young page.

de Lara, Teague – The largest and youngest of Bretton's knights. Appears in DEVIL'S DOMINION.

de Lara, Verity Shericus – She is the middle daughter of Antillius Shericus. She later marries Luc de Lara and they become the ancestors of the de Lara family in England. She appears in WARWOLFE.

de Lave, Graham – He is a knight serving the St. Lo family. He appears in BAY OF FEAR.

de la Rosa, Edgar – He is the father of Daniella de la Rosa de Winter, and the father-in-law to Devon de Winter. He is from notorious Fighting de la Rosa family. Appears in SWORDS AND SHIELDS.

de la Rosa, Guy – He is a knight in the service of Christopher de Lohr. Appears in RISE OF THE DEFENDER.

de Leon, Graehm – A knight serving Braxton de Nerra. Appears in THE FALLS OF ERITH.

de Leybourne, Cecily – She is from Cornwall and is in the service as a lady-in-waiting to the Duchess of Colchester. Appears in SHIELD OF KRONOS.

de Leybourne, Henry – He is the father of Rhodes de Leybourne, and is Lord of Tyringham Castle. He appears in LADY OF THE MOON.

de Leybourne, Jareth – Serving King Henry III as part of his Guard of Six. Appears in SILVERSWORD.

de Leybourne, Rhodes – Hero of LADY OF THE MOON. Only son and heir of Henry de Leybourne of Tyringham Castle. He later inherits the title of Lord Tyringham, and of St. Ives, and of Trevalgan. He serves the Earl of Bristol, Bastian de Russe, from BEAST.

de Leybourne, Rhyne – An unscrupulous knight who was in service at Okehampton where Andressa du Bose de Long fostered at. He is the birth father of Andressa's firstborn child, Danae de Long. Appeared in BY THE UNHOLY HAND.

de Leybourne, Samarra le Brecque – Heroine of LADY OF THE MOON. She is female mercenary. Her father was a pirate, and her brother is a pirate. She rules the land and is from Mithian Castle.

de Llion, Allastan de Velt – Heroine of DEVIL'S DOMINION. Daughter of Ajax de Velt & Kellington Coleby de Velt from THE DARK LORD.

de Llion, Amaline – Youngest daughter of Roald de Llion. She dresses and fights like a warrior. Appears in THE RED LION.

de Llion, Berwyn – Bretton's grandfather. Garrison commander of Bronllys Castle. Appears in DEVIL'S DOMINION.

de Llion, Brethwyn de Titouan – Mother of Bretton de Llion. Appears in DEVIL'S DOMINION.

de Llion, Bretton – Hero of DEVIL'S DOMINION. Only son of Morgan & Brethwyn de Llion.

de Llion, Ceri – Bretton's only sibling and sister. Appears in DEVIL'S DOMINION.

de Llion, Gareth – Firstborn child and son of Bretton de Llion & Allaston de Velt de Llion. Appears in DEVIL'S DOMINION.

de Llion, Madeline – Second daughter of Roald de Llion. She dresses and fights like a warrior. Lover of Evon Preece. Appears in THE RED LION.

de Llion, Morgan – Bretton's father. He is the only son of Berwyn de Llion. He suffers from amnesia from a head injury. Appears in DEVIL'S DOMINION.

de Llion, Roald – He is the garrison commander for Four Crosses, and is vassal to Chris de Lohr. He is part Welsh and part English. He is the father of Havilland, Madeline, and Amaline de Llion. They are descendants of Bretton de Llion from DEVIL'S DOMINION.

de Lohr, Alessandria de Shera – Heroine of SILVERSWORD. She is the daughter of Julius de Shera and sister of Aurelius de Shera.

de Lohr, Alys de Titouan – She marries Christopher de Lohr, the grandson of Christopher de Lohr from RISE OF THE DEFENDER. She appears in SHADOWWOLFE.

de Lohr, Alexander – He is a knight sworn to Jasper de Lara. Appears in DARK DESTROYER. His parents are Henry & Elreda de Lohr, descendants of Christopher de Lohr from RISE OF THE DEFENDER.

de Lohr, Arthur – Brother to Christopher de Lohr II. Appears in SILVERSWORD.

de Lohr, Avrielle – Curtis de Lohr's wife. Appears in SILVERSWORD.

de Lohr, Bartholomew – The only son and heir of William & Maude de Lohr. He is flamboyant and eccentric, preferring to be a poet and a thespian. Appears in GREAT PROTECTOR.

de Lohr, Becket – Son of Christopher de Lohr, Earl of Worcester, and older brother of Tobias de Lohr. Appears in THE RED LION.

de Lohr, Brend – Son of William de Lohr, who is the brother of Christopher de Lohr, and older brother of Thad de Lohr. Appears in THE RED LION.

de Lohr, Brielle – Daughter of Christopher & Dustin de Lohr. First appears in RISE OF THE DEFENDER. Also appears in A BLESSED DE LOHR CHRISTMAS and DEVIL'S DOMINION.

de Lohr, Caroline – Daughter of David and Emilie de Lohr. First appears in RISE OF THE DEFENDER. She also appears in A BLESSED DE LOHR CHRISTMAS.

de Lohr, Chadwick – Hero of SILVERSWORD. He is nicknamed 'Silversword' because of the spectacular sword his grandfather, David de Lohr (STEELHEART), gave to him. He is the son of Daniel de Lohr (SHADOWMOOR) and inherits the title of Lord Thornden of Denstroude Castle and Whitehill Castle. He also will inherit the Earldom of Canterbury. The firstborn child and heir of Daniel & Liselotte de Lohr. First appears in SHADOWMOOR.

de Lohr, Christin – Oldest child and daughter of Christopher & Dustin de Lohr. First appears in RISE OF THE DEFENDER.

Appears in A BLESSED DE LOHR CHRISTMAS, DEVIL'S DOMINION and STEELHEART.

de Lohr, Christina – Youngest daughter of David and Emilie de Lohr. She first appears in A BLESSED DE LOHR CHRISTMAS.

de Lohr, Christopher – Hero of RISE OF THE DEFENDER. He is a knight in service to King Richard with the title of Defender of the Realm. He is in charge of all King Richard's crown troops. Another nickname given to him by King Richard is Lion's Claw. He is the brother of David de Lohr and Deborah de Lohr. He becomes the Earl of Hereford and Worcester. Son of Myles de Lohr and Val du Reims. In LORD OF WINTER he is a young general in Juston de Royans' army. As a young child, he was Juston de Royans' squire. Appears in ARCHANGEL, DEVIL'S DOMINION, SHADOWMOOR, STEELHEART, SPECTRE OF THE SWORD, SHIELD OF KRONOS, GODSPEED, BY THE UNHOLY HAND, THE MOUNTAIN DARK, and A BLESSED DE LOHR CHRISTMAS. He is an older man in UNENDING LOVE.

de Lohr, Christopher II – Grandson of Christopher de Lohr (RISE OF THE DEFENDER). He is heir to the earldom of Worcester. He marries Alys de Titouan. He appears in SHADOWWOLFE, SILVERSWORD, and SHADOWWOLFE.

de Lohr, Chris – He is the grandson of Christopher de Lohr from RISE OF THE DEFENDER, descended from the oldest son, Curtis. He appears in A WOLFE AMONG DRAGONS.

de Lohr, Colleen – Daughter of David and Emilie de Lohr. First appears in RISE OF THE DEFENDER. She also appears in A BLESSED DE LOHR CHRISTMAS and STEELHEART.

de Lohr, Curtis – Son of Christopher and Dustin de Lohr. First appears in RISE OF THE DEFENDER. He also appears as an infant in SPECTRE OF THE SWORD, and an older boy in A

BLESSED DE LOHR CHRISTMAS. e appears as an older man in SILVERSWORD.

de Lohr, Daniel – Hero of SHADOWMOOR. The only son and heir of David de Lohr (Steelheart), Earl of Canterbury. His title is Lord Thorndon. He is a knight and is known as a wanderer. He first appears in RISE OF THE DEFENDER. He also appears in STEELHEART and A BLESSED DE LOHR CHRISTMAS. He is a young knight in UNENDING LOVE. He also appears as an older man in NIGHTHAWK.

de Lohr, David – Hero of STEELHEART. Son of Myles de Lohr & Val du Reims. Younger brother to Christopher de Lohr, and older brother to Deborah de Lohr Olmquist. His nickname is Lion's Cub. Married to Emilie Hampton and through her he inherits to earldom of Canterbury. He is also Baron Thornden. He was also given the small barony of Kington by his brother Christopher, one which Christopher inherited, and through that is Lord Broxwood. He is young knight in service to Juston de Royans alongside his brother, Christopher, in LORD OF WINTER. Also appears in RISE OF THE DEFENDER, ARCHANGEL, SHADOWMOOR, SPECTRE OF THE SWORD, SHIELD OF KRONOS, GODSPEED, BY THE UNHOLY HAND, THE MOUNTAIN DARK, STARLESS, and A BLESSED DE LOHR CHRISTMAS. In UNENDING LOVE he is an older man. He is the grandfather of Adalind de Aston du Bois, wife of Maddoc du Bois.

de Lohr, Douglas – Second-in-Command of the Earl of Cornwall's army, under Thomas de Bretagne. Appears in TENDER IS THE KNIGHT.

de Lohr, Dru – Third child of Chris and Kaedia de Lohr. First appears in A WOLFE AMONG DRAGONS.

de Lohr, Dustin Barringdon – Heroine of RISE OF THE DEFENDER. She marries Christopher de Lohr. She is the only child of Arthur &

Mary Barringdon, and is the heiress to Lioncross Abbey. Appears in DEVIL'S DOMINION, STEELHEART, SPECTRE OF THE SWORD, and A BLESSED DE LOHR CHRISTMAS.

de Lohr, Edward – The only son and heir of Philip de Lohr. He is the first cousin to Christopher, David, and Deborah de Lohr. Appears in RISE OF THE DEFENDER and STEELHEART.

de Lohr, Elreda Augustine von Hault – She is the mother of Alexander de Lohr and is a Teutonic princess. Appears in DARK DESTROYER.

de Lohr, Emilie Hampton – Heroine of STEELHEART. Married to David de Lohr. Her father is Lyle Hampton, Earl of Canterbury. Appears in RISE OF THE DEFENDER, ARCHANGEL SHADOWMOOR, and A BLESSED DE LOHR CHRISTMAS. She appears in UNENDING LOVE and is a little older. She is the grandmother of Adalind de Aston du Bois, wife of Maddoc du Bois.

de Lohr, Henry – He is the father of Alexander de Lohr. Appears in DARK DESTROYER. Henry is a descendant of Christopher de Lohr from RISE OF THE DEFENDER.

de Lohr, James – A knight serving Drake de Winter. Appears in SWORDS AND SHIELDS. Appears in THE QUESTING in service to Cortez de Bretagne. He is the great-grandson of Christopher de Lohr through his son, Curtis de Lohr.

de Lohr, Kade – Fourth child of Chris and Kaedia de Lohr. First appears in A WOLFE AMONG DRAGONS.

de Lohr, Kaedia – Wife of Chris de Lohr. She is Welsh-born. She appears in A WOLFE AMONG DRAGONS.

de Lohr, Katrine – Firstborn child of Chad and Alessandria de Lohr. First appears in SILVERSWORD.

de Lohr, Kristoph – He is a Breton from Lohreac and is Gaetan de Wolfe's second-in-command. He is married to Gaetan's sister, Adalie. Kristoph and Adalie become the ancestors of the de Lohr family in England. He appears in WARWOLFE.

de Lohr, Liselotte l'Audacieux – Heroine of SHADOWMOOR. Daughter of Etzel l'Audacieux, Lord of Shadowmoor.

de Lohr, Maude – She is the wife of William de Lohr and adopted mother to Arissa de Lohr. She and William are the natural parents of Bartholomew and Regine de Lohr. Appears in GREAT PROTECTOR.

de Lohr, Michaela Maud – She is the third child and daughter of David & Emilie de Lohr. First appears in STEELHEART.

de Lohr, Morgan – Oldest child of Chris and Kaedia de Lohr. He appears in A WOLFE AMONG DRAGONS.

de Lohr, Myles – He is Brac Penden's second-in-command at Rochester Castle. At the beginning of this novel Myles was single and had not yet married Val du Reims. They eventually marry and have Christopher and David de Lohr. He appears in WHILE ANGELS SLEPT.

de Lohr, Myles – Great-grandson of Christopher de Lohr from RISE OF THE DEFENDER. He is the Earl of Hereford. He and his wife Agnes de Lohr raise Vietta de Lohr as their own daughter. Appears in SCORPION.

de Lohr, Myles – Son of Christopher and Dustin de Lohr. He first appears in RISE OF THE DEFENDER. He also appears in A BLESSED DE LOHR CHRISTMAS.

de Lohr, Perrin – Youngest brother of Chad and Stefan de Lohr. Appears in SILVERSWORD and IMMORTAL SEA.

de Lohr, Peter Myles de Vries – He is the illegitimate son of Christopher de Lohr and Amanda de Fortlage. He is a miniature version of Christopher. Appears in RISE OF THE DEFENDER and A BLESSED DE LOHR CHRISTMAS.

de Lohr, Philip – He is the brother of Myles de Lohr, who is the father of Christopher, David, and Deborah de Lohr. He is distinguished, fair, and brilliant, and is a confidant of King Richard. Appears in RISE OF THE DEFENDER and STEELHEART.

de Lohr, Rebecca – Daughter of Christopher and Dustin de Lohr. First appears in RISE OF THE DEFENDER. She also appears in A BLESSED DE LOHR CHRISTMAS.

de Lohr, Rees – Second oldest child of Chris and Kaedia de Lohr. First appears in A WOLFE AMONG DRAGONS.

de Lohr, Regine – Youngest daughter of William & Maude de Lohr. Appears in GREAT PROTECTOR.

de Lohr, Rhianne – Youngest child and daughter of Chris and Kaedia de Lohr. First appears in A WOLFE AMONG DRAGONS.

de Lohr, Richard – Son of Christopher and Dustin de Lohr. First appears in RISE OF THE DEFENDER. He also appears in A BLESSED DE LOHR CHRISTMAS.

de Lohr, Stefan – Younger brother of Chad de Lohr. Appears in SILVERSWORD.

de Lohr, Thad – Son of William de Lohr, who is the brother of Christopher de Lohr, and younger brother of Brend de Lohr. Appears in THE RED LION.

de Lohr, Tobias – Younger son of Christopher de Lohr, Earl of Worcester, and younger brother of Becket de Lohr. Appears in THE RED LION.

de Lohr, Valeria "Val" du Reims – She is a female knight in service to her brother, Tevin du Reims. At the beginning of this novel she was single. She eventually married Myles de Lohr and they became the parents of Christopher and David de Lohr. She appears in WHILE ANGELS SLEPT.

de Lohr, Vietta – Twin sister of Annavieve Fitz Roderick. Bastard daughter of the one of the last Prince of Wales, Rhordi ap Gruffydd and Lady Alys Marshall. She is raised as a child of Myles and Agnes de Lohr, and is the great-great-granddaughter of Christopher de Lohr from RISE OF THE DEFENDER. Appears in SCORPION.

de Lohr, William – Earl of Berkshire. He is Arissa de Lohr's adopted father. William is married to Maude de Lohr. They are also the parents of Bartholomew and Regine de Lohr. Appears in GREAT PROTECTOR.

de Lohr, William – Youngest brother of Christopher de Lohr II and Arthur de Lohr. Appears in SILVERSWORD.

de Londres, Nicholas – He is the favorite nephew of King Alexander. He appears in THE RED FURY.

de Long, Andressa du Bose – Heroine of BY THE UNHOLY KNIGHT. She was living at St. Blitha Convent after her greedy aunt stole her inheritance and dumped her at the convent. She fostered at Okehampton.

de Long, Carlton – A knight in service to William de Lohr. He is husband to Maxine de Long. They are the parents of Penelope de Long. Appears in GREAT PROTECTOR.

de Long, Ceri – Third child of Maxton and Andressa de Long. She appears in BY THE UNHOLY HAND.

de Long, Danae – Firstborn child of Andressa de Long. She was pregnant by Rhyne de Leybourne before she married Maxton de Long. Maxton claims her as his child. She appears in BY THE UNHOLY HAND.

de Long, Maxine – Wife of Carlton de Long, a knight in service to William de Lohr. They are the parents of Penelope de Long. Appears in GREAT PROTECTOR.

de Long, Maxton – Hero of BY THE UNHOLY HAND. He is also known as Maxton of Loxbeare. He is also known as one of the Executioner Knights; part of the Unholy Trinity, and is in the service of William Marshal. He was a younger knight serving Juston de Royans, and was part of his Unholy Trinity in LORD OF WINTER.

de Long, Melisandra – Firstborn child of Maxton and Andressa de Long. She appears in BY THE UNHOLY HAND.

de Long, Penelope – Best friends with Arissa de Lohr. She marries Daniel Ellsrod, a knight serving William de Lohr. Appears in GREAT PROTECTOR.

de Longley, Adam – Second son of John de Longley. A knight serving William de Wolfe. Later becomes Earl of Teviot. Appears as a younger man in THE WOLFE, and as an older man in A JOYOUS DE WOLFE CHRISTMAS, BLACKWOLFE, and THE BEST IS YET TO BE.

de Longley, Alexander – Firstborn son and heir to John de Longley. Appears in THE WOLFE.

de Longley, Analiese – Older daughter of John de Longley. Appears in THE WOLFE.

de Longley, Charlotte – Christian Hage's betrothed. Appears in KINGDOM COME.

de Longley, John – Earl of Teviot. Appears in THE WOLFE.

de Mandeville, Bruis – He is a son of Edmund de Mandeville, and is the brother of Julia de Mandeville de Witt. Appears in SWORDS AND SHIELDS.

de Mandeville, Edmund – He is the leader of the ragtag barbaric army of the de Mandevilles. They have a long and bitter grudge against the du Reim family. He is quite barbaric and insane. Appears in SWORDS AND SHIELDS.

de Mandeville, Geoff – One of Braxton de Nerra's knights. Appears in THE FALLS OF ERITH.

de Mandeville, Glenn – He is the oldest son of Edmund de Mandeville, and is the brother of Julia de Mandeville de Witt. Appears in SWORDS AND SHIELDS.

de Marmande, Desmond – He is a young knight in service to Lord Eynsford. He appears in VESTIGES OF VALOR.

de Marsh, Broderick – A knight in THE WOLFE.

de Meynell, Witton – Ally of Samuel de Tiegh. He appears in STARLESS.

de Milne, Blakeney– Captain of the Guard at Elswick Castle and son-in-law of Roger and Anne de Clare. Appears in THE FALLS OF ERITH.

de Montfort, Constance Gray – She is the mother of Gray de Montfort Serroux. She was married to Simon de Montfort's son and comes from the Northumberland Grays. Appears in THE FALLS OF ERITH.

de Montfort, Simon – He is the Earl of Leicester. He is also the biological father of Davyss de Winter through his affair with Katharine de Winter. He is also godfather to Davyss. Appears in LESPADA, THE THUNDER LORD, THE THUNDER WARRIOR, and THE THUNDER KNIGHT.

de Mora, Delaine-Navarre – She is the wife of Owen de Mora, and lives with him in Blackthorn Forest when they were expelled from their lands. She appears in THE PROMISE.

de Mora, Owen – He is the Lord of Blackthorn Forest when he was expelled from his lands as Lord Geddington. He is the leader of the thieves in the forest. His wife is Lady Delaine-Navarre of Guillaume. He appears in THE PROMISE.

de Moray, Artur – Bose de Moray's uncle. He is a trainer and helper to his nephew. He is a tiny old man with a crippled arm. Appears in THE GORGON.

de Moray, Atia Shericus – She is the youngest daughter of Antillius Shericus. She later marries Marc de Moray and they become the ancestors of the de Moray family in England. She appears in WARWOLFE.

de Moray, Bose – Hero of THE GORGON. Former Captain of the Guard under young King Henry III. His nickname is "The Gorgon" because he's dreadful on the battlefield. He marries Summer du Bonne and are the parents of Garran de Moray and Douglass de Moray. He is father-in-law to Tiberius de Shera. Appears in THE THUNDER WARRIOR, THE THUNDER KNIGHT, and SILVERSWORD.

de Moray, Dag – Bose de Moray's first cousin. He is a former knight who became a priest. Appears in THE GORGON.

de Moray, Garran Kermit – Baron Ashington. He is the firstborn son of Bose de Moray and Summer du Bonne de Moray. He first appears in THE GORGON. He named his daughter after his mother, Summer de Moray. He is a younger man in SILVERSWORD. He is a knight in service to Gallus de Shera in THE THUNDER LORD, THE THUNDER WARRIOR, and THE THUNDER KNIGHT. He is an older man in FRAGMENTS OF GRACE.

de Moray, Garret – Hero of SHIELD OF KRONOS. Captain of the Household Guard for King Richard. He is the father of Bose de

Moray from THE GORGON. His titles are Lord Ravendark and Lord Lockerley of Ravendark Castle.

de Moray, Lyssia du Bose – Heroine of SHIELD OF KRONOS. Lady-in-waiting to the Duchess of Colchester. She is the mother of Bose du Moray from THE GORGON.

de Moray, Marc – He is the former Sheriff of Rouen. He marries Atia Shericus (later de Shera), and they become the ancestors of the de Moray family in England. He appears in WARWOLFE.

de Moray, Remy – A muscular young man, he is the second mate to Constantine le Brecque and first mate to Lucifer. Appears in LEADER OF TITANS and SEA WOLFE.

de Moray, Rickard – He is the older brother of Garret de Moray. He is Captain of the Guard for the Duke of Colchester. Appears in SHIELD OF KRONOS.

de Moray, Rolf – Captain of King Henry's Household Troops. Appears in THE WOLFE.

de Moray, Summer du Bonne – The heroine of THE GORGON. Youngest daughter of Edward du Bonne. She stutters and thinks it's a handicap. Because of that, her family hides her so that no one can hear her imperfection. Summer and Bose de Moray are the parents of Garran de Moray. She is the grandmother of Summer de Moray from FRAGMENTS OF GRACE. She also appears in THE THUNDER KNIGHT.

de Moray, Tristiana de Dere – She is the wife of Rickard de Moray and appears in SHIELD OF KRONOS.

de Moreville, Neely – Captain of the Guard for the St. James troops. He is powerful, but calm man. He has always been in love with Sheridan St. James. Appears in LORD OF THE SHADOWS.

de Morville, Calum – He is Valor de Nerra's second-in-command at Selborne Castle. He appears in VESTIGES OF VALOR.

de Morville, Celesse – She is the wife of Calum de Morville. She appears in VESTIGES OF VALOR.

de Morville, Hugh – One of the group of four knights who served King Henry II, and who assassinated the Archbishop of Canterbury. His brother is Calum de Morville, who is the second-in-command to Valor de Nerra. He appears in VESTIGES OF VALOR.

de Motte, Daniel – Bastard son of Daniel de Troiu and Miranda le Londe de Motte. He is a commander at Deauxville Mount. Appears in BLACKWOLFE.

de Motte, Jess – A knight serving Lionel Harringham at the Lyceum. He appears in THE CENTURION.

de Motte, Miranda le Londe – Mother of Daniel de Motte. She is the daughter of Baron Rochedale. She is also known as Lady Chessington. She was a court courtesean in THE WOLFE, and appeared in that novel. Appears in BLACKWOLFE.

de Motte, Thaddeus – Stepfather of Daniel de Motte. He is married to Miranda le Londe. He is an older knight and is known as Lord Chessington. He appears in BLACKWOLFE.

de Moyon, Brendt – Youngest son of Emberley & Julian de Moyon. Appears in ARCHANGEL.

de Moyon, Julian – 3rd Baron Buckland. First husband of Emberley de Russe. Father of Romney, Orin, Brendt, and Lacy de Moyon. Appears in ARCHANGEL as the antagonist.

de Moyon, Lacy – Youngest daughter of Emberley & Julian de Moyon. Appears in ARCHANGEL.

de Moyon, Olin – Baron Buckland, Gregoria de Moyon's brother. Apppears in LEADER OF TITANS.

de Moyon, Orin – Second son of Emberley & Julian de Moyon. Appears in ARCHANGEL.

de Moyon, Romney – 4th Baron Buckland, Oldest child of Emberley & Julian de Moyon. Appears in ARCHANGEL.

de Nantes, Grace Fitzherbert – She is the Duchess of Colchester. Lyssia du Bose and her aunt Rose de Barenton serve her as ladies-in-waiting. Appears in SHIELD OF KRONOS.

de Nantes, Jago – He is the Duke of Colchester and is first cousin to King Richard. His father is Geoffrey of Nantes (the younger brother of King Richard) and his mother is a washerwoman's daughter. During the Crusades he was known as "Alfaar," which means "The Rat." Appears in SHIELD OF KRONOS.

de Nerra, Annalora de Gare – Wife of Deston de Nerra, and mother of Ellowynn de Nerra. Appears in LORD OF WAR: BLACK ANGEL.

de Nerra, Auston – Second son of Braxton & Gray de Nerra. Appears in THE FALLS OF ERITH.

de Nerra, Braxton – Hero of THE FALLS OF ERITH. He is a knight bannerette and leads his mercenary army. He is the youngest son of Thomas de Nerra.

de Nerra, Charlotte – She is the daughter of Val & Vesper de Nerra. She appears in REALM OF ANGELS.

de Nerra, Cullen – Hero of THE PROMISE. Son of Val & Vesper de Nerra from VESTIGES OF VALOR. He marries Theodora "Teddy" de Rivington. He also appears in REALM OF ANGELS and BY THE UNHOLY HAND.

de Nerra, Dair – A grandson of Thomas de Nerra. Appears in THE FALLS OF ERITH.

de Nerra, Davis – The second son of Thomas de Nerra. Appears in THE FALLS OF ERITH.

de Nerra, Deston – Firstborn child and son of Braxton and Gray de Nerra. First appears in THE FALLS OF ERITH. Also appears in

LORD OF WAR: BLACK ANGEL. Son of Braxton and Gray de Nerra from THE FALLS OF ERITH. He is the father of Ellowyn de Nerra, the heroine of LORD OF WAR: BLACK ANGEL.

de Nerra, Gabriel – Younger twin son of Valor & Vesper de Nerra. He first appears in VESTIGES OF VALOR. He also appears in REALM OF ANGELS.

de Nerra, Gavin – Firstborn twin son of Valor & Vesper de Nerra. He first appears in VESTIGES OF VALOR. He is a young knight in SHIELD OF KRONOS, and also appears in GODSPEED.

de Nerra, Gray de Montfort Serroux – Heroine of THE FALLS OF ERITH. Great grand-daughter of Henry II and grand-daughter of Simon de Montfort. Her first husband was Guy Serroux. Her second husband was Braxton de Nerra. She also appears in LORD OF WAR: BLACK ANGEL.

de Nerra, Laurence – A grandson of Thomas de Nerra. Appears in THE FALLS OF ERITH.

de Nerra, Margaretha Byington – Valor de Nerra's mother. She appears in VESTIGSE OF VALOR.

de Nerra, Robert – The oldest son of Thomas de Nerra. He was once a powerful knight but has crippling arthritis. Appears in THE FALLS OF ERITH.

de Nerra, Roderick – A grandson of Thomas de Nerra. Appears in THE FALLS OF ERITH.

de Nerra, Sophia – Youngest daughter of Val & Vesper de Nerra. She appears in REALM OF ANGELS.

de Nerra, Steven – The third oldest son of Thomas de Nerra. He is the most volatile of the de Nerra brothers. Appears in THE FALLS OF ERITH.

de Nerra, Theo – Youngest child of Val & Vesper de Nerra. He appears in REALM OF ANGELS.

de Nerra, Theodora "Teddy" de Rivington – Heroine of THE PROMISE. She is the only child of Bradford and Antoinette de Rivington.

de Nerra, Thomas – The 4th Baron of Gilderdale. He is the father of Robert, Davis, Steven, and Braxton. Appears in THE FALLS OF ERITH.

de Nerra, Valor – Hero of VESTIGES OF VALOR. He is the Itinerant Justice of Hampshire and owner of Selborne Castle. He later becomes Baron Gliderdale and owner of Black Fell Castle. He is the commander of the House of de Percy's Troops. He is the direct ancestor of Braxton de Nerra. He also appears in REALM OF ANGELS.

de Nerra, Vesper d'Avignon – Heroine of VESTIGES OF VALOR. She also appears in REALM OF ANGELS.

de Nerra, Willew – Amelia de Velt's mother. She appears in WITH DREAMS.

de Neville-Aubrey, William Tygor – He is the firstborn son of Avalyn and Brogan d'Aurilliac, but Avalyn was pregnant with "Ty" when she married her first husband, Charles Aubrey, so Ty is therefore the heir of Charles Aubrey's wealthy estate and barony. He first appears in VALIANT CHAOS.

de Neville, Anne – She is age 13 and is the youngest daughter of Richard and Anne de Neville. Appears in VALIANT CHAOS.

de Neville, Anne Beauchamp – Countess of Warkwick. She is Richard de Neville's wife. Her sister was Avalyn du Brant's mother. She is known as "The Peacemaker." Appears in VALIANT CHAOS.

de Neville, Richard – Earl of Warwick. He is a shrewd, calculating, and powerful man; known to all as "The Kingmaker." He is the uncle of Avalyn du Brant d'Aurilliac. Appears in VALIANT CHAOS.

de Noble, Elyse – Daughter of Raymond de Noble, commander at de Cleveley's settlement. Appears in BLACK SWORD.

de Noble, Raymond – Commander for de Cleveley. Appears in BLACK SWORD.

de Norgaret, Frances –She is the wife of Nikolas de Nogaret. Appears in LESPADA.

de Nogaret, Nikolas – A knight in the service of Davyss de Winter. He is married to Frances de Nogaret. Appears in LESPADA.

de Norville, Adele – Youngest daughter of Hector and Evelyn de Norville. Appears in NIGHTHAWK and THE BEST IS YET TO BE.

de Norville, Adonis – Son of Paris & Caladora Scott de Norville. Appears in SCORPION, A JOYOUS DE WOLFE CHRISTMAS, and THE BEST IS YET TO BE.

de Norville, Ajax – He is the son of Adonis and Wesleigh de Norville. He appears in THE BEST IS YET TO BE.

de Norville, Aline – She is the young daughter of Hector and Evelyn de Norville. She appears in THE BEST IS YET TO BE.

de Norville, Angelia – She is the oldest child of Adonis and Wesleigh de Norville. She appears in THE BEST IS YET TO BE.

de Norville, Apollo – Son of Paris & Caladora Scott de Norville. Appears in SERPENT and in NIGHTHAWK as a knight in service to Patrick de Wolfe. He also appears in A JOYOUS DE WOLFE CHRISTMAS, A WOLFE AMONG DRAGONS, BLACKWOLFE, and THE BEST IS YET TO BE.

de Norville, Atreus – Oldest son of Hector and Evelyn de Norville. Appears in NIGHTHAWK, STORMWOLFE, and BLACKWOLFE.

de Norville, Caladora Scott – Cousin to Jordan Scott & Jemma Scott. Marries Paris de Norville in THE WOLFE. She also appears in BLACKWOLFE.

de Norville, Evelyn de Wolfe – Daughter of William and Jordan de Wolfe, she is married to Hector de Norville. Appears in NIGHTHAWK, BLACKWOLFE, and THE BEST IS YET TO BE.

de Norville, Hector – Son of Paris & Caladora de Norville. Appears in NIGHTHAWK as a knight in service to his brother-in-law, Patrick de Wolfe. He married Evelyn de Wolfe, sister of Patrick. He also appears in DARKWOLFE, A JOYOUS DE WOLFE CHRISTMAS, A WOLFE AMONG DRAGONS, STORMWOLFE, BLACKWOLFE, and THE BEST IS YET TO BE.

de Norville, Hermes – Second son of Hector and Evelyn de Norville. Appears in NIGHTHAWK, STORMWOLFE, and BLACKWOLFE.

de Norville, Lane – An older man and sergeant for the Earl of Norfolk's battalion. Appears in THE SAVAGE CURTAIN.

de Norville, Lesander – He is the young son of Hector and Evelyn de Norville. He appears in THE BEST IS YET TO BE.

de Norville, Lisbet – Oldest daughter of Hector and Evelyn de Norville. Appears in NIGHTHAWK, BLACKWOLFE, and THE BEST IS YET TO BE.

de Norville, Moira Hage – She is the daughter of Kieran and Jemma Hage. She marries Apollo de Norville. She appears in THE BEST IS YET TO BE.

de Norville, Nathaniel – Youngest child of Paris & Caladora de Norville. He is a shorter knight. He appears in BLACKWOLFE.

de Norville, Paris – Hero of THE BEST IS YET TO BE. He is also a main character in THE WOLFE. Marries Caladora Scott. Appears in UNENDING LOVE as a young knight and in THE

CENTURION. Appears in SERPENT, NIGHTHAWK, SHADOWWOLFE, DARKWOLFE, A WOLFE AMONG DRAGONS, STORMWOLFE, and BLACKWOLFE as an older man. He is the father-in-law of Scott de Wolfe and Troy de Wolfe.

de Norville, Paris (the younger) – He is the son of Adonis and Wesleigh de Norville, and is the twin brother of Talos de Norville. He appears in THE BEST IS YET TO BE.

de Norville, Steven – A knight who served Peter Courtnay and then John de Vere. Appears in THE DARK ONE: DARK KNIGHT.

de Norville, Talos – He is the son of Adonis and Wesleigh de Norville, and is the twin brother of Paris (the younger). He appears in THE BEST IS YET TO BE.

de Norville, Wesleigh de Lara – She is the wife of Adonis de Norville. She appears in THE BEST IS YET TO BE.

de Paura, Anyu – Lady of Baiadepaura Castle in 1060 A.D. She appears in BAY OF FEAR.

de Paura, Fautus – Lord of Baiadepaura Castle in 1060 A.D. He appears in BAY OF FEAR.

de Percy, William – He is the military commander for Agnes de Percy. He appears in VESTIGES OF VALOR.

de Poyer, Caledon – Twin son of Keller & Chrystobel de Poyer. First appears in NETHERWORLD.

de Poyer, Chrystobel d'Einen – Heroine of NETHERWORLD. She was awarded with Nether Castle to Keller de Poyer by William Marshal. She is the daughter of Trevyn d'Einen, former lord of Nether Castle.

de Poyer, Ewan – A knight in service to Kaspian St. Hever. Older brother of Reece de Poyer. Appears in QUEEN OF LOST STARS.

de Poyer, Genevieve – Daughter of Keller & Chrystobel de Poyer. First appears in NETHERWORLD.

de Poyer, Iselle – Daughter of Keller & Chrystobel de Poyer. First appears in NETHERWORLD.

de Poyer, Keller – Hero of NETHERWORLD. He was awarded Nether Castle by William Marshal and became Lord Carnedd. He was given Chrystobel d'Einen as part of the contract. His family has held the title of High Sheriff of Leicester for over a century. He is also the Lord Protector of the King's interest in Powys. Appears in DEVIL'S DOMINION. Ally of Christopher de Lohr. He appears in THE WHISPERING NIGHT, and was the garrison commander at Pembroke Castle before his story happens in Netherworld.

de Poyer, Kenan – He is a knight serving Valor de Nerra. He appears in VESTIGES OF VALOR.

de Poyer, Kent – Serving King Henry III as part of his Guard of Six. Appears in SILVERSWORD.

de Poyer, Laria – Sister of Charlisa de Poyer du Reims. She appears in DARK STEEL.

de Poyer, Reece – A knight in service to Kaspian St. Hever. Younger brother of Ewan de Poyer. Appears in QUEEN OF LOST STARS.

de Poyer, Stafford – Twin son of Keller & Chrystobel de Poyer. First appears in NETHERWORLD.

de Poyer, Syler – He is in service to Shrewsbury, and is a cousin of Dastan du Reim's wife. He appears in DARK STEEL.

de Poyer, Tallys – Youngest son of Keller & Chrystobel de Poyer. First appears in NETHERWORLD.

de Puiset, Hugh – Bishop of Durham. He appears in LORD OF WINTER.

de Reigate, Gavril – He is an older knight serving Tevin du Reims. He appears in WHILE ANGELS SLEPT.

de Reyne, Annabella – Daughter of Creed & Carington de Reyne. Appears in GUARDIAN OF DARKNESS.

de Reyne, Brodie – He is a knight, and appears in DARKWOLFE.

de Reyne, Carington Kerr – Heroine of GUARDIAN OF DARKNESS. An honorable hostage promised to the safekeeping of Lord Richard d'Umfraville to ensure peace between England and Scotland. She is from the warring Scot clan of Clan Kerr.

de Reyne, Cathlina de Lara – Heroine of THE FALLEN ONE. She is the middle daughter of Saer and Rosalund de Lara. Cousin to Tate de Lara.

de Reyne, Cora – Daughter of Creed & Carington de Reyne. Appears in GUARDIAN OF DARKNESS.

de Reyne, Cormac – Oldest son of Creed & Carington de Reyne. Appears in GUARDIAN OF DARKNESS.

de Reyne, Creed – Hero of GUARDIAN OF DARKNESS. A colossal knight in service to his brother, Ryton, at Prudhoe Castle. Younger brother of Ryton de Reyne. He later inherited the title of Baron Hartlepool and later became chief of Clan Kerr and inherited Throston Castle upon his father-in-law's passing.

de Reyne, Eryx – Hero of WITH DREAMS. He is the garrison commander of Corchester Castle. He found the Theodosia Sword.

de Reyne, Frederica de Titouan – Heroine of WITH DREAMS. She is from Wales and was staying with her de Velt relatives at Pelinom Castle.

de Reyne, Gaira – Daughter of Creed & Carington de Reyne. Appears in GUARDIAN OF DARKNESS.

de Reyne, Hayes – He is a big knight in the service of William de Wolfe. He appears in BLACKWOLFE.

de Reyne, Justus – The father of Mathias and Sebastian de Reyne. Appears in THE FALLEN ONE.

de Reyne, Lancelot "Lance" – He is a Breton from Morlaix and becomes the ancestor of the de Reyne family in England. He appears in WARWOLFE.

de Reyne, Magnus – Firstborn son of Mathias and Cathlina de Reyne. Appears in THE FALLEN ONE. He is a knight in service to Brandt de Russe. He marries Brandt de Russe's daughter from his first marriage, Rosalind de Russe. Appears in LORD OF WAR: BLACK ANGEL.

de Reyne, Mathias – Hero of THE FALEN ONE. He was the head of Mortimer's army when Mortimer rebelled against King Edward for his throne. Instead of being executed like Mortimer was after he was captured, Mathias, his brother, and father were stripped of their knighthood, lands, and titles. He is redeemed in THE FALLEN ONE, and was given the title of Earl of Bristol, Baron Westbury, and High Warden of the West.

de Reyne, Moira – Daughter of Creed & Carington de Reyne. Appears in GUARDIAN OF DARKNESS.

de Reyne, Ramsey Ryton – Youngest son of Creed & Carington de Reyne. Appears in GUARDIAN OF DARKNESS.

de Reyne, Ridge – He is the personal bodyguard to King Alexander. He appears in THE RED FURY.

de Reyne, Rosalind de Russe – Brandt de Russe's oldest daughter from his first marriage. She later marries Magnus de Reyne. Appears in LORD OF WAR: BLACK ANGEL.

de Reyne, Rossalyn – Daughter of Creed & Carington de Reyne. Appears in GUARDIAN OF DARKNESS.

de Reyne, Ryton – Older brother of Creed de Reyne. Ryton is the commander of Prudhoe's army. Appears in GUARDIAN OF DARKNESS.

de Reyne, Sebastian – Known as Sebastian the Red. He is the youngest brother of Mathias de Reyne. He has a mass of red hair, with a temper quick to ignite. Appears in THE FALLEN ONE.

de Rhydian, Cadelyn "Cadie" "Catherine" – Heroine of THE MOUNTAIN DARK. She is the biological daughter of Owain Dant y Draig; a descendant of the last kings of Rhos, and Nesta ferch Madog; a direct descendant of the last kings of Pengwern. She is also the ward of the Earl of Arundel, Hugh d'Aubigney. She is an underground poetess of naughty poems, and writes under the name of Lady Dark. When living in Scotland, she goes by the name of Catherine.

de Rhydian, Keene – Firstborn son of Kress and Cadie de Rhydian. He first appears in THE MOUNTAIN DARK.

de Rhydian, Kress – He is one of the Executioner Knights and part of the Unholy Trinity. He appears in BY THE UNHOLY HAND.

de Rhydian, Mattox – Second son of Kress and Cadie de Rhydian. He first appears in THE MOUNTAIN DARK.

de Rivington, Antoinette – Mother of Theodora de Rivington. Wife of Bradford. Appears in THE PROMISE.

de Rivington, Bradford – Father of Theodora de Rivington. Husband of Antoinette. Appears in THE PROMISE.

de Roche, Hamlin – A knight serving Roger Mortimer. He has been trying to assassinate young King Edward. Appears in DRAGONBLADE.

de Rosa, Alger – Brother of Bertram de Rosa. He appears in THE WHISPERING NIGHT.

de Rosa, Bertram – He is an older man with green eyes. Along with this two brothers and three sons, they form the formidable warring de Rosa clan. He is the father of Derica de Rosa le Mon. He appears in THE WHISPERING NIGHT.

de Rosa, Daniel – Oldest son of Bertram de Rosa. He appears in THE WHISPERING NIGHT.

de Rosa, Dixon – Son of Bertram de Rosa. He appears in THE WHISPERING NIGHT.

de Rosa, Donat – Son of Bertram de Rosa. He appears in THE WHISPERING NIGHT.

de Rosa, Hoyt – Brother to Bertram de Rosa. He is a great warrior, but he suffered a blow to his head in battle and has periods where he dresses as a woman and becomes Lady Cleo Blossom. He appears in THE WHISPERING NIGHT.

de Rosa, Lon – Brother of Bertram de Rosa. He appears in THE WHISPERING NIGHT.

de Rou, Lucy – She is the wife of Philip de Rou. Appears in LESPADA.

de Rou, Philip – A knight in the service of Davyss de Winter. He is married to Lucy de Rou. Appears in LESPADA.

de Royans, Alycia – Torston and Alyx's oldest daughter. She appears in THE CENTURION.

de Royans, Alyx de Ameland – Heroine of THE CENTURION. She is the daughter of Winslow de Ameland of Makendon Castle.

de Royans, Amalie de Vere – Heroine of TO THE LADY BORN, and sister of Robert de Vere, who was the Earl of Oxford and Duke of Ireland. She is also the mother of Colton de Royans and appears with him in THE IRON KNIGHT.

de Royans, Aubria – She is the firstborn daughter of Weston & Amalie de Royans. Her birth was the result of her mother's brutalization by John Sorrell, first garrison commander at Hedingham Castle. She is loved and accepted by Weston de Royans as if he was her birth father. She first appears in TO THE LADY BORN.

de Royans, Asthon – He is the firstborn son of Juston and Emera de Royans. He appears In LORD OF WINTER.

de Royans, Blossom – Juston and Lizette's oldest daughter in LORD OF WINTER.

de Royans, Brighton – He is a knight in service to Hugh d'Aubigney, the Earl of Norfolk. He is the older brother of Adalind de Aston's best friend, Glennie de Royans. He is the heir of Baron Cononley and is a desperate suitor of Adalind de Aston du Bois. He appears in UNENDING LOVE.

de Royans, Caston – Youngest son of Easton de Royans, Baron Cononley. He is the twin brother of Brighton de Royans (Unending Love). He is a knight in service to his father. Appears in SHADOWMOOR.

de Royans, Cedrica – Juston and Lizette's youngest daughter in LORD OF WINTER.

de Royans, Colton – He is the second-in-command for Lucien de Russe. He is the firstborn son of Weston and Amalie de Royans and first appears in TO THE LADY BORN. He marries Emmaline de Gournay in THE IRON KNIGHT.

de Royans, Easton – Baron Cononley. He is the father of Brighton, Caston, and Glennie de Royans. Appears in SHADOWMOOR.

de Royans, Elizabeth – She is the mother of Weston and Sutton de Royans. She was the only child of Hugh de Busli. Appears in TO THE LADY BORN.

de Royans, Elizabeth – Daughter of Weston & Amalie de Royans. She is named after her grandmother, Elizabeth de Royans, Weston's mother. First appears in TO THE LADY BORN.

de Royans, Emera la Marche – Heroine of LORD OF WINTER. She is the youngest sister of Jessamyn la Marche de la Roarke.

de Royans, Emmaline de Gournay. She is Sophina de Russe's daughter from her first marriage to Edward de Gournay. She marries Colton de Royans in THE IRON KNIGHT.

de Royans, Glennie – Daughter of Easton de Royans, Baron Cononley. She is the best friend of Adalind de Aston (Unending Love). Appears in SHADOWMOOR.

de Royans, Juston – Hero of LORD OF WINTER. He is the High Sheriff of Yorkshire and Baron Cononley, and owns Nethergyll Castle. He is also known as the "Lord of Winter." He is a young knight in THE LION OF THE NORTH.

de Royans, Kingston – Twin son of Weston & Amalie de Royans. First appears in TO THE LADY BORN.

de Royans, Lizette – She was Juston de Royans first wife in LORD OF WINTER. She and their two daughters were killed by Juston's adversary.

de Royans, Paeton – He is the right-hand of Simon de Montfort. He appears in THE THUNDER WARRIOR.

de Royans, Paget de Clifford – She is the daughter of Lord Clifton of Skipton Castle. She marries Sutton de Royans. Appears in TO THE LADY BORN.

de Royans, Ryston – Torston's illegitimate son. He appears in THE CENTURION.

de Royans, Sutton – He is the younger brother of Weston de Royans. He was gifted the barony of Ulster by Amalie de Vere de Royans, and became Baron Tirone. He marries Paget de Clifford. Appears in TO THE LADY BORN.

de Royans, Thornton – Juston's illegitimate son, born to Sybilla d'Evereux. She was the sister of Gillem d'Evereux, who was a knight serving Juston. He was raised by Juston and his second wife, Emera, after Sybilla died. He appears in LORD OF WINTER.

de Royans, Torston – Hero of THE CENTURION. Twin son of Weston & Amalie de Royans. First appears in TO THE LADY BORN. He is the grandson of Juston de Royans of LORD OF WINTER. He also is the captain of The Lyceum's army.

de Royans, Uriah – He is a knight in service to the de Gare family. Appears in THE WARRIOR POET.

de Royans, Weston – Hero of TO THE LADY BORN, and is Baron Cononley of Nethergyll Castle, and Constable of the North Yorkshire Dales. He was also the second garrison commander at Hedingham Castle. He is also Colton de Royans' father and also appears in THE IRON KNIGHT.

de Royans, Wynter – She is the firstborn daughter of Juston and Emera de Royans. She appears in LORD OF WINTER.

de Russe, Achilles – Firstborn son of Lucien & Sophina de Russe. First appears in THE IRON KNIGHT.

de Russe, Adela de Montford – Thid wife of Trenton de Russe. She's the illegitimate daughter of the Duke of Brittany. She appears in DARK MOON.

de Russe, Aramis – Uncle to Bastian. Father of Worthington. Former Duke of Exeter and now Duke of Warminster. Appears in BEAST.

de Russe, Aramis – He is of Flemish ancestry, and is the heir of the Count of Roeselare. He marries Lygia Shericus (later de Shera), and they become the ancestors of the de Russe family in England. He appears in WARWOLFE.

de Russe, Asher "Ash" – Hero of EMMA. He is Baron Westhorpe, and owns Blackmoor Hall.

de Russe, Augustine – Known as "Gus," he is a very big man with a mean streak. He is a quartermaster for Constantine le Brecque's crew. Appears in LEADER OF TITANS.

de Russe, Bastian – Nicknamed "Beast." Hero of BEAST. Guardian Protector of young King Henry VI. Granted Etonbury Castle and title of Baron Henlow and Baron Arlesey. Married Gisella le Bec.

de Russe, Beatrice – Wife of Bastian's Uncle Hugh. She is the mother of Brant and Martin de Russe. Appears in BEAST.

de Russe, Boden – Younger brother of Dane de Russe. He serves his brother at Shrewsbury. Appears in DARK MOON, DARK STEEL, and A DE RUSSE CHRISTMAS MIRACLE.

de Russe, Brant – Bastian's cousin and brother of Martin de Russe. Appears in BEAST.

de Russe, Brandt – Hero of LORD OF WAR: BLACK ANGEL. Brandt's nickname was "The Black Angel," because of his war tactics. He is the Duke of Exeter, Lord of the Western Gates, and Baron Guildford and Waverley.

de Russe, Braxton de Nerra – Father of Bastian. Wife was Aderyn. Appears in BEAST.

de Russe, Cort Henry Hubert – Firstborn son of Gaston & Remington de Russe. Appears in THE DARK ONE: DARK KNIGHT, DARK MOON, DARK STEEL, and A DE RUSSE CHRISTMAS MIRACLE.

de Russe, Cynthia – Wife to Aramis de Russe. Mother of Worthington de Russe. Appears in BEAST.

de Russe, Dane Stoneley – Hero of DARK STEEL. Remington and Guy Stoneley's only son and child together. He is like his mother in personality and is very protective of his mother. First appears in THE DARK ONE: DARK KNIGHT. He is later adopted by Gaston de Russe. As an adult, he is Lord Blackmore of Blackmore Castle. He becomes Duke of Shrewsbury and Lord of the Trinity Castles upon the death of Garreth de Lara and his marriage to the heiress, Grier de Lara. Also appears in DARK MOON and A DE RUSSE CHRISTMAS MIRACLE.

de Russe, Darrien – A knight in service to Simon de Montfort. Appears in LESPADA.

de Russe, Ellowyn "Wynny" de Nerra – Heroine of LORD OF WAR: BLACK ANGEL. She is the grand-daughter of Braxton de Nerra from THE FALLS OF ERITH.

de Russe, Emma Fairweather – Hero of EMMA. She was of noble birth, but was reduced to hiring on as a maid.

de Russe, Erik – A knight serving King Richard. He is the brother of Emberley de Russe, heroine of ARCHANGEL. He is best friends with Gart Forbes and appears alongside Gart Forbes in LORD OF WINTER.

de Russe, Gage – Younger son of Gaston and Remington de Russe. He appears in DARK MOON and A DE RUSSE CHRISTMAS MIRACLE.

de Russe, Gaston – Hero of THE DARK ONE: DARK KNIGHT. A feared warrior during his time. Earned his nickname of 'The Dark One.' First married to Mari-Elle and then to Remington Stoneley. Best friend of Matthew Wellesbourne. His title is the Duke of Warminster of Deverill Castle. Also appears in WALLS OF BABYLON, THE WHITE LORD OF WELLESBOURNE, DARK MOON, DARK STEEL, and A DE RUSSE CHRISTMAS MIRACLE.

de Russe, Gilliana – Younger daughter of Gaston and Remington de Russe. She appears in DARK MOON and A DE RUSSE CHRISTMAS MIRACLE.

de Russe, Gisella le Bec – Nicknamed "Gigi." Heroine of BEAST. Daughter of Richmond le Bec of GREAT PROTECTOR.

de Russe, Grier de Lara – Heroine of DARK STEEL. Only child and heiress of Garreth de Lara. She becomes the Duchess of Shrewsbury and Lady of the Trinity Castles. Also appears in A DE RUSSE CHRISTMAS MIRACLE.

de Russe, Hugh – Youngest of Bastian's uncles. He married Beatrice and they are the parents of Brant de Russe and Martin de Russe. Appears in BEAST.

de Russe, Hughston – He is a powerful man and is a close ally with Hugh Bigod and Simon de Montfort. He resides at Braidwood Manor, the London home of the de Russe family, and it's where the opposing barons meet. He appears in THE THUNDER LORD, THE THUNDER WARRIOR, and THE THUNDER KNIGHT.

de Russe, Jorden – A knight and friend to Chad de Lohr. Appears in SILVERSWORD.

de Russe, Lucien – Hero of THE IRON KNIGHT. He's nicknamed the "Iron Knight." He was gifted the barony of Tytherington and given Spelthorne Castle by King Henry. He is the eldest son of Aramis de Russe and will inherit the dukedom of Exeter and was born Baron Exminster. He is also the Sheriff of Cranborne.

de Russe, Lygia Shericus – She is widowed, and is the oldest daughter of Antillius Shericus. She later marries Aramis de Russe, and they become the ancestors of the de Russe family in England. She appears in WARWOLFE.

de Russe, Lysabel Wellesbourne – Heroine of DARK MOON. She is the eldest daughter of Matthew and Alixandrea Wellesbourne (hero of THE WHITE LORD OF WELLESBOURNE). Her first marriage was to Benoit de Wilde. They have two daughters from that marriage. Her second marriage is to Trenton de Russe. She also appears in A DE RUSSE CHRISTMAS MIRACLE.

de Russe, Marc – A knight serving Christopher de Lohr. Appears in SHADOWMOOR.

de Russe, Margarethe – Brandt de Russe's youngest daughter from his first marriage. She joins a convent in England. Appears in LORD OF WAR: BLACK ANGEL.

de Russe, Mari-Elle – Gaston de Russe's first wife. Mari-Elle and Gaston are the parents of Trenton de Russe. Appears in THE DARK ONE: DARK KNIGHT and in THE WHITE LORD OF WELLESBOURNE.

de Russe, Martin – The father of Patrick and Nicholas de Russe. He is an uncle to Gaston through his brother Brant. Appears in THE DARK ONE: DARK KNIGHT and BEAST.

de Russe, Matthieu – Younger son of Gaston and Remington de Russe. He appears in DARK MOON and A DE RUSSE CHRISTMAS MIRACLE.

de Russe, Maxim – A knight in THE LION OF THE NORTH. He is the son of Bastian & Gisella de Russe from BEAST.

de Russe, Nicholas – Cousin to Gaston and serves in his knight corps. Son of Martin de Russe. Brother to Patrick de Russe. He marries Skye Halsey. Appears in THE DARK ONE: DARK KNIGHT.

de Russe, Patrick – Cousin to Gaston and serves in his knight corps. Son of Martin de Russe. Brother to Nicholas de Russe. He was in love with Rory Halsey before her death. Appears in THE DARK ONE: DARK KNIGHT and THE WHITE LORD OF WELLESBOURNE.

de Russe, Rafe – He is Lucien de Russe's oldest son and appears in THE IRON KNIGHT.

de Russe, Raphael – Oldest son of Trenton & Lysabel de Russe. He first appears in DARK MOON.

de Russe, Remington Halsey Stoneley – Heroine of THE DARK ONE: DARK KNIGHT. First married to Guy Stoneley, and then to Gaston de Russe. She also appears in DARK MOON and A DE RUSSE CHRISTMAS MIRACLE.

de Russe, Robert – Firstborn son of Skye & Nicholas de Russe. Appears in THE DARK ONE: DARK KNIGHT.

de Russe, Skye Halsey – Remington de Russe's youngest sister. She marries Nicholas de Russe. Appears in THE DARK ONE: DARK KNIGHT.

de Russe, Sophina Seavington de Barenton de Gournay – Heroine of THE IRON KNIGHT. She's a widow with a daughter named Emmaline de Gournay.

de Russe, Susanna – She is Lucien de Russe's daughter who was born with a weak spine and legs. She appears in THE IRON KNIGHT.

de Russe, Trenton – Hero of DARK MOON. The only son of Gaston and Mari-Elle de Russe. He is known as the Crown's Own Agent, and is one of four master assassins for King Henry VIII. He is the heir of Gaston de Russe for the dukedom of Warminster. He is also the Earl of Westbury. Appears in THE DARK ONE: DARK KNIGHT, THE WHITE LORD OF WELLESBOURNE, DARK STEEL, and A DE RUSSE CHRISTMAS MIRACLE.

de Russe, Worthington – Son of Aramis de Russe and is Viscount Westbury. Appears in BEAST.

de Rydal, Ovid – Lord of Goring Hall. Husband to Margaret, and together they have 11 children. Their son and heir is Tad de Rydal. Appears in GREAT PROTECTOR.

de Rydal, Margaret – Wife of Ovid de Rydal. Together they have 11 children. Their son and heir is Tad de Rydal. Appears in GREAT PROTECTOR.

de Rydal, Tad – A handsome knight, and heir of Ovid & Margaret de Rydal. Appears in GREAT PROTECTOR.

de Ryes, Adeliza de Russe – Oldest twin daughter of Gaston & Remington de Russe. Appears in THE DARK ONE: DARK KNIGHT and A DE RUSSE CHRISTMAS MIRACLE.

de Ryes, Norman – Second-in-command to Thomas de Wolfe at Wark Castle. His sister is married to Thomas de Wolfe.

de Rhydian, Kress – Hero of THE MOUNTAIN DARK. He is one of the Executioner Knights and part of the Unholy Trinity. He is from a wealthy noble family. He also appears in LORD OF WINTER as a young knight serving Juston de Royans. He also appeared in BY THE UNHOLY HAND.

de Saix, Juno – She is the daughter of Wardell de Saix, and appears in THE IRON KNIGHT.

de Saix, Laurent – He is a knight and good friend of Lucien de Russe. He appears in THE IRON KNIGHT.

de Saix, Wardell – He is the Earl of Holderness. He is the father of Juno de Saix and Laurent de Saix and appears in THE IRON KNIGHT.

de Sansen, August – Lord of Larrigan Castle. He is the father of Lyonette de Sansen. He appears in LADY OF THE MOON.

de Sauster, Bogomil – He is an older man and soldier serving Henry de Leybourne. He is the only soldier of his father that Rhodes likes. He appears in LADY OF THE MOON.

de Serreaux, Torran – Captain of King Henry's Six. Appears in SILVERSWORD.

de Shera, Antillius Decimus (Shericus) – He is descended from the Third Legion of Roman soldiers, and is the leader of their village called Tertium. He is an older widowed father with three daughters. He later marries a Norman woman and has sons with her, and becomes the ancestor of the de Shera family in England. He appears in WARWOLFE.

de Shera, Antoninus – Son of Tiberius and Douglass de Shera. Appears in THE THUNDER KNIGHT.

de Shera, Antoninus – He is the youngest brother of Tatius de Shera. He appears as a young man in THE MOUNTAIN DARK. He is the father of Gallus, Maximus, and Tiberius de Shera (the Lords of Thunder).

de Shera, Atilius – He is a younger brother of Tatius de Shera. He commands the de Shera armies. He appears in THE MOUNTAIN DARK.

de Shera, Augustus – Firstborn son of Maximus and Courtly de Shera. Appears in THE THUNDER KNIGHT. He is a knight serving Chris de Lohr. Appears in A WOLFE AMONG DRAGONS.

de Shera, Bhrodi – Hero of SERPENT. Hereditary King of Anglesey, with Welsh royalty from his mother and is the Earl of Coventry on his father's side. Father is Gallus de Shera and mother is Jeniver ferch Gaerwen of THE THUNDER LORD. His nickname is The Serpent. Appears as a young boy in SILVERSWORD. He also appears in THE THUNDER WARRIOR, THE THUNDER KNIGHT, and A WOLFE AMONG DRAGONS.

de Shera, Bose – Son of Tiberius and Douglass de Shera. Appears in THE THUNDER KNIGHT.

de Shera, Bowen – He is a young squire serving his cousin William de Wolfe. Bowen's parents are Bhrodi and Penelope de Wolfe de Shera. Appears in SWORDS AND SHIELDS.

de Shera, Cassius – Illegitimate son of Maximus de Shera. He is the son of Rose, who was the daughter of the castle smithy. He marries Sable de Moray. Appears in THE THUNDER KNIGHT and in DARKWOLFE.

de Shera, Charlotte – Daughter of Tiberius and Douglass de Shera. Appears in THE THUNDER KNIGHT.

de Shera, Charlotte "Honey" de Lohr – She is the youngest daughter of Christopher and Dustin de Lohr from RISE OF THE DEFENDER. She married Antoninus de Shera and they are the parents of Gallus, Maximus, and Tiberius de Shera. She is an older woman in THE THUNDER LORD and THE THUNDER WARRIOR.

de Shera, Courtly de Lara – Heroine of THE THUNDER WARRIOR. Wife of Maximus de Shera. Appears in THUNDER KNIGHT and SILVERSWORD.

de Shera, Douglass de Moray – Heroine of THE THUNDER KNIGHT. Daughter of Bose and Summer de Moray from THE GORGON. Younger sister of Garran de Moray. Appears in SILVERSWORD.

de Shera, Elizabetha – Daughter of Maximus and Courtly de Shera. Appears in THE THUNDER KNIGHT.

de Shera, Fabius – He is a younger brother of Tatius de Shera. He appears in THE MOUNTAIN DARK.

de Shera, Gallus – Hero of THE THUNDER LORD. Husband of Jeniver de Shera. He is the oldest brother of Maximus and Tiberius. His titles are the Earl of Coventry and the Lord Sheriff of Worcester. He and his wife Jeniver are the parents of Bhrodi de Shera, hero of SERPENT. Through his wife, Jeniver, he inherits the titles of the hereditary kings of Anglesey. He also appears in THE THUNDER WARRIOR, THE THUNDER KNIGHT, and SILVERSWORD.

de Shera, Jeniver Tacey ferch Gaerwen – Heroine of THE THUNDER LORD. Wife of Gallus de Shera and is a Welsh princess. Her father was the hereditary king of Anglesey. She and Gallus are the parents of Bhrodi de Shera, hero of SERPENT. She also appears in THE THUNDER WARRIOR, THE THUNDER KNIGHT, and SILVERSWORD.

de Shera, Josephine – Twin daughter of Tiberius and Douglass de Shera. Appears in THE THUNDER KNIGHT.

de Shera, Justus – Son of Maximus and Courtly de Shera. Appears in THE THUNDER KNIGHT.

de Shera, Kellen – Son of Maximus and Courtly de Shera. Appears in THE THUNDER KNIGHT.

de Shera, Leeton – He previously was Captain of the Guard for the Earl of Derby and now is a knight in service to Christopher de Lohr. Appears in RISE OF THE DEFENDER and STEELHEART.

de Shera, Lily – She is the youngest daughter of Gallus de Shera and his first wife, Catheryn. She appears in THE THUNDER LORD, THE THUNDER WARRIOR, and THE THUNDER KNIGHT.

de Shera, Lucius – Son of Maximus and Courtly de Shera. Appears in THE THUNDER KNIGHT.

de Shera, Marcus – Son of Tiberius and Douglass de Shera. Appears in THE THUNDER KNIGHT.

de Shera, Magnus – Son of Tiberius and Douglass de Shera. Appears in THE THUNDER KNIGHT.

de Shera, Maximus – Hero of THE THUNDER WARRIOR. Husband to Courtly de Shera. He is the middle brother of Gallus and Tiberius de Shera. His title is Baron Allesley. He also appears in THE THUNDER LORD, THE THUNDER KNIGHT, and SILVERSWORD.

de Shera, Micheline le Bec – Sister of Mara le Bec. She is wife to Edmund de Cleveley first and then to Spencer de Shera. Appears in THE DARKLAND.

de Shera, Penelope de Wolfe – Heroine of SERPENT. Daughter of William de Wolfe from THE WOLFE. The most beautiful of all the de Wolfe daughters. Trained as a knight by her father. She also appears in NIGHTHAWK and A JOYOUS DE WOLFE CHRISTMAS as a young child, and in BLACKWOLFE at age 16. She appears in A WOLFE AMONG DRAGONS.

de Shera, Perri – Young son of Bhrodi and Penelope de Shera. Appears in A WOLFE AMONG DRAGONS.

de Shera, Sable de Moray – She is the youngest daughter of Bose and Summer de Moray. She marries Cassius de Shera. She appears in THE THUNDER KNIGHT and in DARKWOLFE.

de Shera, Tatius – He is the Earl of Ellesmere, and was betrothed to Cadelyn of Vendotia. He resides at The Paladin. He is the oldest brother of Atilius, Fabius, and Antoninus de Shera. He appears in THE MOUNTAIN DARK.

de Shera, Tertius – Isobeau de Shera de Wolfe's brother. Appears in THE LION OF THE NORTH.

de Shera, Thomasina – Twin daughter of Tiberius and Douglass de Shera. Appears in THE THUNDER KNIGHT.

de Shera, Tiberius – Hero of THE THUNDER KNIGHT. Husband of Douglass de Moray de Shera. He is the youngest brother of Gallus and Maximus de Shera. His title is Lord Lockhurst of Keresley Castle. He also appears in THE THUNDER LORD, THE THUNDER WARRIOR, and SILVERSWORD.

de Shera, Titus – Son of Maximus and Courtly de Shera. Appears in THE THUNDER KNIGHT.

de Shera, Violet – She is the oldest daughter of Gallus de Shera and his first wife, Catheryn. She appears in THE THUNDER LORD, THE THUNDER WARRIOR, and THE THUNDER KNIGHT.

de Shera, William – Young son of Bhrodi and Penelope de Shera. Appears in A WOLFE AMONG DRAGONS.

de Sherrington, Alexander "Sherry" – He is a massively huge knight, and is in the service of William Marshal in BY THE UNHOLY HAND, THE MOUNTAIN DARK, and STARLESS.

de Sotheby, St. Alban – He is an older knight and best friend of Brogan d'Aurilliac. He is now infirmed with a joint disease in his old age. Appears in VALIANT CHAOS.

de Soto, Amaro – He is a Spanish pirate sailing on the Santa Margarita. He is called "Diabolito," meaning "Little Demon." He appears in SEA WOLFE.

de Soulant, Edward – Baron Craven of Castle Kinlet. He is the father of Alisanne de Soulant. Appears in LORD OF LIGHT.

de Soulant, John Adam – He is Edward de Soulant's brother. He later became known as Father Joseph Ari. He was a knight serving as a healer in the Order of the Hospitallers of St. John the Baptist. Roane de Garr "healed" him of his eye affliction. Appears in LORD OF LIGHT.

de Tarquins, Burle – An older knight in the service at Prudhoe Castle. Appears in GUARDIAN OF DARKNESS.

de Tiegh, Byron – Baron Coverdale, Keir St. Hever's commander. He appears in FRAGMENTS OF GRACE.

de Tiegh, Samuel – Baron Coverdale, and twin brother of Susanna de Tiegh de Dere. He appears in STARLESS.

de Titouan, Dylan – He is the youngest son of Renard and Orlaith de Titouan. Appears in SPECTRE OF THE SWORD.

de Titouan, Effington de Velt– Daughter of Jax & Kellington de Velt. Marries Rod de Titouan. Appears in DEVIL'S DOMINION.

de Titouan, Orlaith de Llion – She is the mother of Rhys du Bois from her forced liaison with the Duke of Navarre. She married Renard de Titouan and became the parents of Rod, Carys, and Dylan. Appears in SPECTRE OF THE SWORD.

de Titouan, Renard – He is the stepfather to Rhys du Bois, and with Rhys' mother, Orlaith, they have three children – Rod, Carys and Dylan. Appears in SPECTRE OF THE SWORD.

de Titouan, Rhett – He is the older brother to Renard de Titouan. Appears in SPECTRE OF THE SWORD.

de Titouan, Riston – A knight serving Dennis d'Vant. He has dark hair and blue eyes. Appears in TENDER IS THE KNIGHT.

de Titouan, Rod – First cousin to Bretton de Llion and the younger half-brother of Rhys du Bois from SPECTRE OF THE SWORD. Marries Effington de Velt, daughter of Ajax & Kellington de Velt. Appears in DEVIL'S DOMINION and SPECTRE OF THE SWORD.

de Tormo, Ferdinand – He is a priest at St. Denys chapel. He is the younger brother of Otho de Tormo. He appears in A DE RUSSE CHRISTMAS MIRACLE.

de Tormo, Otho – A papal envoy who helps Remington & Gaston de Russe with their annulments. Older brother of Ferdinand de Tormo. Appears in THE DARK ONE: DARK KNIGHT.

de Tracy, William – One of the group of four knights who served King Henry II, and who assassinated the Archbishop of Canterbury. He appears in VESTIGES OF VALOR.

de Troiu, Daniel – From Deauxville Mount. Antagonist in THE WOLFE.

de Troiu, Declan – A knight who served Titus de Wolfe. He later became a traitor and murdered Titus in THE LION OF THE NORTH.

de Troyes, Ransom – Cpatain of the Guard at Wellesbourne Castle. He appears in DARK MOON.

de Ufford, Robert – Earl of Suffolk. Appears in DRAGONBLADE.

de Vahn, George – A knight serving Nathaniel du Rennic in SHADOWWOLFE.

de Vaston, Acacia – Middle child of the Duke of Savernake. Appears in GODSPEED.

de Vaston, Bentley Ashbourne – He is a senior knight to Dashiell du Reims in GODSPEED. He later becomes Lily de Vaston's second husband and inherited the title of Duke of Savernake and later changes his name to Bentley Ashbourne de Vaston when he inherited the dukedom. He also appears in HIGH WARRIOR.

de Vaston, Edward – He is the Duke of Savernake, and is the father of Lily, Acacia, and Belladonna. He is senile. Appears in GODSPEED.

de Vaston, Lily – Oldest daughter of the Duke of Savernake. First married to Clayton le Cairon. She later marries Bentley Ashbourne. Appears in GODSPEED.

de Vaston, Merrick Edward – Oldest child and firstborn son of Bentley and Lily de Vaston. He is the Earl of Collingbourne. Appears in GODSPEED.

de Vauden, Edmund – He was the Earl of Northumbia. His daughter and heiress, Adelaide de Vauden, was married for one day to Thomas de Wolfe. He appeared in STORMWOLFE.

de Vaughn, Anthony – Bradford de Rivington's captain of his army at Cerenbeau Castle. Appears In THE PROMISE.

de Vaux, Kerr – He is a knight in service to Kress de Rhydian. He is half Scottish and half English. He appears in THE MOUNTAIN DARK.

de Velt, Ajax "Jax" – Hero of THE DARK LORD. He's a fearsome warlord with two different color eyes. He appears in DEVIL'S DOMINION. Father of Allastan de Velt, heroine of DEVIL'S DOMINION. He also appears in THE DARK LORD'S FIRST CHRISTMAS.

de Velt, Annalyla St. Lo – Heroine of BAY OF FEAR.

de Velt, Anthony – Twin brother of Max de Velt. He is a knight in service to Christopher de Lohr. Appears in RISE OF THE DEFENDER and STEELHEART.

de Velt, Amelia de Nerra – Wife of Broderick de Velt and daughter of Willew de Nerra. She appears in WITH DREAMS.

de Velt, Beauson – A knight in Saer de Lara's castle. Appears in THE FALLEN ONE.

de Velt, Blaize – He is the oldest son and child of Tenner & Annalyla de Velt. He first appears in BAY OF FEAR.

de Velt, Broderick – Lord of Pelinom Castle. He appears in WITH DREAMS.

de Velt, Cassia – She is the sister of Mars de Velt and aunt to Valeria. Appears in OF LOVE AND LEGEND.

de Velt, Cassian – Youngest child and son of Jax & Kellington de Velt. Appears in DEVIL'S DOMINION and A BLESSED DE LOHR CHRISTMAS.

de Velt, Coleby (Cole) – The oldest child of Jax & Kellington de Velt. Appears in THE DARK LORD. Appears in DEVIL'S DOMINION.

de Velt, Julian – Second oldest child and son of Jax & Kellington de Velt. Spitting image of Jax de Velt with one eye brown and the other eye with a splash of green. Appears in DEVIL'S DOMINION.

de Velt, Kellington Coleby – Heroine of THE DARK LORD. Daughter of the garrison commander Keats Coleby of Pelinom Castle. Appears in DEVIL'S DOMINION. Mother of Allastan de Velt, heroine of DEVIL'S DOMINION. She also appears in THE DARK LORD'S FIRST CHRISTMAS.

de Velt, Lucan – He is a knight serving Keir St. Hever. He has considerable strength and skill. Appears in FRAGMENTS OF GRACE.

de Velt, Mars – Father of Romulus and Valeria de Velt. Warden of the Tyne Vale. Appears in OF LOVE AND LEGEND.

de Velt, Max – Twin brother of Anthony de Velt. He is a knight in service to Christopher de Lohr. Appears in RISE OF THE DEFENDER, STEELHEART, A BLESSED DE LOHR CHRISTMAS, SHIELD OF KRONOS, and THE MOUNTAIN DARK.

de Velt, Morgan – An English mercenary fighting for the Scots for the Earl of Moray. He was previously in the service to Roger Mortimer and is an enemy to King Edward III. He is also a first cousin to Joselyn Seton and Kynan MacKenzie. He appears in THE SAVAGE CURTAIN.

de Velt, Tenner – Hero of BAY OF FEAR. He is the grandson of Ajax de Velt from his father's side, and from Christopher de Lohr on his mother's side. He is the Captain of the Earl of Tiverton's army.

de Venter, Cabot – He is a young knight in the service of Christopher de Lohr. He first appears in A BLESSED DE LOHR CHRISTMAS.

de Vere, Anne – Wife of John de Vere. Appears in THE DARK ONE: DARK KNIGHT.

de Vere, Dodge – He is an evil, pompous, and arrogant knight, the bastard son of Sir Aubrey de Vere. He is also a bounty hunter. Appears in LORD OF LIGHT.

de Vere, John – Earl of Oxford and friend of Gaston de Russe. He accepts Trenton de Russe and Dane Stoneley to foster at his castle to train as pages. Appears in THE DARK ONE: DARK KNIGHT.

de Vesci, Gilbert – Baron of Northumberland at Alnwick Castle. Appears in THE DARK LORD. He gave Ajax de Velt a castle and some lands to leave him alone.

de Ville, Margot – Bose de Moray's former mother-in-law. She is an angry shrew, who is thin and frail. Appears in THE GORGON.

de Weese, Bridget "Lady Antonia" de Weese – She is Morley's half-sister. She appears in THE CENTURION.

de Wilde, Benoit – First husband to Lysabel Wellesbourne. He was the Sheriff of Ilchester. He appears in DARK MOON.

de Wilde, Brencis – Youngest child of Benoit de Wilde and Lysabel Wellesbourne. She first appears in DARK MOON.

de Wilde, Cynethryn – Oldest child of Benoit de Wilde and Lysabelle Wellesbourne. She first appears in DARK MOON.

de Winter, Dair du Reims – The firstborn son and heir of Drake and Elizaveta de Winter. First appears in SWORDS AND SHIELDS.

de Winter, Dallan – The youngest son of Davyss and Devereux de Winter. He is very close to his parents, especially to his mother, Devereux. Appears in SWORDS AND SHIELDS.

de Winter, Daniella de la Rosa – She is married to Devon de Winter. She is from the Fighting de la Rosa Family. Appears in SWORDS AND SHIELDS.

de Winter, Daveigh – He is the Earl of Ardmore and is Baron Cressingham. He is Bric MacRohan's liege in HIGH WARRIOR.

de Winter, Davyss – Hero of LESPADA. He is an enormous man. He is quick-tempered, conceited and arrogant at the beginning the novel. He is the illegitimate son of Simon de Montfort and Katharine de Winter, but was raised as the oldest son of Grayson & Katharine de Winter. He is a vassal to King Henry III. He inherits the title of the Earl of Thetford and Breckland Castle through his mother. Also appears in SWORDS AND SHIELDS, SILVERSWORD, THE THUNDER LORD, THE THUNDER WARRIOR, and THE THUNDER KNIGHT. He is best friends with the de Shera brothers, Gallus, Maximus, and Tiberius.

de Winter, Denis – He is a descendant of the Visigoths. He brought the sword "Lespada" with him when he came to England with William the Conqueror. He appears in WARWOLFE.

de Winter, Denys –Son of Davyss & Devereux de Winter. He looks like his Uncle Hugh. First appears in LESPADA. He is the largest of the de Winter boys. Also appears in SWORDS AND SHIELDS.

de Winter, Devereux Allington – Heroine of LESPADA. She is the only child of St. Paul & DeHaven Allington. She is mistress of the House of Hope, a poorhouse that provides for the needy. Also appears in SWORDS AND SHIELDS.

de Winter, Devon – Youngest twin son of Davyss & Devereux de Winter. First appears in LESPADA. Twin brother of Drake de Winter. He is the spitting image of Drake. Devon is married to Daniella de la Rosa. Appears in SWORDS AND SHIELDS.

de Winter, Drake – Hero of SWORDS AND SHIELDS. Eldest twin son of Davyss & Devereux de Winter. First appears in LESPADA. By marriage to Elizaveta du Reims he inherits the earldom of the Earls of East Anglia and Thunderbey Castle. In THE QUESTING he is in service to Cortez de Bretagne.

de Winter, Elizaveta du Reims – Heroine of SWORDS AND SHIELDS. She is the only child of Christian du Reims and Agnes Maxwell du Reims.

de Winter, Grayson – He is the father of Davyss de Winter. He was the best friend of Antoninus de Shera, father of Gallus, Maximus, and Tiberius. He also has been in love with Honey de Shera for years. He does not appear in his son's novel, LESPADA, as he had passed away before Davyss met his wife. He appears in THE THUNDER LORD, THE THUNDER WARRIOR, and THE THUNDER KNIGHT.

de Winter, Hugh – Youngest son of Grayson & Katharine de Winter. He is a vassal to King Henry III. He is married to Roger Mortimer's daughter, Isolde. Appears in LESPADA and SILVERSWORD.

de Winter, Katharine – Wife of Grayson de Winter and mother of Davyss and Hugh de Winter. She is overbearing and bitter at times. She carries the wealth of the de Winter fortune. Appears in LESPADA.

de Winter, Katharine – Daughter of Davyss & Devereux de Winter. First appears in LESPADA.

de Winter, Keeva Da Goish – She is the wife of Daveigh de Winter, and is a cousin to Bric MacRohan in HIGH WARRIOR.

de Winter, Range – He is a royal messenger and a big knight. Appears in TO THE LADY BORN.

de Winter, Rose – She is the firstborn child and daughter of Devon and Daniella de Winter. First appears in SWORDS AND SHIELDS.

de Winter, Warenne – Earl of Thetford. Best friend of Atticus de Wolfe. A descendant of Davyss de Winter from LESPADA. The firstborn de Winter son carries the Lespada sword with him and

Warenne has it with him it at all times in THE LION OF THE NORTH.

de Witney, Graciela Mortimer – Mother of Aubrielle de Witney. Sister to Garson Mortimer and cousin to Roger Mortimer. Appears in ISLAND OF GLASS.

de Witt, Anthony – One of four master assssins, in partnership with Trenton de Russe, for King Henry VIII. He appears in DARK MOON.

de Witt, Emma – Oldest daughter of Stanton & Vivian de Witt. Appears in GUARDIAN OF DARKNESS.

de Witt, Julia de Mandeville – Wife of the garrison commander at Spexhall Castle. Her family has had a long-held grudge against the du Reim family. Appears in SWORDS AND SHIELDS.

de Witt, Oliver – A knight in service to Roland Fitzroy. Appears in SHADOWMOOR.

de Witt, Stanton – A knight in the service at Prudhoe Castle. His wife is Vivian. They have one child, Emma de Witt. Appears in GUARDIAN OF DARKNESS.

de Witt, Vivian – Wife of Stanton de Witt. Appears in GUARDIAN OF DARKNESS.

de Witt, Watcyn – Garrison Commander at Spexhall Castle. He is married to Julia de Mandeville de Witt. Appears in SWORDS AND SHIELDS.

de Wolfe, Acacia – Oldest twin daughter of Troy de Wolfe and his first wife, Helene de Norville de Wolfe. She perishes in an accident in SHADOWWOLFE and DARKWOLFE.

de Wolfe, Adelaide de Vauden – She was married for one day to Thomas de Wolfe, before her death. She was the only child and heiress of the Earl of Northumbria, Edmund de Vauden. She appears in STORMWOLFE.

de Wolfe, Alexander – Youngest son of Scott & Avrielle de Wolfe. He appears in SHADOWWOLFE.

de Wolfe, Alys de Royans – Wife of Gerard de Wolfe. Her parents are Torston & Alyx de Royans. She appears in BLACKWOLFE.

de Wolfe, Andreas – Firstborn son of Troy and Helene de Wolfe. He appears in DARKWOLFE, A JOYOUS DE WOLFE CHRISTMAS, and STORMWOLFE.

de Wolfe, Andrew – Scott de Wolfe's youngest son by his first wife, Athena. He perishes with his mother, and appeared in SHADOWWOLFE and DARKWOLFE.

de Wolfe, Arista – Youngest twin daughter of Troy de Wolfe and his first wife, Helene de Norville de Wolfe. She perishes in an accident in SHADOWWOLFE and DARKWOLFE.

de Wolfe, Artus – Former neglected orphan at the Edenside Foundling Home. He is adopted by Thomas & Maitland de Wolfe in STORMWOLFE.

de Wolfe, Asmara ferch Cader – Heroine of A WOLFE AMONG DRAGONS. She is the second wife of James de Wolfe/Blayth the Strong. She is also known as the Dragon Princess and is a female Welsh warrior. She is the beautiful eldest daughter of Cader ap Macsen.

de Wolfe, Asteria – She is the young daughter of Edward and Cassiopeia de Norville. She appears in THE BEST IS YET TO BE.

de Wolfe, Athena de Norville – First wife of Scott de Wolfe. She is the daughter of Paris & Caladora de Norville. She appears in SHADOWWOLFE and DARKWOLFE.

de Wolfe, Athena – Newborn daughter of William & Lily de Wolfe. She is the granddaughter of Scott de Wolfe and his first wife, Athena de Wolfe. She appears in SHADOWWOLFE.

de Wolfe, Atticus – Hero of THE LION OF THE NORTH. Younger brother of Titus de Wolfe. Married his brother's widow, Isobeau de Shera de Wolfe. Leads Northumberland's army after Titus' death.

de Wolfe, Avrielle du Rennic – Heroine of SHADOWWOLFE. She is the daughter of Gordon Huntley, and the sister of Jeremy Huntley. Her first husband was Nathaniel du Rennic, Commander of Castle Canaan. She also appears in BLACKWOLFE.

de Wolfe, Beatrice – Scott de Wolfe's youngest daughter by his first wife, Athena. She perishes with her mother, and appeared in SHADOWWOLFE and DARKWOLFE.

de Wolfe, Brighton de Favereux – Heroine of NIGHTHAWK. Illegitimate child of King Magnus Haakonsson, King of the Northmen, and Juliana de la Haye. Known as "Bridey" to her friends and family. She also appears in BLACKWOLFE.

de Wolfe, Caria – A Welsh princess who is being raised incognito by William and Jordan de Wolfe. She was born to Tacey ap Gruffydd, who was married to the last prince of Wales. She appears in STORMWOLFE.

de Wolfe, Cassiopeia de Norville – Heroine of BLACKWOLFE. She is the only surviving daughter of Paris & Caladora de Norville. She also appeared in A JOYOUS DE WOLFE CHRISTMAS and THE BEST IS YET TO BE.

de Wolfe, Dayne – He is the young child of Edward and Cassiopeia de Wolfe. He appears in THE BEST IS YET TO BE.

de Wolfe, Dyana – Former neglected orphan from the Edenside Foundling Home. She is adopted by Thomas and Maitland de Wolfe in STORMWOLFE.

de Wolfe, Edward – Father of William de Wolfe of THE WOLFE. He is a knight in service to Christopher de Lohr. He is the heir of his father, Robert, Earl of Wolverhampton. Appears in RISE OF THE DEFENDER, DEVIL'S DOMINION, STEELHEART, GODSPEED, and THE MOUNTAIN DARK.

de Wolfe, Edward – Hero of BLACKWOLFE. Son of William & Jordan de Wolfe. He is a silver-tongued skillful negotiator for King Edward. He was gifted the barony of Kendal from King Edward, and is known as Lord Kentmere. His castle is known as Seven Gates Castle. He also appears in SERPENT, SPECTRE OF THE SWORD, A JOYOUS DE WOLFE CHRISTMAS, and THE BEST IS YET TO BE.

de Wolfe, Gaetan – Hero of WARWOLFE. A tactical mastermind for the Duke of Normandy, and the leader of William the Conqueror's 10 generals. He is sometimes referred to as "Gates," like his descendant, Gates de Wolfe (from Dark Destroyer). On his father's side he is descended from the kings of Breton. He is titled the 1st Earl of Wolverhampton from William the Conqueror. Gaetan and Ghislaine become the ancestors of the de Wolfe family in England.

de Wolfe, Gareth – Firstborn son of Troy and Rhoswyn de Wolfe. He first appears in DARKWOLFE.

de Wolfe, Gates – Hero of DARK DESTROYER. He earned the nickname of "Dark Destroyer" because on the battlefield he is dark and destructive to men and is greatly feared by men. To women he is dark and a destroyer of hearts because women are his weakness and his downfall. A great leader among men, Gates is the great-grandson of William De Wolfe of THE WOLFE.

de Wolfe, Genevieve Efford – Heroine of SEA WOLFE. She was a captive first of Constantine le Brecque and then Lucifer's captive. She is the sister of Vivienne Efford. She also appeared in LEADER OF TITANS.

de Wolfe, Gerard – Nephew of William de Wolfe. Gerard's father is William's oldest brother. He is titled Lord Essington. He appears in BLACKWOLFE.

de Wolfe, Ghislaine – Heroine of WARWOLFE. In history she is referred to as The Beautiful Maid of Mercia. She is the sister of the Earl of Mercia, Edwin of Mercia. She is a warrior woman and fights in her brother's battles.

de Wolfe, Giselle – She is the wife of Robert de Wolfe, the Earl of Wolverhamptom. She is the Countess of Wolverhampton. She appears in THE WOLFE.

de Wolfe, Helene de Norville – First wife of Troy de Wolfe. Her parents are Paris & Caladora de Norville. She appeared in SHADOWWOLFE and DARKWOLFE.

de Wolfe, Helene – She is the oldest child and daughter of Edward and Cassiopeia de Wolfe. She appears in THE BEST IS YET TO BE.

de Wolfe, Hestia – She is the young daughter of Edward and Cassiopeia de Wolfe. She appears in THE BEST IS YET TO BE.

de Wolfe, Isobeau de Shera – The heroine of THE LION OF THE NORTH. Widow of Titus de Wolfe and wife to Atticus de Wolfe. A descendant of Maximus de Shera from THE THUNDER WARRIOR.

de Wolfe, James –He is also known as Blayth the Strong. Hero of A WOLFE AMONG DRAGONS. He was first married to Rose Hage de Wolfe, and then married Asmara ap Cader. He is the younger son of William and Jordan de Wolfe. He is young knight in DARKWOLFE and appears in A JOYOUS DE WOLFE CHRISTMAS, STORMWOLFE, BLACKWOLFE, and THE BEST IS YET TO BE.

de Wolfe, James – A great knight at Templehurst Castle. A descendant of Edward de Wolfe from RISE OF THE DEFENDER. Appears in THE DARK ONE: DARK KNIGHT.

de Wolfe, Jeremy – Oldest son of Scott & Avrielle de Wolfe. He appears in SHADOWWOLFE.

de Wolfe, Jordan Scott – Heroine of THE WOLFE. Wife of William de Wolfe. Appears in SERPENT, NIGHTHAWK, SHADOWWOLFE, DARKWOLFE, A JOYOUS DE WOLFE CHRISTMAS, A WOLFE AMONG DRAGONS, STORMWOLFE, and BLACKWOLFE. She is an older woman when she appears in THE BEST IS YET TO BE.

de Wolfe, Kathalin de Lara – She is the heroine of DARK DESTROYER. She is the daughter of Jasper & Rosamund de Lara.

de Wolfe, Leonidas – He is a young child of Edward and Cassiopeia de Wolfe. His nickname is "Leo." He looks like his father, Edward de Wolfe. He appears in THE BEST IS YET TO BE.

de Wolfe, Liam Alexander Edward – Firstborn son of Gates & Kathalin de Wolfe. Appears in DARK DESTROYER.

de Wolfe, Lily de Lohr – She is the daughter of Christopher & Alys de Lohr. She marries William de Wolfe, oldest son and heir of Scott & Athena de Wolfe. Appears in SHADOWWOLFE.

de Wolfe, Maitland de Ryes Bowlin – Heroine of STORMWOLFE. She was the widow of Henry Bowlin. She is the sister of Norman de Ryes, second-in-command to Thomas de Wolfe at Wark Castle.

de Wolfe, Markus – He is the oldest son of Patrick and Brighton de Wolfe. First appears in NIGHTHAWK. Also appears in STORMWOLFE.

de Wolfe, Marybelle – Former neglected orphan from the Edenside Foundling Home. She is adopted by Thomas and Maitland de Wolfe in STORMWOLFE.

de Wolfe, Morgan – He is the nephew of the Earl of Wolverhampton. He is also a knight serving Caius d'Avignon. Appears in STARLESS.

de Wolfe, Nathaniel – Middle son of Scott & Avrielle de Wolfe. He appears in SHADOWWOLFE.

de Wolfe, Nora – Former neglected orphan from the Edenside Foundling Home. She is adopted by Thomas and Maitland de Wolfe in STORMWOLFE.

de Wolfe, Patrick – Hero of NIGHTHAWK. First appears in THE WOLFE. Third son of William & Jordan de Wolfe, and is the biggest and most powerful of the de Wolfe brothers. He becomes Lord Westdale of Penton Castle, and is Lord Protector to King Henry and Garrison Commander of Berwick Castle. Known as "Atty" to his family. Also appears in SERPENT, DARKWOLFE, A JOYOUS DE WOLFE CHRISTMAS, A WOLFE AMONG DRAGONS, STORMWOLFE, and BLACKWOLFE.

de Wolfe, Phin – Former neglected orphan from the Edenside Foundling Home. He is adopted by Thomas and Maitland de Wolfe in STORMWOLFE.

de Wolfe, Phoebe – She is the second oldest daughter of Edward and Cassiopeia de Wolfe. She appears in THE BEST IS YET TO BE.

de Wolfe, Renard – Former neglected orphan from the Edenside Foundling Home. He is adopted by Thomas and Maitland de Wolfe in STORMWOLFE. He is the twin brother of Roland de Wolfe.

de Wolfe, Rhoan – Hero of SEA WOLFE, he is also known as "Lucifer," he is the oldest son of the Earl of Wolverhampton. He is the best assassin in Constantine le Brecque's fleet. He is Viscount Essington, and is also the heir of Wolverhampton. He also appears in LEADER OF TITANS.

de Wolfe, Rhoswyn Whitton Kerr – Heroine of DARKWOLFE. She is the second wife of Troy de Wolfe, and is the only child of Keith Kerr, chief of Clan Kerr. She was raised as a warrior. She also appears in BLACKWOLFE.

de Wolfe, Robert – He is the oldest son and heir of Edward de Wolfe (from RISE OF THE DEFENDER), and is the older brother of William de Wolfe. He is the Earl of Wolverhampton. He appears in THE WOLFE.

de Wolfe, Roland – Former neglected orphan from the Edenside Foundling Home. He is adopted by Thomas and Maitland de Wolfe in STORMWOLFE.

de Wolfe, Rose Hage – She is the daughter of Kieran and Jemma de Wolfe. She marries James de Wolfe in A JOYOUS DE WOLFE CHRISTMAS. She also appears in BLACKWOLFE.

de Wolfe, Rowan – Son of James "Blayth" de Wolfe. He appears in STORMWOLFE.

de Wolfe, Scott – Hero of SHADOWWOLFE. Eldest son and heir of of William & Jordan de Wolfe. Twin brother to Troy de Wolfe. He was a young knight in the service of Gallus de Shera. He appears in THE THUNDER LORD, THE THUNDER WARRIOR, THE THUNDER KNIGHT, SERPENT, NIGHTHAWK, WITH DREAMS, DARKWOLFE, A JOYOUS DE WOLFE CHRISTMAS, A WOLFE AMONG DRAGONS, STORMWOLFE, and BLACKWOLFE. He is later titled as ord Bretherdale and owns Ravenstone Castle. His nicknames are ShadowWolfe and Black Adder. His first wife is Athena de Norville, daughter of Paris de Norville. His second wife is Avrielle Huntley du Rennic de Wolfe.

de Wolfe, Solomon – Father of Titus and Atticus de Wolfe in THE LION OF THE NORTH.

de Wolfe, Titus – Older brother of Atticus de Wolfe. Murdered by Simon de la Londe and Declan de Troiu in THE LION OF THE NORTH. First husband of Isobeau de Shera.

de Wolfe, Thomas – Hero of STORMWOLFE. Youngest son of William & Jordan Scott de Wolfe. He marries Maitland de Ryes Bowlin. His title is Earl of Northumbria, through his short first marriage to Adelaide de Vauden. Also appears in SCORPION, SERPENT, NIGHTHAWK, A JOYOUS DE WOLFE CHRISTMAS, and BLACKWOLFE.

de Wolfe, Thomas – Second son of Scott & Athena de Wolfe. Appears in SHADOWWOLFE.

de Wolfe, Troy – Hero of DARKWOLFE. Son of William & Jordan de Wolfe. Twin brother to Scott de Wolfe. His first wife was Helene de Norville. Aggressive and deadly, he is known as the darkest Wolfe of all. After she passed away, he married Rhoswyn Kerr. As a young knight he was in the service of Gallus de Shera. He becomes the owner of Monteviot Tower after his marriage to Rhoswyn Kerr. He also appears in THE THUNDER LORD, THE THUNDER WARRIOR, THE THUNDER KNIGHT, SERPENT, NIGHTHAWK, SHADOWWOLFE, A JOYOUS DE WOLFE CHRISTMAS, A WOLFE AMONG DRAGONS, STORMWOLFE, and BLACKWOLFE.

de Wolfe, William – Hero of THE WOLFE. Also known as The Wolfe of the North. Husband of Jordan Scott de Wolfe. Later becomes Baron Killham with Castle Questing as his hold, King's Champion, and Warden of the North Border. He is also titled as the Earl of Warenton. As a newly married knight, he appears in UNENDING LOVE and THE CENTURION. Appears in SERPENT. He is in his middle years when he appears in THE

THUNDER LORD, THE THUNDER WARRIOR, and THE THUNDER KNIGHT. He is in his older years when he appears in NIGHTHAWK, SHADOWWOLFE, DARKWOLFE, A JOYOUS DE WOLFE CHRISTMAS, A WOLFE AMONG DRAGONS, STORMWOLFE, and BLACKWOLFE. He is in his 90s when he appears in THE BEST IS YET TO BE.

de Wolfe, William "Will" – He is the Earl of Warenton, and the heir of Scott de Wolfe, who was the firstborn son of William de Wolfe, otherwise known as "The Wolfe." He is a cunning fighter, like his father Scott and his grandfather William. Appears in SWORDS AND SHIELDS, SHADOWWOLFE, and STORMWOLFE. He marries Lily de Lohr, daughter of Christopher (grandson of Christopher de Lohr from RISE OF THE DEFENDER) and Alys de Lohr.

de Worth, Charles – Captain of the Household Troops under King Richard II. He is seeking vengeance against King Henry IV for having an affair with his wife and having an illegitimate daughter together. Appears in GREAT PROTECTOR.

de Worth, Ellyn Glendower – She is the wife of Captain of the Household Troops to King Richard II, Charles de Worth. She is the sister of David Glendower, and they are cousins to Owen Glendower, the Welshman leading the resistance against King Henry IV. She has an affair with Prince Henry before he became king and they have a daughter together, Arissa, who is being raised by the de Lohr family. Appears in GREAT PROTECTOR.

de Worth, Niles – A knight serving Edmund de Cleveley. Appears in THE DARKLAND.

Delamere, Arica de Russe – Youngest twin daughter of Gaston & Remington de Russe. Appears in THE DARK ONE: DARK KNIGHT and A DE RUSSE CHRISTMAS MIRACLE.

Dietrich, Frederick "Bud" – Archeologist with Rory. He is very good-looking and is in love with Rory. He appears in THE CRUSADER and KINGDOM COME.

Douglas, Alasdair Baird – He is an agent/messenger/assassin from the Holy Father in Rome, and appears in BY THE UNHOLY HAND.

Douglas, Arn – Son of one of the Black Douglas'. Older brother of William Douglas. Appears in SWORDS AND SHIELDS.

Douglas, Mac – Younger brother of Roger Douglas. Appears in THE WARRIOR POET.

Douglas, Roger – Ruler of Clan Douglas. He is related to the St. Johns and the de Gares. Appears in THE WARRIOR POET.

Douglas, William – Son of one of the Black Douglas'. Younger brother of Arn Douglas. Appears in SWORDS AND SHIELDS.

Doyle, Hubert – Captain at Ripley Castle in service to Alex Ingilsby. He served under King Edward and then with Gaston de Russe. Appears in THE DARK ONE: DARK KNIGHT.

du Bexley, Eloise – Heiress of the du Bexley holdings. Only daughter of Sir Barnabas and Felicia du Bexley. Appears in SILVERSWORD.

du Bexley, Felicia – Lady of Bexley Manor. Appears in SILVERSWORD.

du Bois, Adalind de Aston – Heroine of UNENDING LOVE. She is the daughter of Christina de Lohr de Aston, and is the oldest granddaughter of David de Lohr.

du Bois, Avarine – She is the mother of twin girls born out of wedlock from her affair with Davyss de Winter. Appears in LESPADA.

du Bois, Cathlina Elizabeau – Third child of Maddoc and Adalind du Bois. She first appears in UNENDING LOVE.

du Bois, Elizabeau de Treveighan – Heroine of SPECTRE OF THE SWORD. She is the illegitimate daughter of Geoffrey of Brittany, who was the son of King Henry II and his wife Eleanor. She was named successor to the throne after her half-brother Arthur's death.

du Bois, Jean-Pierre – A knight serving Scott de Wolfe in SHADOWWOLFE.

du Bois, Lizabetha – She is the niece of Marianne Langdon. She helped her aunt nurse Christopher de Lohr back to health. Appears in RISE OF THE DEFENDER.

du Bois, Maddoc – Hero of UNENDING LOVE. Son of Rhys du Bois (now changed to de Foix) and his first wife, Gwyneth. He is Captain of the Guard of Canterbury troops for David de Lohr. Appears in SHADOWMOOR and SPECTRE OF THE SWORD.

du Bois, Macsen de Lorh – Second son of Maddoc and Adalind du Bois. He first appears in UNENDING LOVE.

du Bois, Margaret – Christian St. John's former betrothed. She's also known as 'Marble-head Maggie.' Appears in THE WARRIOR POET.

du Bois, Rhoslyn – Youngest child and daughter of Maddoc and Adalind du Bois. She first appears in UNENDING LOVE.

du Bois, Rhun – A knight and friend of Chad de Lohr. He is the son of Maddoc du Bois (from UNENDING LOVE). Appears in SILVERSWORD.

du Bois, Rhys – Hero of SPECTRE OF THE SWORD. He also appears in KINGDOM COME as a knight in charge of an army Kieran Hage took over to the Crusades. He makes in appearance in NETHERWORLD while in the service of Christopher de Lohr and comes to Nether Castle to lend military aid to Keller de Poyer. He also appears as a young knight in SHIELD OF KRONOS. Rhys is the illegitimate son of the Duke of Navarre. He marries Elizabeau de Treveighan, who is the illegitimate daughter of

Geoffrey of Brittany, who was the son of King Henry II and Queen Eleanor. When they move to France they take his birth father's legal last name, which is de Foix. He is an older man when he appears in UNENDING LOVE with his son, Maddoc du Bois.

du Bois, Rory – Firstborn child of Rhys and Elizabeau du Bois. First appears in SPECTRE OF THE SWORD.

du Bois, Stefan – Oldest son of Maddoc and Adalind du Bois. He first appears in UNENDING LOVE. He is a knight in service to Gallus de Shera in THE THUNDER LORD, THE THUNDER WARRIOR, and THE THUNDER KNIGHT.

du Bonne, Anson – Son of Baron Lulworth of Chaldon Castle. He is a knight serving Patrick de Wolfe. Appears in NIGHTHAWK.

du Bonne, Edward – The weak-willed father of Stephan, Ian, Lance, and Summer du Bonne. Appears in THE GORGON.

du Bonne, Genisa Rilaux du Bonne – She is the wife of Stephan du Bonne, and is very chatty. Appears in THE GORGON.

du Bonne, Ian – Middle son of Edward du Bonne. He is a knight with a wicked sense of humor. Appears in THE GORGON.

du Bonne, Lance – Youngest son of Edward du Bonne. He is a knight with a wicked sense of humor. Appears in THE GORGON.

du Bonne, Stephan – Oldest son of Edward du Bonne. He is a knight who is charming and handsome, and is very protective of his sister, Summer. He married Genisa Rilaux. Appears in THE GORGON.

du Bose, Ridge – He is an older and seasoned knight, and father of Victoria du Bose, of Shadoxhurst Castle. He appears in UNENDING LOVE.

du Bose, Victoria – She was a friend to Adalind de Aston. She is the daughter of Ridge du Bose of Shadoxhurst Castle. She appears in UNENDING LOVE.

du Guerre, Jathan – He is a fighting priest, and is the chronicler of the Book of Battle. He appears in WARWOLFE.

du Lesseps, Eynsford – Son of heir of Baron Wallingsford of Preston Castle in Oxfordshire. He is a dramatic and unaccomplished knight, and is an unwanted suitor for Adalind de Aston's hand. Appears in UNENDING LOVE.

du Ponte, St. Michael – A wealthy merchant and an unscrupulous man, who is corrupt and greedy. He is the nephew of King Henry's wife, Joan. Appears in THE IRON KNIGHT.

du Reims, Agnes Maxwell – Elizaveta's mother. Agnes helps her own mother in espionage by using Eilzaveta to spy on the de Winter family. Agnes is weak-willed and easily controlled by her mother, Mabelle l'Arressengale Maxwell. Appears in SWORDS AND SHIELDS.

du Reims, Arabel – She is the invalid daughter of Tevin du Reims, and his first wife, Louisa. She was born with spina bifida. She appears in WHILE ANGELS SLEPT.

du Reims, Belladonna de Vaston – Heroine of GODSPEED. She is the youngest child of the Duke of Savernake, Edward de Vaston.

du Reims, Cantia du Bexley Penden – Heroine of WHILE ANGELS SLEPT. First wife of Brac Penden.

du Reims, Charlisa de Poyer – Wife of Daston du Reims. She is a cousin to Syler de Poyer. She appears in DARK STEEL.

du Reims, Christian –He is the Earl of East Anglia and is Elizaveta's father. Appears in SWORDS AND SHIELDS.

du Reims, Dashiell – Hero of GODSPEED. He is Viscount Winterton and is heir to the earldom of East Anglia. He also appears in HIGH WARRIOR and BY THE UNHOLY HAND.

du Reims, Daston – Captain of Shrewsbury's army. Husband of Charlisa de Poyer du Reims. He appears in DARK STEEL.

du Reims, Elizabetha – Daughter of Tevin & Cantia du Reims. Appears in WHILE ANGELS SLEPT.

du Reims, Gerid – A knight in service to David de Lohr. He is second-in-command of the Canterbury troops. Appears in SHADOWMOOR and UNENDING LOVE.

du Reims, Grayton – Bretton's second-in-command. Appears in DEVIL'S DOMINION.

du Reims, Kinnon – Youngest son of Tevin & Cantia du Reims. Appears in WHILE ANGELS SLEPT.

du Reims, Louisa Solveig – She was Tevin du Reims' first wife and came from an illustrious Saxon family; the House of Hesse. She left her husband and her newborn daughter, Arabel du Reims, and ran off with her lover. She appears in WHILE ANGELS SLEPT.

du Reims, Rik – Son of the Earl of East Anglia. A knight who appears in THE LION OF THE NORTH.

du Reims, Talus – Firstborn son of Tevin & Cantia du Reims. First appears in WHILE ANGELS SLEPT.

du Reims, Tarran – Son of Tevin & Cantia du Reims. Appears in WHILE ANGELS SLEPT.

du Reims, Teo – He is the bastard son of the Duke of Reims and is from Reims. He appears in WARWOLFE. He is the ancestor of the du Reims family in England.

du Reims, Tevin – Hero of WHILE ANGELS SLEPT. He was first Viscount Winterton and then became the Earl of East Anglia. He is the brother of Valeria du Reims de Lohr, the mother of Christopher and David de Lohr. He also appears in VESTIGES OF VALOR.

du Reims, Tobin – Oldest child and firstborn son of Dashiell and Belladonna du Reims. Appears in GODSPEED.

du Reims, Tristen – Son of Tevin & Cantia du Reims. Appears in WHILE ANGELS SLEPT.

du Reims, William – A knight who serves under Victor St. John. Appears in BLACK SWORD.

du Rennic, Nathaniel – He was the commander at Castle Canaan, and was the first husband of Avrielle Huntley du Rennic. He appeared in SHADOWWOLFE.

du Rennic, Sophia – She is Avrielle's oldest daughter from her husband Nathaniel du Rennic. She appears in SHADOWWOLFE.

du Rennic, Sorcha – She is the newborn child of Avrielle and her first husband, Nathaniel du Rennic. She was born after her father's death. She appears in SHADOWWOLFE.

du Rennic, Stephen – He is the oldest son and heir of Avrielle and her first husband, Nathaniel du Rennic. He appears in SHADOWWOLFE.

Dudley, Thomas "Dud" – He is a young and newly knighted man in the service of Marcus Burton. Appears in RISE OF THE DEFENDER, STEELHEART, A BLESSED DE LOHR CHRISTMAS, and SHIELD OF KRONOS.

Dunkeld, Alexander – He is the King of Scotland. Hugh de Carron, father of Josephine de Carron, and King Alexander shared the same grandfather, so he is a cousin to Josephine. He appears in THE RED FURY.

Dunkeld, Marie de Coucy – She is the Queen of Scotland, and is wife to King Alexander. She appears in THE RED FURY.

Edlington, George – Father of Robert Edlington, and grandfather of Sophie Edlington. Appears in THE QUESTING.

Edlington, Robert – He is the first husband of Diamantha Edlington in THE QUESTING. He perished in Scotland after the Battle of Falkirk.

Edlington, Sophie – She is the only daughter of Robert & Diamantha Edlington in THE QUESTING. She later marries Liam de Lara, the adopted brother of Tate de Lara.

Efford, Vivienne – Tiny, thin, and dark-haired captive of Constantine le Brecque. She is the sister of Genevieve Efford. Appears in LEADER OF TITANS.

Eggardon, Bruce – The Marquis of Cerne and Edward du Bonne's liege. Appears in THE GORGON.

Ellsrod, Aloria de Gare – Tall and big-boned lady-in-waiting to Jordan Scott de Wolfe. Marries Dienwald Ellswood in THE WOLFE.

Ellsrod, Daniel – A knight serving William de Long. He has an aggressive attitude. He marries Penelope de Long. Appears in GREAT PROTECTOR.

Ellsrod, Dienwald – A knight and main character in THE WOLFE. He also appears in STORMWOLFE, BLACKWOLFE, and THE BEST IS YET TO BE as an older man.

Ellsrod, Edric – Son of Dienwald and Aloria Ellsrod. He appears in STORMWOLFE.

Ellsrod, Garr – Son of Edric Ellsrod, and grandson of Dienwald Ellsrod. He appears in STORMWOLFE.

Ellsrod, Hugh – Son of Edric Ellsrod, and grandson of Dienwald Ellsrod. He appears in STORMWOLFE.

Eynsford, Maude – She is the lady of the manor where Vesper d'Avignon fosters at. She appears in VESTIGES OF VALOR.

Farnum, Tate – A knight serving Bose de Moray. Appears in THE GORGON.

Falco, Quintus Aquinus – A fellow soldier with Lucius Aentillius. He took over the command of their group when their leader, Euricus, was injured in battle. He appears in WITH DREAMS.

ferch Maddoc, Eolande – Grier de Lara de Russe's best friend at the St. Idloes in Wales. She is from Welsh nobility and is the sister of Davies ap Maddoc. Appears in DARK STEEL.

ferch Madog, Nesta – She is the alleged mother of Cadelyn of Vendotia. It is later revealed she is a sister of the real Nesta, and is known as a zealot. She appears in THE MOUNTAIN DARK.

FitzJohn, Ivor – Earl of Tiverton. He is the bastard grandson of King John. He appears in BAY OF FEAR.

Flavius, Antonius – An Italian knight serving in Gaston de Russe's knight corps. He marries Jasmine Halsey, the sister of Remington de Russe. Appears in THE DARK ONE: DARK KNIGHT.

Flavius, Jasmine Halsey – Remington de Russe's sister. Marries Antonius Flavius, a knight serving Gaston de Russe. Appears in THE DARK ONE: DARK KNIGHT.

Flavius, Mary Halsey – Jasmine's bastard child from her rape by Guy Stoneley. Antonius Flavius adopts as his own when he married Jasmine. Appears in THE DARK ONE: DARK KNIGHT.

Flavius, Sophia – Firstborn daughter of Jasmine & Antonius Flavius. Appears in THE DARK ONE: DARK KNIGHT.

Fitz Gerald, Marc – A knight in THE WOLFE.

Fitz Hammond, Barric – He is the cohort of King John. Appears in THE PROMISE.

Fitz Robert, Isabella – Otherwise known as Hawisa of Goucester. She was married to Prince John. Appears in SHIELD OF KRONOS.

Fitz Walter, Bruce – He is the Lord of Nottingham Castle. He is the estranged father of Mary Fitz Walter Barringdon, and is the grandfather of Dustin de Lohr. He is a supporter of Prince John. Appears in RISE OF THE DEFENDER and STEELHEART.

Fitz Walter, Ralph – He is the first cousin of Mary Fitz Walter Barringdon, who is the mother of Dustin de Lohr. He is a knight in service to Prince John. He is a confidant of Prince John, and is his right-hand man. He was given the title of Sheriff of Nottingham by Prince John. Appears in RISE OF THE DEFENDER and STEELHEART.

Fitzroy, Roland – Lord Bramley. He claims to be the nephew of King Henry, as his half-sister is Joan of Wales, King John's bastard daughter. She is the niece of King Henry. Appears in SHADOWMOOR.

FitzUrse, Reginald – One of the group of four knights who served King Henry II, and who assassinated the Archbishop of Canterbury. He appears in VESTIGES OF VALOR.

Forbes, Ackerley – A knight who serves Kenton le Bec in WALLS OF BABYLON. Known as part of the "Trouble Trio."

Forbes, Alexander – He is the father of Jackston Forbes, and is Lord Daviot. He appears in THE HIGHLANDER'S HIDDEN HEART.

Forbes, Brydon – Oldest son of Gart & Emberley Forbes. Appears in ARCHANGEL. He appears in UNENDING LOVE as a young knight serving his father, Gart Forbes. He is a master of tactics and planning.

Forbes, Donnan – He is the oldest son and heir of Jackston and Rora Forbes in THE HIGHLANDER'S HIDDEN HEART. He becomes the 3rd Lord Daviot of Blackbog Castle in Scotland.

Forbes, Emberley de Russe de Moyon – Heroine of ARCHANGEL. Maiden name de Russe. First married to Julian de Moyon.

Forbes, Gabriel "Gart" – Hero of ARCHANGEL. Marries Emberley de Russe de Moyon. He is in the service of David de Lohr during ARCHANGEL. Appears in NETHERWORLD to Nether Castle to lend military aid to Keller de Poyer. In LORD OF WINTER he was 18 years old and was serving as a squire to Juston de Royans. He is a young knight in SHIELD OF KRONOS and GODSPEED.

He appears as an older man in UNENDING LOVE and is now Lord Gallox. He also appears in BY THE UNHOLY HAND.

Forbes, Jackston – Hero of THE HIGHLANDER'S HIDDEN HEART. He's the 2nd Lord Daviot of Blackbog Castle in 1368 A.D. He came back to his family's home as one of the heroes of the Battle of Crecy.

Forbes, Rora – Heroine of THE HIGHLANDER'S HIDDEN HEART. She was an indentured servant to Lizelle Menzies, and later marries Jackston Forbes.

Gainsborough, John – William Payton-Forrester's Second-in-Command at Beverly. Appears in THE WOLFE.

Glendower, David – Brother to Ellyn Glendower de Worth, and uncle to Arissa de Lohr. He is a cousin of Owen Glendower. Appears in GREAT PROTECTOR.

Glendower, Owen – The Welshman resisting England's rule over Wales. He is the cousin of David Glendower and his sister Ellyn Glendower. Appears in GREAT PROTECTOR.

Godinez, Miguel – He is known as Miguel the Pirate. He is the father of Patrizia Godinez. Appears in TENDER IS THE KNIGHT.

Godinez, Patrizia – She is a Spanish lady who makes a living as a seamstress. She is in service to Ryan de Bretagne. She is the daughter of Miguel the Pirate, or Miguel Godinez. Appears in TENDER IS THE KNIGHT.

Godwinson, King Harold II – He was the king of England when William the Conqueror defeated him at the Battle of Hastings. His wife, Queen Edith, was the sister of Ghislaine of Mercia. He appears in WARWOLFE.

Gordon, Ysabella – She is the Mother Prioress at Coldingham Priory. She is the sister of Richard Gordon, who is the leader of Clan Gordon. Appears in NIGHTHAWK.

Gordon, Richard – He is the leader of Clan Gordon and is brother to the Mother Prioress of Coldingham Priory, Ysabella Gordon. Appears in NIGHTHAWK.

Grantham, Alan – A knight serving Stephen Pembury. He appears in THE SAVAGE CURTAIN.

Gray, Jason – A knight in THE WOLFE.

Grey, Emma – She is the daughter of Lord Grey of Chillingham Castle. Appears in IMMORTAL SEA.

Guillaume, Dessa-Etienne of, – She is Lady de Mora's younger sister. She is bold and ill-mannered. Appears in THE PROMISE.

Haaksonsson, Magnus – King of the Northmen, and father of Brighton de Favereux. Appears in NIGHTHAWK.

Hage, Alec – He is the oldest son of Kieran and Jemma Hage. He is a knight in service to his brother-in-law, Patrick de Wolfe. He married Katheryn de Wolfe. Appears in NIGHTHAWK, A JOYOUS DE WOLFE CHRISTMAS, A WOLFE AMONG DRAGONS, STORMWOLFE, BLACKWOLFE, and THE BEST IS YET TO BE.

Hage, Andrew – Kieran's 4th oldest brother. He serves his father Jeffrey as Captain of Southwell's army, along with his brother Christian. Appears in KINGDOM COME.

Hage, Annavieve Fitz Roderick – Bastard daughter of the one of the last Prince of Wales, Rhordi ap Gruffydd and Lady Alys Marshall. Heroine of SCORPION.

Hage, Axel – Middle son of Alec and Katheryn Hage. Appears in NIGHTHAWK, A WOLFE AMONG DRAGONS, and STORMWOLFE.

Hage, Bud – Young orphaned servant. His birth name is John but Rory immediately renamed him "Bud" in honor of her colleague

Bud Dietrich. He is the older brother of David Hage. Later adopted by Kieran & Rory. Appears in KINGDOM COME.

Hage, Christian – Kieran's 3rd oldest brother. He serves his father Jeffrey as Captain of Southwell's army, along with his brother Andrew. He is like his father Jeffrey; hot-headed and brash. Betrothed to Charlotte de Longley of Northwood Castle. Appears in KINGDOM COME.

Hage, Christoph – Youngest son of Alec and Katheryn Hage. Appears in NIGHTHAWK and A WOLFE AMONG DRAGONS.

Hage, Daniel Anthony Christopher – 18th Earl of Newark. Appears in KINGDOM COME.

Hage, David – Young orphaned servant. He was called "Little Mouse" by his older brother John (Bud Hage), but Rory immediately named him David Hage, in honor of her colleague David Peck. Later adopted by Kieran & Rory. Appears in KINGDOM COME.

Hage, Edward – Oldest son of Alec and Katheryn Hage. Appears in NIGHTHAWK, A WOLFE AMONG DRAGONS, and STORMWOLFE.

Hage, Eleanor du Reims – Second child of Tevin & Cantia du Reims. She marries Geoffrey Hage and they became the parents of Keiran Hage, hero of THE CRUSADER and KINGDOM COME. Appears in WHILE ANGELS SLEPT.

Hage, Gavan – A knight second-in-command to Richmond le Bec. Appears in GREAT PROTECTOR.

Hage, Jeffrey – Kieran's father, the 5th Earl of Newark. He is a cruel and competitive man, given to yelling and ranting. He is over-emotional and brilliant, and hot-headed and brash. Appears in KINGDOM COME.

Hage, Jemma Scott – Heroine of THE BEST IS YET TO BE. She is also a main character in THE WOLFE. Known as "Banshee."

Marries Kieran Hage. Mother of Kevin Hage, hero of SCORPION. Appears in SCORPION, NIGHTHAWK, and BLACKWOLFE.

Hage, Katheryn de Wolfe – Younger sister of Patrick de Wolfe, and is married to Alec Hage. Appears in NIGHTHAWK and BLACKWOLFE.

Hage, Kevin – Hero of SCORPION and is a mercenary and paid assassin in that novel. Son of Keiran and Jemma Scott Hage of THE WOLFE. Appears in NIGHTHAWK as a knight in service to Patrick de Wolfe. He also appears in A JOYOUS DE WOLFE CHRISTMAS and A WOLFE AMONG DRAGONS.

Hage, Kieran – Great-uncle of Kieran Hage of THE WOLFE and SCORPION. This Kieran is the hero of THE CRUSADER and KINGDOM COME. His titles are Viscount of Dykemoor and Sewall and is from Southwell Castle. He is also Baron Hawksbury, Baron Mere and Heyrose, and is the hereditary lord of Deus Mons. He would have been the 6th Earl of Newark and Sherwood if he stayed with his family. He also owns Peveril Castle, Bucklow Castle, and Rainhill Castle. His parents are Jeffrey Hage & Eleanor Britton du Reims (her father is Tevin du Reims from WHILE ANGELS SLEPT).

Hage, Kieran – Great-nephew of Kieran Hage from THE CRUSADER and KINGDOM COME. A main character in THE WOLFE. Marries Jemma Scott. He appears as a young newlywed in UNENDING LOVE. He and Jemma are the parents of Kevin Hage, the hero of SCORPION. He also appears in his middle age in NIGHTHAWK and BLACKWOLFE. He is an older man in A WOLFE AMONG DRAGONS.

Hage, Margaret de Russe Bigood – Sean Hage's wife. She and Sean have a daughter named Eleanor. Appears in KINGDOM COME.

Hage, Mary Alys – Adopted daughter of Jemma and Kieran Hage in THE WOLFE.

Hage, Nathaniel "Nat" – Younger son of Kieran and Jemma Hage. Appears in NIGHTHAWK and THE BEST IS YET TO BE.

Hage, Rory Elizabeth "Libby" Osgrove – Heroine of THE CRUSADER & KINGDOM COME. A biblical archeologist who spent 14 months excavating Kieran Hage's burial site in Nahariya, Israel. She is also called "Libby" by Kieran because he doesn't like her given name of Rory.

Hage, Sean – Kieran's 2nd oldest brother. He serves King Richard. He is married to Margaret "Maggie" Bigood. Appears in KINGDOM COME.

Hage, Tevin Jeffrey Lucas – Only child of Kieran & Rory Hage. He was raised by Sean & Margaret Hage after Rory disappeared. Appears in KINGDOM COME.

Halsey, Rory – Remington de Russe's sister. She was the prankster and played lots of tricks on Nicholas de Russe. She was in love with Patrick de Russe before her death. Appears in THE DARK ONE: DARK KNIGHT.

Hammer Fist, Iorick – A Northman and Lord of Findlater Castle. Appears in DEEP INTO DARKNESS.

Hampton, Elise – She is the youngest of the Hampton sisters and is the daughter of Lyle Hampton. Appears in STEELHEART.

Hampton, Lyle – He is the Earl of Canterbury, and is the father of Emilie Hampton de Lohr and Nathalie Hampton. Appears in RISE OF THE DEFENDER and STEELHEART.

Hampton, Nathalie – She is the younger sister of Emilie Hampton and daughter of Lyle Hampton, Earl of Canterbury. Appears in RISE OF THE DEFENDER and STEELHEART.

Hampton, Payn – He is the illegitimate son of Lyle Hampton and his daughter's nurse, Lillibet. He was raised by a peasant family. He appears in STEELHEART.

Harringham, Lionel – He is Baron Kielder, and owns The Lyceum. He is also known as "Great Caesar." He appears in THE CENTURION.

Helgeson, Arik – A Norse knight and Gaston de Russe's best friend in the knight corp. They squired together. Appears in THE DARK ONE: DARK KNIGHT.

Horley, Simon – He is a knight serving Tevin du Reims. He appears in WHILE ANGELS SLEPT.

Howard, Kelvin – He is a friend and ally of Christian St. John. Appears in THE WARRIOR POET.

Huntley, Gordon Huntley – A knight serving Nathaniel du Rennic. He is also the father of Avrielle du Rennic de Wolfe. Appears in SHADOWWOLFE.

Huntley, Jeremy – A knight serving Nathaniel du Rennic. He is also the brother of Avrielle du Rennic de Wolfe, who was the first wife of Nathaniel du Rennic. Appears in SHADOWWOLFE.

Ibn ad-Din, Yusef Ibn Ahmed – A Saracen and one of Salah-ad Din's cousins, a servant of the great Saracen general El-Hajidd. He had been at the head of the peace delegation from El-Hajidd that had presented Kieran and the other English knights with the crown of thorns reputed to have belonged to Jesus Christ. He follows Kieran to England and is one of his most trusted friends. Appears in KINGDOM COME.

ibn Aziz, Al-Zayin – He is cousin to Salah ah-din, the commander of the Muslim armies in Jerusalem during the Crusades. He becomes Garret de Moray's companion in England. Appears in SHIELD OF KRONOS.

Ingilsby, John – Lord of Ripon Castle. He battles for Chloe de Geld, known as "The Goddess" at all cost. Appears in FRAGMENTS OF GRACE.

Ingilsby, Alex – An older knight who owns Ripley Castle. He has always been in love with Remington Stoneley even though he is married to Anne Ingilsby. Appears in THE DARK ONE: DARK KNIGHT.

Ingilsby, Anne – Wife of Alex Ingilsby, Lady of Ripley Castle. Appears in THE DARK ONE: DARK KNIGHT.

Inglesbatch, William – He is a legacy knight serving the de Neville family. He is a great knight with a great sword hand. Appears in VALIANT CHAOS.

Kaleef – Alchemist in Nahariya who creates the elixir potion that put Kieran Hage to sleep. Appears in KINGDOM COME.

Kerr, Artis – Fergus Kerr's son. Appears in DARKWOLFE.

Kerr, Douglas – Laird of Clan Kerr at Luckenburn Tower. He is a cousin to Torston de Royans. He appears in THE CENTURION.

Kerr, Dunsmore – Fergus Kerr's son. Appears in DARKWOLFE.

Kerr, Edna – She is Douglas Kerr's mother. She appears in THE CENTURION.

Kerr, Fergus – Younger brother of Keith Kerr, and father of Artis Kerr and Dunsmore Kerr. He appears in DARKWOLFE.

Kerr, Finlay – Son of Nevin Kerr. He appeared in BLACKWOLFE.

Kerr, Keith – Chief of Clan Kerr, and father of Rhoswyn Kerr. He is the chief of a smaller offshoot of Clan Kerr. He is known as 'Red Keith' because of his fiery temper and not for the color of his hair. He appears in DARKWOLFE.

Kerr, Michael Kerr – He is Douglas Kerr's young son. He appears in THE CENTURION.

Kerr, Nevin – He is the leader of his Scottish clan. He appears in BLACKWOLFE.

Kerr, Sian – Laird Etterick, Head of the warring Scot clan of Clan Kerr. Appears in GUARDIAN OF DARKNESS.

Kerry, Breck – An unscrupulous and unethical knight. Appears in THE GORGON.

Kerry, Duncan – An honest knight and younger brother of Breck Kerry. He is well-liked by his peers. Appears in THE GORGON.

Kessler, Jeffrey – Captain of Lioncross Abbey before Christopher de Lohr married Dustin Barringdon. He is a seasoned German warrior. Appears in RISE OF THE DEFENDER, A BLESSED DE LOHR CHRISTMAS, and THE MOUNTAIN DARK.

Kluge, Ranulf – Oldest of William de Wolfe's knights in THE WOLFE in 1240 A.D.

Kluge, Ranulf – A muscular knight. He appears in FRAGMENTS OF GRACE in 1291 A.D.

L'Ancresse, Apollo –One of the Titan Generals, and cousin to Jax de Velt. Appears in THE DARK LORD.

l'Audacieux, Brynner – Oldest son and heir of Etzel l'Audacieux. He is a former knight who is perpetually drunk. Appears in SHADOWMOOR.

l'Audacieux, Etzel – Father of Brynner, Liselotte, and Gunnar. He is the Lord of Shadowmoor. Appears in SHADOWMOOR.

l'Audacieux, Gunnar – Youngest son of Etzel l'Audacieux. Appears in SHADOWMOOR.

l'Breaux, Everett – A knight in the service of Kenneth St. Hever. Appears in ISLAND OF GLASS.

l'Ebreux, Cairn – First husband of Madelayne Gray l'Ebreux. He was the second-in-command at Lavister Crag Castle. Appears in QUEEN OF LOST STARS.

l'Evereux, John – He is a knight in service to St. Michael du Pont. Appears in THE IRON KNIGHT.

la Londe, Dennis – He is a French mercenary and assassin, who is an ally of Howard Terrington, Lord Ryesdale. He appears in THE WHITE LORD OF WELLESBOURNE.

la Londe, Jules – A knight in service to Roland Fitzroy. Appears in SHADOWMOOR.

Lancaster, Henry IV, King – He was the Duke of Hereford, the grandson of King Edward III, and King Richard II's cousin, and is also known as Henry Bolingbroke. He appears in GREAT PROTECTOR.

Lancaster, Henry VI, King – He is nine years old when he appears in BEAST.

Langdon, Marianne – She is the wife of the Earl of Langdon. She lives with her husband and the rest of their people in Sherwood Forest. She also helped nurse Christopher de Lohr back to health. Appears in RISE OF THE DEFENDER.

Langdon, Rob "Rob of the Hood" – He is the Earl of Langdon, who was displaced from his Castle at Tickhill by Prince John and now lives in Sherwood Forest with the rest of his displaced people. He is the husband of Marianne Langdon and leads his band of robbers. They usually steal from Prince John's supporters. He helped to save Christopher de Lohr's life. Appears in RISE OF THE DEFENDER.

Langdon, Simon – He is the only son and heir of Rob, the Earl of Langdon. He is a young boy who later goes to foster at Lioncross Abbey. Appears in RISE OF THE DEFENDER.

Langton, Stephen – He is the archbishop of Canterbury. Appears in GODSPEED.

le Bec, Alec – A knight in THE LION OF THE NORTH.

le Bec, Arissa de Lohr – Heroine of GREAT PROTECTOR. Illegitimate daughter of Henry IV and Ellyn Glendower de Worth.

She is given a protector, Richmond le Bec, who guards her as she's raised by the de Lohr family.

le Bec, Brentford – He is a knight serving the Earl of Derby. Appears in STEELHEART.

le Bec, Gannon – Brother to Gisella le Bec. A knight who serves Bastian. Marries Sparrow Summerlin. Appears in BEAST.

le Bec, Kenton – Hero of WALLS OF BABYLON. Grandson of Richmond le Bec from GREAT PROTECTOR. He inherits the Dunscar Barony and owns Steelmoor Castle in Yorkshire. He is the commander at Babylon Castle. Appears in THE LION OF THE NORTH. Known as Warwick's attack dog.

le Bec, Nicola Aubrey-Thorne – Heroine of WALLS OF BABYLON. Widow of Lord Gaylord Thorne. Marries Kenton le Bec.

le Bec, Richmond – Hero of GREAT PROTECTOR. Henry IV's greatest knight. Assigned as a protector guardian of King Henry's illegitimate daughter, Arissa de Lohr. He also appears in THE IRON KNIGHT and TO THE LADY BORN.

le Bec, Sparrow Summerlin – Best friend of Gisella le Bec. Marries her brother Gannon le Bec. Appears in BEAST.

le Bec, Stefan – A knight in service to Brandt de Russe. Appears in LORD OF WAR: BLACK ANGEL.

le Bec, Stephan – Firstborn and oldest son of Richmond & Arissa le Bec. First appears in GREAT PROTECTOR.

le Brecque, Constantine – Hero of LEADER OF TITANS. Bastard son of Henry V. His title is Earl of West Wales. He is a leader of pirates.

le Brecque, Gregoria de Moyon – Heroine of LEADER OF TITANS. She is the sister of Baron Buckland.

le Breton, Richard – One of the group of four knights who served King Henry II, and who assassinated the Archbishop of

Canterbury. He is heavy-set, and is the oldest knight in the group of four assassins. He appears in VESTIGES OF VALOR.

le Cairon, Clayton – He is the husband of Lily de Vaston le Cairon, the oldest daughter of the Duke of Savernake. Appears in GODSPEED.

le Crughnan, Dalton – He is a knight serving Marcus Burton. Appears in RISE OF THE DEFENDER.

le Foix, Armand – A Gascon knight, part of the Armagnacs specializing in espionage, kidnappings, and assassinations. Appears as the antagonist in BEAST.

le Londe, Dennis – A French mercenary who is known as "Dennis the Destroyer." He is in the paid service of Prince John and is an unscrupulous knight. Appears in RISE OF THE DEFENDER and STEELHEART.

le Mon, Allan – Garren's father, baron of Anglecynn and Ceri. He and Bertram de Rosa squired together when they were younger, and Allan saved Bertram's life as a young man. He appears in THE WHISPERING NIGHT.

le Mon, Aneirin – Daughter of the peasant woman, Mair. She is later adopted by Garren and Derica. Appears in THE WHISPERING NIGHT.

le Mon, Austin – Youngest son of Garren & Derica le Mon. He first appears in THE WHISPERING NIGHT.

le Mon, Dallan – A knight who goes into the service of Brandt de Russe. Appears in LORD OF WAR: BLACK ANGEL.

le Mon, Davin – Middle son of Garren & Derica le Mon. He first appears in THE WHISPERING NIGHT.

le Mon, Derica de Rosa – Heroine of THE WHISPERING NIGHT. She is the daughter of Bertram de Rosa, and is the only daughter in a family of three sons.

le Mon, Gabrielle le Mon – Garren le Mon's oldest sister. She has been blind since birth, and is a nun, known as Sister Mary Felicitas. She appears in THE WHISPERING NIGHT.

le Mon, Garren – Hero of THE WHISPERING NIGHT, and heir to the barony of Anglecynn and Ceri and owns Chateroy Castle. His wife inherited the marcher lordship of Knighton Castle, Hopton Castle, and Clun Castle. He is a massive knight, and protégé of William Marshal.

le Mon, Gerik – A knight who serves Kenton le Bec in WALLS OF BABYLON. Known as part of the "Trouble Trio."

le Mon, Lily – Youngest daughter of Garren & Derica le Mon. She first appears in THE WHISPERING NIGHT.

le Mon, Roselyn – Oldest daughter of Garren & Derica le Mon. She first appears in THE WHISPERING NIGHT.

le Mon, Sian – Son of the peasant woman, Mair. He is later adopted by Garren and Derica. Appears in THE WHISPERING NIGHT.

le Mon, Trevor – A knight from the le Mon family of Chateroy Castle, who are descendants of the Kings of Anglecynn. Appears in BLACK SWORD.

le Mon, Weston – Oldest son of Garren & Derica le Mon. He first appears in THE WHISPERING NIGHT.

le Sander, Kerk – Hero of IMMORTAL SEA. In NIGHTHAWK he is a captain in the service of Sir Henry Grey of Chillingham Castle. In LEADER OF TITANS he is an excellent knight and shipmate to Constantine le Brecque during this time period in history.

le Somes, Amadeo – Ajax de Velt's second-in-command. Appears in THE DARK LORD. He is possessive, ambitious, and controlling.

le Somes, Robbin – A knight serving Eryx de Reyne. He appears in WITH DREAMS.

le Tourneau, Julia – She is a ward of Richard & Anne d'Umfraville. Appears in GUARDIAN OF DARKNESS.

le Tourneaux, Eugene – A Yorkist knight who loses against Gaston de Russe in a fight. Appears in THE DARK ONE: DARK KNIGHT.

le Vay, Lionel – Baron Wyresdale. Father of Lily le Vay. Appears in THE DARKLAND.

le Vay, Lily – Daughter of Baron Wyresdale, Lionel le Vay. Appears in THE DARKLAND.

le Velle, Atreus – One of the Titan Generals and is Jax's most treasured man. Appears in THE DARK LORD. He is cousin to Tor de Barenton.

Levington, Adrian – One of four master assassins, in partnership with Trenton de Russe; for King Henry VIII. He appears in DARK MOON.

Linhope, Amethyst – Sister of Emerald Linhope de la Haye. Appears in THE JEWEL'S EMBRACE.

Linhope, Garnet – Sister of Emerald Linhope de la Haye. Appears in THE JEWEL'S EMBRACE.

Linhope, Lammy – She is an older widow and mother of Sapphire, Garnet, Amethyst, and Emerald Linhope de la Haye. She appears in THE JEWEL'S EMBRACE.

Linhope, Sapphire – Sister of Emerald Linhope de la Haye. Appears in THE JEWEL'S EMBRACE.

Linley, Helene – Lord Linley's daughter. Appears in DARK DESTROYER. She bore the bastard son of Gates de Wolfe.

Linley, Huw – Lord Linley is the father of Helene Linley. Appears in DARK DESTROYER.

Linley, Wolfe – The bastard son of Gates de Wolfe. He looks exactly like Gates' father, Edward de Wolfe. Appears in DARK DESTROYER.

Longbow, Stewart – A senior knight serving Scott de Wolfe in SHADOWWOLFE.

Longchamp, William – He is the Bishop of Ely, and is King Richard's chancellor. Appears in RISE OF THE DEFENDER and STEELHEART.

Longespee, Roger – Viscount Twyford, oldest son of William Longespee, and is his heir. Appears in SCORPION. Male lover of Victor de Ferrers, Duke of Dorset, who was Annavieve Fitz Roderick's first husband.

Longespee, William – Earl of Salisbury and cousin of King Edward I. Father of Roger Longespee. Appears in SCORPION.

Lovell, Francis – Lord Chamberlain of the Royal Household to King Richard III, and is his closest advisor. He is young, intellectual, and loyal. He appears in THE WHITE LORD OF WELLESBOURNE.

Lucas, Clarence – Rory's birth father. He was married with four children and had a one-night stand with Sylvia Osgrove. He was a Marine. Appears in THE CRUSADER.

MacBeth, Raleigh "Leigh" – He is the Scottish pirate captain of the "Beast of the Sea." He appears in BAY OF FEAR.

MacDougall, Shaw – Hero of SAVAGE OF THE SEA, Book 1, from Eliza Knight. Appears in LEADER OF TITANS.

MacKay, Beaux – One of four Lions of the Highlands and is called "The White Dragon." He is the heir to the Clan MacKay. He is handsome and gently, but is deadly with a sword. Appears in THE RED LION.

MacKenzie, Connell "the Crazed" – Older brother of Eva MacKenzie. He is the eldest son and heir of Somerlad MacKenzie. Appears in THE RED LION.

MacKenzie, Eva – Sister to Connell "the Crazed" MacKenzie. She is a siren with loose morals. Appears in THE RED LION.

MacKenzie, Kynan Lott – He is first cousin to Joselyn Seton. Their mothers were de Velt sisters. He is a Scottish rebel and appears in THE SAVAGE CURTAIN.

MacKenzie, Padriag – Second son of Somerled MacKenzie, and next chief of Clan MacKenzie after the death of his older brother and his father. He is well-liked and is wise and reasonable. Appears in THE RED LION.

MacKenzie, Somerled – Chief of Clan MacKenzie, and father to Connell and Eva. Appears in THE RED LION.

MacRohan, Bric – Hero of HIGH WARRIOR. Bric is a part of his cousin Keeva Da Goish de Winter's dowry. He is the Captain of the Guard for the House of de Winter. He is a big Irish knight, known as the High Warrior. Appears also appears in GODSPEED, BY THE UNHOLY HAND, THE MOUNTAIN DARK, and STARLESS.

MacRohan, Conor – He is the firstborn son and child of Bric and Eiselle MacRohan in HIGH WARRIOR.

MacRohan, Eiselle de Gael – Heroine of HIGH WARRIOR. She is the bastard great-granddaughter of the Earl of East Anglia (Geoffrey de Gael from WHILE ANGELS SLEPT). She is also a cousin to Dashiell du Reims.

Magnesson, Arik – He is Gaston de Russe's right hand man. He appears in THE WHITE LORD OF WELLESBOURNE.

Magnusson, Wallace – A former knight who became a priest. He saved a young Tate de Lara and now serves as his majordomo at Harbottle Castle. Appears in DRAGONBLADE and THE SAVAGE CURTAIN.

Malcolm, Ian – A knight serving Stephen Pembury. He appears in THE SAVAGE CURTAIN.

Marion, Stephen – A knight serving Marcus Burton at Somerhill Castle. Appears in RISE OF THE DEFENDER and STEELHEART.

Marshall, Alys – Annavieve Fitz Roderick and Vietta de Lohr's birth mother. Nicknamed Mimsy, and was the nurse to the Earl of Hereford's children. Appears in SCORPION.

Marshal, William – Earl of Pembroke. He is King Richard's administrator and marshal. Appears in LORD OF THE SHADOWS, RISE OF THE DEFENDER, STEELHEART, THE WHISPERING NIGHT, BY THE UNHOLY HAND, THE PROMISE, THE MOUNTAIN DARK, and STARLESS.

Martin, Corwin – A knight serving Edmund de Cleveley. Husband to Valdine Martin. Appears in THE DARKLAND.

Martin, Valdine – Wife to Corwin Martin. She is a twin to Wanda. Appears in THE DARKLAND.

Matts, Sir – An older knight serving in Gaston's knight corps. Appears in THE DARK ONE: DARK KNIGHT.

Maxwell, Davey – He is a cousin of Eustace Maxwell. Appears in SWORDS AND SHIELDS.

Maxwell, Eustace – Lord of Caerlaverock, and nephew of Mabelle's deceased husband, Argyle Maxwell. He leads the Clan Maxwell. Appears in SWORDS AND SHIELDS.

Maxwell, John – Nephew of Eustace Maxwell, and a relative of Mabelle's deceased husband, Argyle Maxwell. He is the older brother of Robert Maxwell. Appears in SWORDS AND SHIELDS.

Maxwell, Mabelle l'Arressengale – She's a Frenchwoman who married a Scottish man named Argyle Maxwell of the Clan Maxwell from Scotland. She's Agnes' mother and Elizaveta's grandmother. She is a vindictive old woman who uses her granddaughter to spy on the de Winter family. Appears in SWORDS AND SHIELDS.

Maxwell, Robert – Nephew of Eustace Maxwell, and a relative of Mabelle's deceased husband, Argyle Maxwell. He is the younger brother of John Maxwell. Appears in SWORDS AND SHIELDS.

McCorkle, Farl – A large burly Irish knight serving Bose de Moray. Appears in THE GORGON.

McCullough, Emma – She is the wife of Nels McCullough and resides at Somerhill Castle. Appears in RISE OF THE DEFENDER.

McCullough, Nels – He is an older knight serving Marcus Burton at Somerhill Castle. Appears in RISE OF THE DEFENDER.

McKenna, Abner – Son of Dunbar McKenna. Antagonist in THE WOLFE.

McKenna, Dunbar – Laird of Clan McKenna. Antagonist in THE WOLFE.

Mercia, Alary of – He is the younger bastard brother of Edwin, Morcar, Edith, and Ghislaine, and is sometimes called Alary the Dark or Alary the Insane. He was exiled by his brother Edwin. He appears in WARWOLFE.

Merlin, Peter – A sergeant-at-arms serving Cortez de Bretagne. Appears in THE QUESTING.

Menzies, Lizelle – Childhood friend of Jackston Forbes. As a child she was spoiled and annoying. As an adult she became more spoiled and demanding. She appears in THE HIGHLANDER'S HIDDEN HEART.

Menzies, Robert – He is the father of Lizelle Menzies. He appears in THE HIGHLANDER'S HIDDEN HEART.

Michaleen, Shain – Second-in-command to Devlin de Bermingham. Keeper of the Blade. Childhood friend of Devlin's. Appears in BLACK SWORD.

Michaelson, Debra – Present day visitor on the tour guide of Blackmoor Hall. She appears in EMMA.

Moncrief, Stanley – A knight serving Scott de Wolfe in SHADOWWOLFE.

Montgomery, Justine de Carron – Youngest sister of Josephine de Carron. She is the chatelaine of Castle Torridon, and is also a self-proclaimed 'white witch.' She marries Sully Montgomery, and appears in THE RED FURY.

Montgomery, Raymond – A knight serving Scott de Wolfe in SHADOWWOLFE.

Montgomery, Sully – He is Captain of the Guard at Castle Torridon. He later inherits the castle and the title of Earl of Ayr when Josephine gifts the land and titles to her sister, Justine, who in turn marries Sully. He appears in THE RED FURY.

Moresby, Vanessa – Niece to the king's master chamberlain. Court whore. Appears in THE WOLFE.

Mortimer, Garson – Earl of Wexham. Uncle to Aubrielle de Witney, who is his heiress. Cousin to Roger Mortimer. Appears in ISLAND OF GLASS.

Mortimer, Roger – Earl of March, and lover to Queen Isabella. Appears in DRAGONBLADE and LESPADA.

Muir, Donald – He is a neighboring friend of the de Carron family. He appears in THE RED FURY.

Munro, Ainsley – She is the wife of George Munro the Elder, and is the mother of George Munro the Younger, Jamison, Robert, and Hector. Appears in THE RED LION.

Munro, George the Elder – He is the Chief of Clan Munro. He is the father of George the Younger, Jamison, Robert, and Hector. Appears in THE RED LION.

Munro, George the Younger – He is the eldest son and heir of George the Elder Munro. He is not a warrior. He studied religion, Latin, and literature in France. Appears in THE RED LION.

Munro, Havilland de Llion – Heroine of THE RED LION and DEEP INTO DARKNESS. Oldest daughter of Roald de Llion. She dresses like a warrior and fights like one. Her father raised her and her two sisters as warriors.

Munro, Heather Monroe – A present-day journalist for World's Best Haunts reality TV show. She marries Jim Munro. Appears in DEEP INTO DARKNESS.

Munro, Hector – The youngest son of George Munro the Elder. Appears in THE RED LION.

Munro, Jamison – Hero of THE RED LION and DEEP INTO DARKNESS. He is one of the four Lions of the Highlands, and is called "The Red Lion." He is the second son of George the Elder Munro. He became chief of Clan Munro upon the death of his elder brother, George the Younger Munro. He also inherits Foulis Castle.

Munro, Jim – The Assistant Deputy Chief Constable of Police, Scotland. He marries Heather Monroe. Appears in DEEP INTO DARKNESS.

Munro, Robert "Robbie" – He is the third son of George Munro. He is a reckless womanizer. Appears in THE RED LION.

Nelson, Adam – A knight serving Lord Alex Ingilsby. Appears in THE DARK ONE: DARK KNIGHT.

Neville, Richard – Earl of Warwick – Liege of Kenton le Bec in WALLS OF BABYLON.

Normandy, Duke of, or William the Conqueror – He conquers England and becomes King William I. He appears in WARWOLFE.

O'Byrne, Brandon – From the Clan O'Byrne. Son of Daniel O'Bryne. A warring clan that fights against Black Sword. Appears in BLACK SWORD.

O'Byrne, Daniel – From the Clan O'Byrne. Father of Brandon O'Byrne. A warring clan that fights against Black Sword. Appears in BLACK SWORD.

O'Murphy, Kelly – One of Shaw's captains. He is Irish by birth, but is a Scottish pirate. Appears in SEA WOLFE.

Olmquist, Deborah de Lohr – She is the younger sister of Christopher & David de Lohr. She marries Gowen Olmquist. She and Gowen are the parents of Michael Olmquist. Appears in RISE OF THE DEFENDER, STEELHEART, and A BLESSED DE LOHR CHRISTMAS.

Olmquist, Gowen – He is the village scholar and becomes the bookkeeper at Lioncross Abbey. He marries Deborah de Lohr. Gowen & Deborah are the parents of Michael Olmquist. Appears in RISE OF THE DEFENDER. He also appears in A BLESSED DE LOHR CHRISTMAS.

Olmquist, Michael – He is the firstborn son of Gowen & Deborah de Lohr Olmquist. He is the nephew of Christopher and David de Lohr. Appears in RISE OF THE DEFENDER.

Orry, Tommy – Second-in-command and distant cousin to Richard Gordon of Clan Gordon. He was the childhood sweetheart of Ysabella Gordon. Appears in NIGHTHAWK.

Orsini, Giulia – She is also known has the Mother Abbess from St. Blitha Convent. She is also an older nun, and is the leader of the murderess nuns in BY THE UNHOLY HAND.

Osgrove, Sylvia – Rory's mother, and niece of Uriah Becker. She is a brow-beating mother who was never happy nor satisfied with anything Rory ever did. Appears in THE CRUSADER.

Payton-Forrester, Connor – He is the son of William de Wolfe's friend, William Payton-Forrester. He appears in BLACKWOLFE.

Payton-Forrester, Corbett – Son of William Payton-Forrester from THE WOLFE. He is the garrison commander for the Earl of Pembroke, William de Valence at Gwendraith Castle. Appears in A WOLFE AMONG DRAGONS.

Payton-Forrester, William – Captain of Beverley. The most beautiful man ever created. He married a Scottish woman. Appears in THE WOLFE.

Peck, David – Archeologist with Rory and Bud. Appears in THE CRUSADER and KINGDOM COME.

Pembury, Ashton – Firstborn daughter of Stephen & Joselyn Pembury. First appears in THE SAVAGE CURTAIN.

Pembury, Cade Alexander Seton – Son of Jocelyn Seton, the result of a rape. Stephen Pembury adopts him when he marries Cade's mother, Joselyn. Appears in THE SAVAGE CURTAIN. He marries Cate de Lara, daughter of Tate & Toby de Lara.

Pembury, Gabriel – He is a knight serving Lucien de Russe in THE IRON KNIGHT.

Pembury, Joselyn de Velt Seton – Heroine of THE SAVAGE CURTAIN. Her mother is a de Velt, and her father was the commander of the Scottish forces at Berwick Castle.

Pembury, Kenneth – He is a knight from Bayhall. Appears in TO THE LADY BORN.

Pembury, Michael – He is a knight serving Keir St. Hever. He marries Summer de Moray, daughter of Garran de Moray. Appears in FRAGMENTS OF GRACE and THE QUESTING. Stephen and Summer are the parents of Stephen Pembury, hero of THE SAVAGE CURTAIN.

Pembury, Remington – Firstborn son of Stephen & Joselyn Pembury. First appears in THE SAVAGE CURTAIN.

Pembury, Sebastian – Son of Stephen & Joselyn Pembury. First appears in THE SAVAGE CURTAIN.

Pembury, Stephen – Hero of THE SAVAGE CURTAIN. He is the Commander of Berwick Castle, and Guardian Protector of Berwick for King Edward III. His title is Baron Lamberton and will become Baron Pembury through his father. He owns Ravensdowne Castle. His father is Michael of Pembury, and his mother is Summer de Moray, daughter of Garan de Moray, son of Bose of de Moray of THE GORGON. Appears as a knight serving Tate de Lara in DRAGONBLADE. Also appears in THE FALLEN ONE.

Pembury, Summer de Moray – Daughter of Garran de Moray. She's a healer. She marries Michael Pembury and they are the parents of Stephen Pembury of ISLAND OF GLASS. Appears in FRAGMENTS OF GRACE.

Penden, Brac – First husband of Cantia Penden in WHILE ANGELS SLEPT. He is the son of the Steward of Rochester Castle. He and Cantia were childhood sweethearts.

Penden, Charles – Father of Brac Penden. He appears in WHILE ANGELS SLEPT.

Penden, Huntington "Hunt" – Only son and heir of Brac and Cantia Penden. He appears in WHILE ANGELS SLEPT.

Penden, Knox – He is from the great Stewards of Rochester. He is a young knight in SHIELD OF KRONOS.

Penn, Caelen – One of Ajax de Velt's knights. Appears in THE DARK LORD.

Percy, Henry – An earl of Northumberland. He is also known as "Hotspur." He sides with Owen Glendower against Henry IV. Appears in GREAT PROTECTOR.

Plantagenet, Edward – Prince Edward, known as the "Black Prince." In this novel he is the Prince of Wales at age 26. Appears in LORD OF WAR: BLACK ANGEL.

Plantagenet, Edward I, King – He is tall and lanky. He was Prince Edward in LESPADA. He is King Edward in SCORPION, SERPENT, THE LEGEND, and SWORDS AND SHIELDS.

Plantagenet, Edward III, King – He is tall and thin and masquerades as a squire serving Tate de Lara to stay one step ahead of Roger Mortimer's assassins in DRAGONBLADE. He is a young king in THE SAVAGE CURTAIN.

Plantagenet, Eleanor, Queen – She is from Provence, and is married to King Henry III. She appears in THE WOLFE.

Plantagenet, Eleanor, Queen – She is from Castille, and was Princess Eleanor in LESPADA. She is Prince Edward's wife. She later becomes Queen Eleanor when Prince Edward is crowned Edward I.

Plantagenet, George – Duke of Clarence. He is the younger brother of King Edward. He marries Isobel de Neville, daughter of Richard and Anne de Neville. He appears in VALIANT CHAOS.

Plantagenet, Henry II, King – He appears in VESTIGES OF VALOR. His temper is legendary.

Plantagenet, Henry III, King – He is a short man with a droopy eyelid. He appears in LESPADA, THE WOLFE, SILVERSWORD, THE GORGON, TENDER IS THE KNIGHT, and NIGHTHAWK.

Plantagenet, Isabella – From Angouleme, queen to King John. A lover of Julian de Moyon. Appears in ARCHANGEL.

Plantagenet, Isabella – Wife of King Edward II. Mother of King Edward III. Lover to Roger Mortimer, Earl of March. Her brother is the king of France. Appears in DRAGONBLADE.

Plantagenet, Isobel de Neville – She is age 18 in this novel, and marries George, Duke of Clarence, who is King Edward's younger brother. She is the daughter of Richard and Anne de Neville, and is the first cousin of Avalyn du Brant d'Aurilliac. She appears in VALIANT CHAOS.

Plantagenet, John, King – He was Prince John in KINGDOM COME, RISE OF THE DEFENDER, STEELHEART, and SHIELD OF KRONOS. He was the brother of King Richard the Lionheart, and is the son of King Henry II. In LORD OF THE SHADOWS he became King John. He also appears in BY THE UNHOLY HAND and THE PROMISE.

Plantagenet, Richard – Earl of Cornwell. He is the brother to King Henry III. He is the birth father of Ryan de Bretagne. Appears in TENDER IS THE KNIGHT.

Plantagenet, Richard I, King – Known as the Lionheart. He is brother to Prince John, and is the son of King Henry II. He appears in RISE OF THE DEFENDER and STEELHEART.

Plantagenet, Richard III, King – He is short, pale, and thin, and is not a military tactician. He appears in THE WHITE LORD OF WELLESBOURNE.

Pompeius, Euricus Lollius – The leader of the Roman soldiers at Hadrian's Wall. He was a spoiled man-child with no military acumen. He appears in WITH DREAMS.

Preece, Evon – A Welsh rebel and eldest son and heir of Lord Preece. He is the lover of Madeline de Llion. Appears in THE RED LION.

Preece, Morys – A Welsh rebel and younger son of Lord Preece. He is the younger brother to Evon Preece. Appears in THE RED LION.

Roald, Sir – The oldest knight in Gaston's knight corps. Appears in THE DARK ONE: DARK KNIGHT.

Ross, Adgar – A knight serving Bose de Moray. Appears in THE GORGON.

Ross, Caspian – One of the four Lions of the Highlands, and is called "The Black Falcon." He is a fearsome warrior with a bulky with a muscular build and is strong like an ox. Appears in THE RED LION.

Russe, Ash – Present day heir of Blackmoor Hall. He appears in EMMA.

Russell, Coraline Hampton – Sister of Lyle Hampton. She is the Countess of Orford. Appears in STEELHEART.

Sadgill, _____ – A Cumbrian warlord. He appears in SHADOWWOLFE.

Sauxures, Atlas – One of the Titan Generals. Appears in THE DARK LORD.

Scott, Cord – Jemma Scott Hage's brother. Appears in THE WOLFE.

Scott, Malcom – The black sheep and bastard son of Dunbar McKenna. Appears in THE WOLFE.

Scott, Thomas – Jordan Scott de Wolfe's father. Laird of the Clan Scott. Appears in THE WOLFE.

Sedgewick, Anne – She is the wife of Baron Miles Sedgewick. Appears in RISE OF THE DEFENDER and STEELHEART.

Sedgewick, Miles – He is an older knight and still fights in his older age. He fought in wars with Myles de Lohr. Appears in RISE OF THE DEFENDER and STEELHEART.

Seton, Alexander – Father of Joselyn Seton. He was the commander of the Scottish forces at Berwick Castle. He appears in THE SAVAGE CURTAIN.

Seton, Julia de Velt – Mother of Joselyn Seton. Appears in THE SAVAGE CURTAIN.

Sheffield, John – He is a knight serving Weston de Royans. Appears in TO THE LADY BORN.

Sherford, Thomas – He is Lord Wembury and close friend of Olin de Moyan, Baron Buckland. Appears in LEADER OF TITANS.

Skye, Morgan – An older knight serving Bose de Moray. Appears in THE GORGON.

Sorrell, John – He was the first garrison commander at Hedingham Castle. He brutalized Amalie de Vere before he was replaced as commander by Weston de Royans. Appears in TO THE LADY BORN.

St. Erth, Lyonette de Sansen – She is the daughter of Lord August de Sansen of Larrigan Castle. She was betrothed to Rhodes de Leybourne, but elopes with Tavish St. Erth instead. She appears in LADY OF THE MOON.

St. Erth, Tavish – He is a young soldier serving August de Sansen. He elopes with Lyonette de Sansen. He appears in LADY OF THE MOON.

St. Hever, Aubrielle de Witney – Heroine of ISLAND OF GLASS. Heiress of the Wexham earldom. Also appears in THE SAVAGE CURTAIN.

St. Hever, Brennan – Firstborn child and son of Kenneth & Aubrielle St. Hever. First appears in ISLAND OF GLASS. Also appears in THE SAVAGE CURTAIN. He is a knight in service to Brandt de Russe in LORD OF WAR: BLACK ANGEL. He marries Bridget St. John.

St. Hever, Bridget St. John – A lady-in-waiting to Ellowyn de Russe. She later marries Brennan St. Hever. Appears in LORD OF WAR: BLACK ANGEL.

St. Hever, Cassandra de Geld – She is the oldest daughter of Anton and Blanche de Geld. She marries Kurtis St. Hever, who is the brother to Keir St. Hever. She and Kurtis are the parents of Kenneth St. Hever, who is the hero in ISLAND OF GLASS. Appears in FRAGMENTS OF GRACE.

St. Hever, Chloe de Geld – She is the heroine in FRAGMENTS OF GRACE. She is Lord Exelby's youngest daughter. Also known as "The Goddess." She is the second wife of Keir St. Hever.

St. Hever, Evan – Second child and son of Kenneth & Aubrielle St. Hever. First appears in ISLAND OF GLASS. Also appears in THE SAVAGE CURTAIN. In the epilogue of LORD OF WAR: BLACK ANGEL, he serves as a knight to Brandt de Russe, along with his brother, Brennan.

St. Hever, Frances – Keir's firstborn child with Madeleine. She died with her mother in a fire. Appears in FRAGMENTS OF GRACE.

St. Hever, Isadora de Lara – Younger sister of Courtly de Lara. She appears in THE THUNDER WARRIOR and THE THUNDER KNIGHT. She marries Kirk St. Hever.

St. Hever, Kairn – Firstborn son of Kaspian and Madelayne St. Hever. First appears in QUEEN OF LOST STARS.

St. Hever, Kaspian – Hero of QUEEN OF LOST STARS. Garrison Commander at Lavister Crag Castle. Second husband of Madelayne l'Ebreux.

St. Hever, Keenan – He is the firstborn son of Kirk and Isadora St. Hever. He first appears in THE THUNDER KNIGHT.

St. Hever, Keir – Hero of FRAGMENT OF GRACE. A knight in King Edward's army. Appears in SERPENT and THE QUESTING. Former Captain of the Guard for King Edward. He later becomes garrison commander for Coverdale and is Guardian of the Coverdale barony. He is later titled Lord Sedburg and is Knight of the Shire. His first wife is Madeleine de Gare and his second wife is Chloe de Geld.

St. Hever, Kenneth – Hero of ISLAND OF GLASS. He serves Garson Mortimer, Earl of Wrexham. He previously served Tate de Lara in DRAGONBLADE. From his wife he inherits the title of the 2ⁿᵈ Earl of Wrexham and Kirk Castle, and the Lordship of Tenbury and Highwood House. He is the son of Kurtis & Cassandra St. Hever. Also appears in THE FALLEN ONE and THE SAVAGE CURTAIN.

St. Hever, Kirk – He is a knight second-in-command to Kellen de Lara. Appears in THE THUNDER WARRIOR and THE THUNDER KNIGHT. He marries Isadora de Lara, daughter of Kellen de Lara, and sister to Courtly de Lara de Shera.

St. Hever, Kurtis – He is the older brother of Keir St. Hever. He is Captain of the Guard for Northumberland, serving Yves de Vesci. He marries Cassandra de Geld. They are the parents of Kenneth St. Hever, hero of ISLAND OF GLASS. Appears in FRAGMENTS OF GRACE.

St. Hever, Kye – He is from Normandy, and is a nephew of the Count of Anjou, and is known as "The Hammer." He becomes the ancestor of the St. Hever family in England. He appears in WARWOLFE.

St. Hever, Madelayne Gray l'Ebreux – Heroine of QUEEN OF LOST STARS. Widow of Cairn l'Ebreux, who was Kaspian St. Hever's second-in-command at Lavister Crag Castle.

St. Hever, Madeleine de Gare – Keir's first wife. She died tragically in a fire with her children when their castle was overrun. Appears in FRAGMENTS OF GRACE.

St. Hever, Merritt – Keir's youngest son with Madeleine St. Hever. He died in a fire with his mother and sister.

St. Hever, Witney – Youngest child and only daughter of Kenneth & Aubrielle St. Hever. First appears in ISLAND OF GLASS.

St. James, Alys – Youngest daughter of Henry and Lillian St. James. She is young, impressionable, and very dramatic. Appears in LORD OF THE SHADOWS.

St. James, Lillian – Lady of Bath, wife of Henry St. James, and mother of Sheridan and Alys St. James. Appears in LORD OF THE SHADOWS.

St. James, Lydia Wellesbourne – She is the widowed sister of Adam Wellesbourne. She appears in THE WHITE LORD OF WELLESBOURNE.

St. John, Aidric – Serving King Henry III as part of his Guard of Six. Appears in SILVERSWORD.

St. John, Alexander – Firstborn son of Christian & Gaithlin St. John. First appears in THE WARRIOR POET.

St. John, Barton – He is a big knight and Captain of the Guard for Geurdley Cross. He is Charles Aubrey's right hand man. Appears in VALIANT CHAOS.

St. John, Brome – A knight and Garrison Commander of Conisburgh. Appears in WALLS OF BABYLON.

St. John, Christian – Hero of THE WARRIOR POET. His nickname is the 'Demon of Eden,' and is the Lord of Eden and owns Eden Castle.

St. John, Gaithlin de Gare – Heroine of THE WARRIOR POET. She is the only child of Alex and Alicia de Gare.

St. John, Jasper – He is the nephew of Jean St. John. He is a simpleton. He appears in THE WARRIOR POET.

St. John, Jean – He is the father of Christian and Quinton St. John. He is quick-tempered and irrational. He appears in THE WARRIOR POET.

St. John, Katryne – Sister to Brome St. John, and ward of the Duke of Exeter. Appears in WALLS OF BABYLON.

St. John, Oliver – A knight serving Drake de Winter in SWORDS AND SHIELDS. In THE QUESTING he is in service to Cortez de Bretagne. He is the son of Christian St. John from THE WARRIOR POET.

St. John, Quinton – He is the younger brother of Christian St. John. He appears in THE WARRIOR POET.

St. John, Victor – A commander for the Earl of Kildare. Father of Emllyn Fitzgerald. Appears in BLACK SWORD.

St. Lo, Benton – The town lawman for St. George's Square. He appears in VESTIGES OF VALOR.

St. Maur, Lily – She is the youngest sister of Holly and Rose. She appears in UPON A MIDNIGHT DREAM.

St. Maur, Payn – He is the general of King Henry's army on his Welsh campaign. Appears in TENDER IS THE KNIGHT.

St. Maur, Perot – He is Lord Elvaston, and is the widowed father of Holly, Rose, and Lily. He appears in UPON A MIDNIGHT DREAM.

St. Maur, Rose – She is the middle sister of Holly. She appears in UPON A MIDNIGHT DREAM.

Stoneley, Charles – Guy Stoneley's younger cousin. He is the total opposite of his cousin Guy in personality. Appears in THE DARK ONE: DARK KNIGHT.

Stoneley, Guy – Remington de Russe's first husband. He was an abusive man to his wife and sister-in-laws. Appears in THE DARK ONE: DARK KNIGHT.

Sudeley, Godfrey – He is the bastard half-brother of Preston de Lacy. He is the husband of Victoria Sudeley. He is also a knight for his half-brother. Appears in THE PROMISE.

Sudeley, Victioria – She is the wife of Godfrey Sudeley, and is a lady-in-waiting to Theodora de Rivington. Appears in THE PROMISE.

Summerlin, Alec – Hero of THE LEGEND. He is the youngest son of Brian Summerlin, Baron of Rothwell. He inherits the title of Baron Rothwell and will be lord of Blackstone Castle. Through his wife, Peyton de Fluorney Summerlin, he becomes Lord of St. Cloven.

Summerlin, Aston – He is a senior knight to Dashiell du Reims. Appears in GODSPEED.

Summerlin, Brian – Father of Peter, Paul, Alec, and Thia Summerlin. He is Baron Rothwell. He appears in THE LEGEND.

Summerlin, Celine – Mother of Peter Paul, Alec, and Thia Summerlin. Wife of Brian Summerlin, Baron Rothwell. She appears in THE LEGEND.

Summerlin, Delesse de Winter – She is the wife of Padriag Summerlin. Appears in THE MOUNTAIN DARK.

Summerlin, Kristina – She is a ward of Richard & Anne d'Umfraville. Appears in GUARDIAN OF DARKNESS.

Summerlin, Luc – He served Simon de Montfort and was King Henry III's primary jailor. Appears in SILVERSWORD.

Summerlin, Padriag – Garrison commander at Castle Rising. He is married to Delesse de Winter. Appears in THE MOUNTAIN DARK.

Summerlin, Paul – Second oldest son of Brian & Celine Summerlin. He has the mental capacity of a young child. His wife is Rachel. Appears in THE LEGEND.

Summerlin, Peter – Oldest son of Brian Summerlin, Baron of Rothwell. He was a knight in the Seventh Crusade with Prince Edward. Appears in THE LEGEND.

Summerlin, Peter Albert Brian – The oldest child and son of Alec & Peyton Summerlin. First appears in THE LEGEND. Also appears in THE QUESTING as Cortez de Bretagne's squire.

Summerlin, Peyton de Fluourney – Heroine of THE LEGEND. She's the heiress of St. Cloven, manufacturer of ale. Wife of Alec Summerlin.

Summerlin, Rachel – Wife of Paul Summerlin. Appears in THE LEGEND.

Summerlin, Shaun – A knight and brother-in-law to Warenne de Winter. Appears in THE LION OF THE NORTH.

Summerlin, Thia – Youngest child of Brian & Celine Summerlin. She is a bully. Appears in THE LEGEND.

Summerlin, Toby – Bastard child of Celine Summerlin. Toby's birth is the result of Nigel Warrington raping Celine Summerlin when her husband Brian was away serving King Edward. He serves his half-brother, Alec. Appears in THE LEGEND.

Sutherland, Kendrick – One of the four Lions of the Highlands, and is called "The Gray Fox." He is cunning, silent, and swift in a battle. Appears in THE RED LION.

Sutton, Dagan – He is an older knight serving Tevin du Reims. He appears in WHILE ANGELS SLEPT.

Swantey, John – He is a knight serving Tevin du Reims. He appears in WHILE ANGELS SLEPT.

Swenholm, Olav – He became the Captain of the Guard for King Henry III after Bose de Moray resigned his post. Appears in THE GORGON.

Terrington, Howard – Lord Ryesdale. He is the uncle of Alixandrea St. Ave Wellesbourne. He appears in THE WHITE LORD OF WELLESBOURNE.

Talbot, Nell – Also known as Lilia de Weese died as a young child. Nell Talbot was found to take her place to pretend she was the heiress. She appears in THE CENTURION.

Tillery, Marc – An attorney representing the Hage Family. Appears in KINGDOM COME.

Thorne, Tab – Oldest son of Nicola & Gaylord Thorne. Appears in WALLS OF BABYLON.

Thorne, Teague – Twin son of Nicola & Gaylord Thorne. Appears in WALLS OF BABYLON.

Thorne, Tiernan – Twin son of Nicola & Gaylord Thorne. Appears in WALLS OF BABYLON.

Thorsson, Boden – Hero of THE LEGEND OF THE SPIRIT WATERS. He is a young Northman and only son of Thorsfinn, a powerful chief.

Trevalyn, Bradley – A knight in the service of Kenneth St. Hever. Appears in ISLAND OF GLASS.

Trevor, Emma – Best friends with Arissa de Lohr. Appears in GREAT PROTECTOR.

Trevor, Livia – Widow of Edward Trevor, who was a knight serving William de Lohr when he was killed in battle. They are the parents of Emma Trevor. Appears in GREAT PROTECTOR.

Tristan, Philip Alexander – He goes by the name of "Tristan" in LORD OF WINTER. He is the firstborn illegitimate son of King Henry and his mistress, Princess Alys of France. He is age nine in this novel, and is under the care of Erik de Russe, and is later raised by Juston and his wife, Emera.

Tudor, Elizabeth, Queen – She is the wife of Henry VII. She appears in THE DARK ONE: DARK KNIGHT.

Tudor, Henry VII, King – He appears in THE DARK ONE: DARK KNIGHT.

Tudor, Jasper – Duke of Bedford, and uncle to King Henry VII. Appears in THE DARK ONE: DARK KNIGHT.

Van Rompay, Dureau – Brother of the great French pirate king, Nicolas Van Rompay, and is known as the prince of pirates. He is one of Constantine's greatest enemies.

Van Rompay, Mme. – Wife of Dureau Van Rompay.

Van Vert, Offa – An aged knight who lives at Cilgarren Castle. He appears in THE WHISPERING NIGHT.

von Brunswick, Carys de Titouan – She is the half-sister to Rhys du Bois, and a sister to Rod and Dylan. She marries Prince Conrad von Brunswick, Prince of Alsace. Appears in SPECTRE OF THE SWORD.

von Brunswick, Conrad Ebhardt – He is the Prince of Alsace and was betrothed to Elizabeau. He marries Carys de Titouan instead. Appears in SPECTRE OF THE SWORD.

Warrington, Colin – Oldest son of Nigel Warrington of Wisseyham Keep. He has been trying for years to marry Peyton de Fluorney to gain control of the wealth of St. Cloven. Appears in THE LEGEND.

Warrington, Nigel – Lord of Wisseyham Keep. He is the father of Colin Warrington. Father and son have been trying for years to wrest control of St. Cloven for themselves. Appears in THE LEGEND.

Wellesbourne, Adam – A young knight in THE LION OF THE NORTH. Father of Matthew Wellesbourne from THE WHITE LORD OF WELLESBOURNE, and also father to Mark, Luke, and John Wellesbourne. Husband to Audrey de Russe from BEAST. Appears in BEAST. In THE WHITE LORD OF WELLESBOURNE he is an older man and is widowed.

Wellesbourne, Alixandrea "Alix" Terrington St. Ave – Heroine of
THE WHITE LORD OF WELLESBOURNE. She is the niece of
Lord Ryesdale. She also appears in DARK MOON.

Wellesbourne, Andrew – Father of Adam Wellesbourne, and
grandfather to Matthew from THE WHITE LORD OF
WELLESBOURNE. Appears in THE LION OF THE NORTH and
BEAST. Married to Josephine.

Wellesbourne, Audrey de Russe – Daughter of Bastian & Gisella le
Bec de Russe. Marries Adam Wellesbourne. Appears in BEAST.

Wellesbourne, Bartholomew – He is a Welsh mercenary from the
ancient town of Wellesbourne. He is the ancestor of the
Wellesbourne family in England. He appears in WARWOLFE.

Wellesbourne, Caroline – Wife of Mark Wellesbourne. She appears
in THE WHITE LORD OF WELLESBOURNE.

Wellesbourne, Daniel – Younger son of Matthew and Alixandrea
Wellesbourne. He appears in DARK MOON.

Wellesbourne, John – He is the youngest son of Adam Wellesbourne
and is age 20. He appears in THE WHITE LORD OF
WELLESBOURNE.

Wellesbourne, Luke – He is the third son of Adam Wellesbourne. He
is age 24 in this novel and appears in THE WHITE LORD OF
WELLESBOURNE.

Wellesbourne, Lysabel-Audrey – Firstborn child and daughter of
Matthew & Alix Wellesbourne. She first appears in THE WHITE
LORD OF WELLESBOURNE.

Wellesbourne, Mark – He is the second son of Adam Wellesbourne.
He is married to Caroline Wellesbourne. He later becomes the
Earl of Hereford. He is age 31 in this novel and appears in THE
WHITE LORD OF WELLESBOURNE.

Wellesbourne, Matthew – Hero of THE WHITE LORD OF
WELLESBOURNE. His title is Lord Ettington and owns
Wellesbourne Castle. He is also known as The White Lord of
Wellesbourne. After the Battle of Bosworth he is given the title of
Earl of Hereford. He is the oldest son and heir of Adam
Wellesbourne. Best friend of Gaston de Russe. Appears in WALLS
OF BABYLON, THE DARK ONE: DARK KNIGHT, DARK
MOON, and DARK STEEL.

Wellesbourne, Simon – He is a big knight from Warwickshire.
Appears in TO THE LADY BORN.

Wellesbourne, William – A knight serving Keller de Poyer. Appears
in NETHERWORLD and DEVIL'S DOMINION.

Wellesbourne, William – Youngest son of Matthew Wellesbourne.
Serves Dane de Russe at Shrewsbury. Appears in DARK MOON
and DARK STEEL.

Wenvoe, Neil – Baron of Creekmere. Antagonist in THE FALLS OF
ERITH.

Williams, Eulalie "Lee" – Present day visitor on the tour guide of
Blackmoor Hall. She appears in EMMA.

Wolfe, Larry – Scotland Yard Inspector. He appears in THE
CRUSADER.

Yellowbeard, Magnus – He is the leader of the Northmen and
appears in THE LEGEND OF THE SPIRIT WATERS.

York, Lynn – She's the present-day producer of World's Best Haunts
reality TV show. Appears in DEEP INTO DARKNESS.

Other Main or Secondary Characters – First Name Only

_____, Agnes – An older nun at St. Blitha, and is a murderess at the
convent in BY THE UNHOLY HAND.

_____, Agrippus – Father of Gaius. Appears in OF LOVE AND LEGEND.

_____, Albie – Woodsman. He is the father of Andrew and husband of Mary in THE DARK LORD'S FIRST CHRISTMAS.

_____, Andra – A Welshwoman in the village near Lioncross Abbey. She first appears in A BLESSED DE LOHR CHRISTMAS.

_____, Andrew – Woodman's son. He is the son of Albie and Mary in THE DARK LORD'S FIRST CHRISTMAS.

_____, Chadwick – The royal physician. He was a former knight and friend to Cullen de Nerra. He appears in THE PROMISE.

_____, Dymphna – An older nun at St. Blitha, and is one of the murderesses at the convent. Appears in BY THE UNHOLY HAND.

_____, Eilis – Heroine of THE LEGEND OF THE SPIRIT WATERS. She is the oldest daughter of Bale.

_____, Gaius – Hero in OF LOVE AND LEGEND. A young man who becomes Theodosia Aentillius' second husband.

_____, Hobelar – The leader of the Thurrock Cu or Thorrock's Dogs. He is the head of the thieves and reivers in STORMWOLFE.

_____, Jerald – Known has Big Jerald. He is a former knight to Owen de Mora, and helps to lead the thieves in Blackthorn Forest. He appears in THE PROMISE.

_____, Lily-Elise – Companion to Cadelyn of Vendotia at Castle Rising. Appears in THE MOUNTAIN DARK.

_____, Mary – Wife of Albie and mother of Andrew. She appears in THE DARK LORD'S FIRST CHRISTMAS.

_____, Petronilla – An older nun at St. Blitha and is a murderess at the convent in BY THE UNHOLY HAND.

_____, Robby the Red – He is the cousin to Douglas Kerr. He appears in THE CENTURION.

_____, Sianet – An older Welshwoman living in the village near Lioncross Abbey. She is Andra's mother. She first appears in A BLESSED DE LOHR CHRISTMAS.

_____, Queenie – A cook and helper at the Edenside Foundling Home. She appeared in STORMWOLFE.

_____, Raphael – He is the archangel of physics and healing. He appears in A DE RUSSE CHRISTMAS MIRACLE.

_____, Tibelda – A beguine and companion to Mailtand de Wolfe in STORMWOLFE.

_____, Timothy – One of four master assassins, in partnership with Trenton de Russe; in service to King Henry VIII. He appears in DARK MOON.

_____, Yerik – A cleric at St. Margaret's church. He is the printer and distributor of the naughty cards, disguised as prayer cards, that Cadelyn of Vendotia writes. He appears in THE MOUNTAIN DARK.

Notes

In case you'd like to add your own notes until the next update....

AND MORE NOTES

AND MORE NOTES

AND MORE NOTES

AND MORE NOTES

In conclusion...

As I've said, this guide will be updated as necessary because more books will be added to the Medieval World of Le Veque. I will try to update it at least four times a year. I hope you've enjoyed the outlines and have come to understand the Houses a bit better. Family trees aren't going to work in the case of Le Veque novels because of the extended family ties and inter-relationships – if I drew you a diagram, it would look like a geometric equation. Therefore, this guide is the best way to 'follow the families' and study the character list.

Enjoy using this guide while reading one of any one of my Medieval novels. You can find more information on Le Veque Novels at:

Kathryn Le Veque Novels

www.kathrynleveque.com

KATHRYN LE VEQUE NOVELS

Medieval Romance:

De Wolfe Pack Series:
Warwolfe
The Wolfe
Nighthawk
ShadowWolfe
DarkWolfe
A Joyous de Wolfe Christmas
BlackWolfe
Serpent
A Wolfe Among Dragons
Scorpion
StormWolfe
Dark Destroyer
The Lion of the North
Walls of Babylon
The Best Is Yet To Be

The de Russe Legacy:
The Falls of Erith
Lord of War: Black Angel
The Iron Knight
Beast
The Dark One: Dark Knight
The White Lord of Wellesbourne
Dark Moon
Dark Steel
A de Russe Christmas Miracle
Dark Warrior

The de Lohr Dynasty:
While Angels Slept
Rise of the Defender
Steelheart
Shadowmoor

Silversword
Spectre of the Sword
Unending Love
Archangel
A Blessed de Lohr Christmas

Lords of East Anglia:
While Angels Slept
Godspeed

Great Lords of le Bec:
Great Protector

House of de Royans:
Lord of Winter
To the Lady Born
The Centurion

Lords of Eire:
Echoes of Ancient Dreams
Blacksword
The Darkland

Ancient Kings of Anglecynn:
The Whispering Night
Netherworld

Battle Lords of de Velt:
The Dark Lord
Devil's Dominion
Bay of Fear
The Dark Lord's First Christmas

Reign of the House of de Winter:
Lespada
Swords and Shields

De Reyne Domination:

Guardian of Darkness
With Dreams
The Fallen One

House of d'Vant:
Tender is the Knight (House of d'Vant)
The Red Fury (House of d'Vant)

The Dragonblade Series:
Fragments of Grace
Dragonblade
Island of Glass
The Savage Curtain
The Fallen One

Great Marcher Lords of de Lara
Lord of the Shadows
Dragonblade

House of St. Hever
Fragments of Grace
Island of Glass
Queen of Lost Stars

Lords of Pembury:
The Savage Curtain

Lords of Thunder: The de Shera
Brotherhood Trilogy
The Thunder Lord
The Thunder Warrior
The Thunder Knight

The Great Knights of de Moray:
Shield of Kronos
The Gorgon

The House of De Nerra:
The Promise
The Falls of Erith
Vestiges of Valor
Realm of Angels

Highland Warriors of Munro:
The Red Lion

Deep Into Darkness

The House of de Garr:
Lord of Light
Realm of Angels

Saxon Lords of Hage:
The Crusader
Kingdom Come

High Warriors of Rohan:
High Warrior

The House of Ashbourne:
Upon a Midnight Dream

The House of D'Aurilliac:
Valiant Chaos

The House of De Dere:
Of Love and Legend

St. John and de Gare Clans:
The Warrior Poet

The House of de Bretagne:
The Questing

The House of Summerlin:
The Legend

The Kingdom of Hendocia:
Kingdom by the Sea

The Executioner Knights:
By the Unholy Hand
The Promise (also Noble Knights of de
Nerra)
The Mountain Dark
Starless
A Time of End

Contemporary Romance:

Kathlyn Trent/Marcus Burton Series:
Valley of the Shadow

The Eden Factor

Canyon of the Sphinx

The American Heroes Anthology Series:

The Lucius Robe

Fires of Autumn

Evenshade

Sea of Dreams

Purgatory

Other non-connected Contemporary Romance:

Lady of Heaven

Darkling, I Listen

In the Dreaming Hour

River's End

The Fountain

Sons of Poseidon:

The Immortal Sea

Pirates of Britannia Series (with Eliza Knight):

Savage of the Sea by Eliza Knight

Leader of Titans by Kathryn Le Veque

The Sea Devil by Eliza Knight

Sea Wolfe by Kathryn Le Veque

Note: All Kathryn's novels are designed to be read as stand-alones, although many have cross-over characters or cross-over family groups. Novels that are grouped together have related characters or family groups. You will notice that some series have the same books; that is because they are cross-overs. A hero in one book may be the secondary character in another.

There is NO reading order except by chronology, but even in that case, you can still read the books as stand-alones. No novel is connected to another by a cliff hanger, and every book has an HEA.

Series are clearly marked. All series contain the same characters or family groups except the American Heroes Series, which is an anthology with unrelated characters.

For more information, find it in **A Reader's Guide to the Medieval World of Le Veque.**

Dragonblade Great Marcher Lord of dohara
frog Grace St.Have
Island glass (St. Houia
Savage Curtain Bubury
fallen Doo DePeyno
Queen host Stars

ABOUT KATHRYN LE VEQUE

Medieval Just Got Real.

KATHRYN LE VEQUE is a USA TODAY Bestselling author, an Amazon All-Star author, and a #1 bestselling, award-winning, multi-published author in Medieval Historical Romance and Historical Fiction. She has been featured in the NEW YORK TIMES and on USA TODAY's HEA blog. In March 2015, Kathryn was the featured cover story for the March issue of InD'Tale Magazine, the premier Indie author magazine. She was also a quadruple nominee (a record!) for the prestigious RONE awards for 2015.

Kathryn's Medieval Romance novels have been called 'detailed', 'highly romantic', and 'character-rich'. She crafts great adventures of love, battles, passion, and romance in the High Middle Ages. More than that, she writes for both women AND men – an unusual crossover for a romance author – and Kathryn has many male readers who enjoy her stories because of the male perspective, the action, and the adventure.

On October 29, 2015, Amazon launched Kathryn's Kindle Worlds Fan Fiction site WORLD OF DE WOLFE PACK. Please visit Kindle Worlds for Kathryn Le Veque's World of de Wolfe Pack and find many action-packed adventures written by some of the top authors in their genre using Kathryn's characters from the de Wolfe Pack series. As Kindle World's FIRST Historical Romance fan fiction world, Kathryn Le Veque's World of de Wolfe Pack will contain all of the great story-telling you have come to expect.

Kathryn loves to hear from her readers. Please find Kathryn on Facebook at Kathryn Le Veque, Author, or join her on Twitter @kathrynleveque, and don't forget to visit her website and sign up for her blog at www.kathrynleveque.com.

Please follow Kathryn on Bookbub for the latest releases and sales: bookbub.com/authors/kathryn-le-veque.

Made in the USA
Columbia, SC
26 April 2020